This posthumous selection of related short stories reveals all of John Bell Clayton's principal gifts—of narrative power, of compassion, of insight, of lyric strength—and suggests the major literary figure he would have become. In spite of the excellence of his three novels, in particular the memorable *Six Angels at My Back,* this volume indicates that Clayton was most at home with the short story form.

John Bell Clayton once wrote in a letter to a friend: "I align myself with the obscure, the tongueless, the unwanted and with those who suffer everywhere." These stories reflect his profound concern for people—for their dignity and their right to love and be loved. One of the motivating forces in all of Clayton's writing was his deep desire to bridge the gap of misunderstanding and hate which makes men strangers to one another, and to themselves as well.

Though they display a lively versatility in subject, mood and treatment, all the stories are unified by their setting—the Virginia town of Colonial Springs, the valley hamlets and the mountains beyond. A wide variety of people come to life in these stories: the affluent and the derelict, children and old men, criminals, evangelists, shopkeepe' farmers, sophisticates and the cold-e mountain-bred. All are treated with an hor sympathy and respect.

stories were published pre- publications as *Harper's,* the *ry, Esquire,* etc. One of them, ircle" won the O. Henry d in 1947.

wrote quite like John Bell an individual voice that will ds of his readers forever.

The
Strangers
Were
There

By John Bell Clayton

The
Strangers
Were
There

SELECTED

STORIES

BY **John Bell Clayton**

New York

The Macmillan Company

1957

For Al Hart, Knox Burger, and
All of Martha's and My Good Friends

✑ Part 1

The Town Clock

✑ Part 2

The Village Bells

⌒§ Part 3

The Valley and the Mountains Beyond

❧ Part 1
The Town Clock

An Empty Sunday, the Snow, and the Strangers

DURING THE MORNING the weather had turned sharply colder and a wind had sprung up. By the time he rode downtown on the bus, about the middle of the afternoon, small keen snowflakes were falling. A steady white skim was forming on the asphalt of Main Street, the few cars in the light Sunday traffic already leaving tire marks, but it had not yet become perceptible on the lawns.

The snow looked as if it would stick. Tomorrow he would write a weather story which Mr. Nelson, the managing editor, would probably put on Page One. The lead to the story came to him quickly, automatically, and well rounded:

> "The first snow of the season, riding in on light erratic west winds out of the Alleghenies, started falling on Colonial Springs shortly after three o'clock yesterday afternoon."

Another winter had descended upon the town. It was an old town. Its first few chimneys and first church spires had risen toward the sky a full generation before the American Revolution. It was a frontier village when young George Washington had passed through inspecting forts during the French and Indian War. It had been raided by Shawnees. A hundred years later, a town by then, it had furnished supplies for Stonewall Jackson and Jubal Early and Turner Ashby; the Yankee, Hunter, had burned the cropfields approaching it and Phil Sheridan had tried to take it and been beaten off by Early and a young brigadier general of cavalry named McCantland.

The bus rolled on down the long Main Street. Passing Wine Jug Hill, the Negro section, he noticed less than a dozen Negroes on the pavement. They were long gone from the cotton fields now, far from the corn. On holiday from their jobs as waiters and bellboys and chauffeurs and janitors and cooks and maids and housekeepers, dressed

2

in double-breasted pin-stripe suits or trailing dresses of bright and fashionable material, they were crowded into the beer parlors, cafés, juke-box places in a noisy celebrant week-end life separate from and unknown to the rest of the town—a loud impulsive improvisation with a juke beat and a brassy rhythm charging against the flimsy walls, unpredictable and uninterpretable as a sea swell.

Near the bottom of the grade the bus passed J. Llewellyn Newcomb, just beginning the long climb up the Hill. Wearing a battered derby and a seedy black overcoat, chewing on a cheap cigar, he moved indifferently along in the slanting snow, blinking a little, probably on his way to the Firehouse to play checkers with Dummy Stuart. Once the second or third richest man in Colonial Springs, owner of the furniture factory, director of the principal bank, an honored man of substance, consulted on civic and economic affairs, J. Llewellyn Newcomb had become obsessed with an impossible dream: the building of a fabulous summer resort in an inaccessible hollow of the Alleghenies. He had put crews of men to work on a tremendous wooden structure with ballrooms, façades, huge chandeliers and vast swimming pools. In his imagination it was going to outdo the Homestead or Greenbrier. Actually it became a monumental ruin that began falling down before it was finished. He lost every dollar he had and a good many he did not have. And now J. Llewellyn Newcomb strolled indifferently about the streets, the fantastic dream in his mind unrealized, unexplained, never even mentioned, his face like a mask someone else had discarded.

In the center of town the pavements were deserted. An occasional parked automobile hugged the curb. The night before, the street had been crowded with people from the villages and farms and mountain hollows. Now it had the universally bleak look that descends upon any business section on Sunday. Snow swirled out of the leaden overcast against the locked places of business—the solid old banks, the Colonial Theater, the store fronts. Only the Cavalier Restaurant, the Acme Newsstand and one of the drugstores—the modern one, Hoge's, with maroon leather booths and an onyx fountain—were open. The old-fashioned Wilmer Bros. with its slow-turning ceiling fans was closed. In front of Hoge's a fishtail Cadillac was parked at an arrogant angle. Hoge's was one of the meeting places of the young country club set—girls who went to Sweet Briar or Vassar and young men who were Dekes at the University or perhaps home from Harvard.

He got off the bus at Third Street, flipped up the collar of his topcoat and waited at the curb until the bus pulled away, expelling a bluish gush of exhaust fumes. Third Street ran diagonally to Main exactly four blocks from the Chesapeake and Ohio Railway Station to the Robert E. Lee Hotel. Below Main it passed Court House Square. There, amid the leafless elm and buckeye trees, the commanding bronze figure of General Lee astride Traveller, his hat in his right hand, assailed by the flakes now, faced with that imperturbable gentle resignation not just South but the whole enigmatic contradiction that was and remained and would always be the South.

He stood on the curb after the bus pulled away and glanced back up the length of Main Street. The wind had a whip to it now, and here and there the light snow looped and coiled upon the sidewalk like blown vagrant feathers. He suddenly thought: I often feel the way Main Street looks on Sunday. I wasn't born into bleakness, but somewhere it became my companion and most of the time I don't even know what I am doing in life. I like the snow. I like the rain. I like the dark of the night and I like the empty streets, especially when it snows.

He pulled the snap brim of his brown hat forward a little over his eyes against the soft pelting snow and crossed the street. Keeping close to the buildings, he walked up Third toward the office, which today would be deserted unless the other news reporter, ancient Bernie Price, had come down to write his copy for the metropolitan papers.

He was the only person on Third Street now. The snow fell quietly.

At the next corner Big Bill Collins, the motorcycle cop, came walking out of Ethel Street with his slow stolid tramp, wearing huge black gloves held away from his sides, on his way to the police station to report in.

"Hi, Bill. Anything doin'?" His tone was casual and familiar.

Bill shook his head.

That meant that Wine Jug Hill and Jitney Street had been quiet. These were the two Negro sections, squalid and dense islands in the midst of the town.

He was going along Lawyers Row now, almost a solid block of two-story offices with ATTORNEY AT LAW or LAW FIRM stenciled on each frosted window. The town had sixty-odd lawyers. Into what complications, he had often wondered, could the affairs of a single community of only 20,000 people involve themselves to require the services of more than half a hundred men trained in and dedicated to the art of deviousness and the handling of mountainous minutiae?

On the other side of the street, up toward the hotel corner, a man came out of a small coffee shop. He was a heavy man, walking with a cane. His name was Major Gentry. He had gone away to World War II and had reurned minus his left leg and his right eye; he had left them at Bastogne. From the county and the town more than four thousand other men—farm youths and village youths, college boys and mountain boys, just plain young men of all kinds—had gone and fought in that war. Some had come back with decorations. Many had not returned at all.

As Major Gentry made his slow way on up the street he had the air of a man in an abstracted and solitary search. He was on his way to the Colonial Club to play pool or rummy with the lawyers and the important businessmen and officeholders who ran the community's political life, the kind of men that ran everything, everywhere: polite, sharp, affable and often capable opportunists who had moved gradually up in the hierarchy of public jobs (and business advantage) after making sure the one they had just relinquished was filled by friend or cousin or, more often, son. Over the telephone in the back room calls were placed to Richmond and Washington and Winchester, and every two years the members sent out experienced and knowing men to beat the bushes for votes for whoever it had been decided was going to be elected to every state office from Justice of the Peace to Governor. In such places as the Colonial Club the leading personages of the New South were fabricated as neatly as if cut out of cardboard. Political Virginia had not lost its intelligence; it had simply surrendered its independence. That for which it had fought for four years against a quarter of a million of Lincoln's blue-uniformed soldiers it had given up voluntarily, without a murmur, to one pale dandruffy Senator.

Turning up the areaway between the *Evening Star* office and the building owned by the law firm of Perkins, Chamberlain, and Perkins, he let himself into the empty stereotyping room, went through the press room past the rank toilet and on up the worn stairs and into the chill gray gloom of the little city room. He sat down at his desk with his hat and topcoat still on, opened a pack of cigarettes, took out one and lit it, and rolled a sheet of copy paper into his machine.

He typed out the lead to the weather story and then sat hunched forward, looking at it. A dullness, like a film, seemed to encase his mind. Last night he had been playing poker and drinking in the room over Saul's Drugstore. And the night before that. And very possibly the night before that.

In a moment he pulled the weather story out of the machine, crumpled it up and threw it toward a big square wastepaper basket beside the desk and dilapidated typewriter Bernie Price had used for forty years to write inanities.

Tomorrow he would write it again he knew. He would also go by the Police Court and pick up five or six items about the number of drunks, the traffic violations ("Failing to Come to a Full Halt at an Arterial Street"), the dented fenders, one or two cases of bad checks and another concerning hell-raising between neighboring families on Estes Street. He would also get Marriage Licenses Issued at the City and County Clerks' Offices, hotel registrations, and a story from James Aleck Bell, secretary of the Chamber of Commerce, in which the Chamber would place itself unequivocally behind the proposal to install parking meters on Second Street, N. E. It was not unlikely that Mr. Nelson would ask him to write an editorial favoring the parking meters, because that was the sort of thing the paper would get right behind.

Suddenly he turned both of his hands palm upward and stared at them. There must be, he thought, a better use for these hands. He wondered how many other men in how many cities sometimes paused and looked at their hands and felt a similar frustration. He shoved his hands into his coat pockets.

He had come to the office to write something of his own, but his mind held no order or coherence. Only a few odd fragmentary sights and sounds from the past drifted irrelevantly into his thoughts: the tolling of a village church bell; the feel of cold November rain; an apple orchard; country people clumping into a backwoods store to buy a week's provisions; a buckeye in full soft blossom; the sharp memory of Uncle George Wayland singing "The Lions of Judah" in the First Methodist Church, Colored, his mighty bass voice coming up out of the deeps of the earth with a volcanic righteousness, sweeping despair and sin from the face of the land. Scraps of memory saved for no purpose.

Out of the west window he saw a brief stretch of roofs—tin, composition and slate—all turning uniformly white under the gray overcast. He looked toward the mountains. Out there, in the rich valley, he had been born and had lived as a boy. There lay the grave of his father among the graves of his ancestors who as pioneers and then as fairly prosperous landed people had lived with humility but with independence in their day.

He got up and walked restlessly to the other window, the one over-looking the areaway with its clutter of big trash boxes, and stared directly across the street at an old building cut up into cheap flats, into one of which one afternoon a little gimlet-eyed gambler named Pike Deane had pursued the pouty young trollop who wore white furry-topped shoes and whom Pike Deane used to watch from the shadows of side-street doorways at night. Reputed a dead shot with either shotgun or revolver, he had pushed his way into the flat, shoot-ing six times and hitting everybody else in the room except the man he was after, the Other Man, possibly distracted by the girl, who had yanked off her white-topped shoes and thrown them at him, screech-ing, "You got to quit watchin' me! It ain't nice!"

Across the low roofs he saw a police car round the corner, taking the patrolmen to their various beats. He could not see the driver but it was probably Middleton, who was promoted to the rank of Lieu-tenant after Artie Davis had been caught one night with a Negro woman in a prowl car and fired.

Standing at the window, staring out at the snow, absently biting his lower lip, he tried to visualize the town as a whole, as a picture or a tableau. But he could achieve no such conception. Instead, an odd impression came to him of strangers going their individual ways, brushing shoulders and passing on.

Just then he heard the four measured booms of the Town Clock, iron thunderclaps of winter slightly muffled by the falling snow.

A town, like a man, was a thing of moods. Colonial Springs today was not the same as last night, when the streets were thronged with country people trooping into the dime stores and notions stores and movie houses and poolrooms. And it was entirely different again on those Saturday afternoons in autumn when crowds of fur-coated col-lege girls and their escorts came back from football games at the University or Washington and Lee, taking over the restaurants and drugstores and the Robert E. Lee Hotel with their proprietary, slightly insolent air. Or on Wednesday afternoons when the Military Academy cadets walked proudly and stiffly along, by threes and fours, sharp in their capes and visored caps and knowing that life and the world were simple things. Or on Thursdays when several hundred girls from the Seminary on the eastern outskirts of town filled the pavements with their fresh, confident beauty. And there were the heavy nights of summer, when the very somnolent darkness seemed to possess substance and weight, and the old maple and elm trees along quiet streets held a mystery and a brooding like the thoughts of a mature woman heavy with child.

There it all was: town and village and valley and mountains. In the rolling hill area surrounding the town were the showplace mansions and trim estates of the fox-hunting Northern millionaires who had come and settled there in what was called the Second Invasion of Virginia. Beyond the fox-hunting country lay the orchards and grazing country and farms. And beyond it all were the somber mountains where the big and unpredictable and sometimes violent clans wrested an existence of a sort from steep rocky patches or ran it out of moonshine stills.

There were the rich and the poor and the good and the indifferent. There was a man worth thirty million dollars, and another, a gaunt moonshiner from Jerkumtight Hollow, come on a Saturday night to look at the neon signs, who did not possess thirty. There were the housewives, the merchants, the lawyers, the schoolteachers, the filling-station attendants, the college girls, the golf players on one scale and the pool players on another. There were the churchgoers and the radio listeners and the ne'er-do-wells and the drinkers of cheap wine. On a Sunday night there were a dinner party at the country club and a tryst at a roadside tourist cabin and a prayer meeting at the Lutheran Church and three drunks telling lies in the men's room of the bus depot and a Negro child dying of leukemia on Jitney Street and a young couple getting married and a thousand women preparing supper and an esthetic girl at the Seminary writing what she believed to be a sonnet or a song.

They were the strangers, to one another and to themselves. Each man was ten or fifty men and each woman a thousand in their individual walk toward oblivion. And all of them had in common only that commodity measured out so surely and so inexorably by the Town Clock in the turret above Hoy's Department Store—and that so briefly.

He stood there thinking of some of the people he knew: Judge Estes, presider of Circuit Court; Fleesie, the aged and gentle-natured Negro porter at the hotel; quiet, deep-bosomed Cathy Rule, a nurse; the police justice and the dozens who came before him repeatedly; a retired madam; a former mayor who had started out as a doctor specializing in gonorrhea; J. Llewellyn Newcomb; Doc Goodloe, a deputy of mercy driving his Cadillac around town at all hours of the night; Jake Timmons, sensitive, vulnerable; a rich man named

Crowder who would not stir off his porch to look at the new sports car just delivered to him; a policeman named Emory Barnes. He remembered riding around town with Emory one day looking for the automobile of a prominent doctor who, it developed, had gone out to a riverbank, shot two grains of morphine into a vein while sitting on a diving board, and then gently toppled into the water. He remembered Emory's slow, puzzled remark: "I don't see how a man can kill himself." And within six months, after being told he had cancer, Emory Barnes had stood in front of a mirror, placed his service revolver to his head and pulled the trigger.

With unexpected vividness the face of a pretty young high school girl took sudden form in his mind. When he had first come to the paper there had been another young reporter named Baker, an easygoing, good-looking fellow who had been married for several years. It was Baker who had told him about the girl. She worked in a newsstand owned and run by her father where Baker sometimes loafed. Certainly no older than sixteen, she had an untouched daintiness clothed in that rich young flesh that excites and sometimes inspires. She sat quietly behind the counter at the cash register and gradually Baker realized she was watching his every move, until one day he walked in and asked in a low voice why she was staring at him. And she whispered, in flat and frank want, "You know why." (It was in the fall of the year, with the whole countryside wrapped in the old poetic glory of autumn. Maple trees and elm trees and poplar trees bore their leaves of brilliant crimson and yellow and on the western outskirts of town the old Fair Grounds was deserted and still and secretive at night.)

Quickly he turned from the window and took off his topcoat and hung it on the back of the door and sat back down at the typewriter with his hat still on. Even though it was chilly in the office, he wanted his elbows and forearms free. He rolled another sheet of copy paper in the typewriter and began typing with the free play of wrists, forearms and elbows:

The town lies silent in that great nature-hacked gully of earth between the Alleghenies and the Blue Ridge. The overcast parts and the snow comes. Gently it covers this town of mine. Main Street wears a look of Sunday desertion and near desolation, like a place either long dead or waiting another hundred years to be born. Snow falls on the Negro hovels and the estates of the Northern millionaire foxhunters, the country club and the golf course, the churches,

Upjohn's poolroom, the dingy railroad station, Ginnie's whorehouse, the hospitals, the two cemeteries, fifty moonshine stills out in the county, the sick, the crippled, the well, the dull, the laughing, the unhappy, the poverty-stricken, the rich.

I try to think of all the people around me in this snow. About this time of day and on this kind of day they are in their homes. They have read the newspapers, they have eaten or are going to eat, they are listening to their favorite radio programs, or they are thinking about going to church. Tomorrow I will walk about this town and talk to people. I will talk to some who are intelligent and some who are stupid and a good many in between, and each will speak as if he understood men and women and life itself, at least enough to satisfy him, almost as if he and he alone possessed a Truth private and inviolate, ready to be outraged if it were faintly indicated he stood in eternal contradiction not only to the man next door but to himself. All of my adult life I have been trying to understand. . . .

He stopped, got up and walked abstractedly into Mr. Nelson's empty office; on the typewriter desk in a row were the books Mr. Nelson called his "Bibles"—Webster's Unabridged, Roget's Thesaurus, Bartlett's Familiar Quotations, World Almanacs for the past decade, Who's Who, and the Annual Report of the United States Department of Commerce.

Mr. Nelson felt that things were pretty much all right; of twenty of his editorials, nineteen were of approval to one of mild and cautious disapproval. Mr. Nelson felt that most constituted bodies, from city council to state senate, were on the whole wise and honorable. He was one of the "old" Virginians, in the sense that Virginians themselves used the word—a courtly, kindly man who liked him and often gave him advice. "Your trouble is tryin' to dig too deep," Mr. Nelson often said, "makin' it over-complicated. You're a gentleman and a Southerner by birth and, I think, by instinct, and that's your place. Don't make it any more complicated than you have to. Try to keep it simple—clear—like the lead to a news story. Don't forget you'll be sittin' at this desk some day."

He wondered. It seemed to him that almost every adult he knew had for him a store of advice impossible to follow, virtually all of it designed to have him conform. And he believed this was the common experience of most other young men, until a safe majority of them simply got tired and quit thinking at all. Would he in time go through that mystic process experienced by the thoughtful Southerner wherein his inherent love and his occasional shame for his native region would be resolved, not as one learns to carry brimming pails on each shoulder, but as one achieves a strange synthesis through denial that the pails are there at all and so walks for the rest of his life? Would he someday be sitting at Mr. Nelson's desk getting it all in a convenient capsule from some authoritative source and telling some restless young member of the next generation: "Don't think so much. Accept what I tell you."

Maybe that's the real slogan, he thought, and should be on our every wall, everywhere: "Conform and Survive and Perhaps Be Honored."

He went back out to his own desk and sat down. Abruptly he began writing again:

Men dwarf their own statures. That dehydration of spirit that comes to them—and that may come to me—that convenient surrender of independence for a brief share and stake in the material world and the accepted scheme is the real tragedy. I want to see men, all men, as tall in spirit as buildings. I want them to stand up and cast a shadow. I want to see us all walk with giant strides and speak with voices so sure and strong they move the earth and yet so kindly that the birds weep. But when I look I see dim corporeal entities that come from nowhere, spend some time holding to an odd chaotic truth of a sort and vanish into nothingness. Between what we are and what we could be lies that blank and solid wall of mystery. What puts it there? What is that hiatus, that unbridgable chasm, in each of us and between each other?

The snow sifts down, on me and on the strangers around me. I feel an understanding trying to flow through me, certain of the existence of a profound spirit in all of us, but knowing with all my heart that awful barrier between and within, and so far from being able to level it I feel choked by my own dismal inability and incoherence....

He ripped the sheet out of the typewriter without reading it and dropped it in the bottom left-hand drawer of his desk, on top of perhaps a hundred other such fragments. He rolled another empty sheet into the typewriter and sat looking at it for a long time.

Darkness was filtering into the office now. He thought once of getting up and turning the light on but decided he wanted to sit alone in the dark office. He wrote no more.

When the Town Clock boomed six times he arose, put on his coat and went down the stairs and through the areaway to the street. He stood for a moment in front of the newspaper office, looking up toward the tall clean outline of the Robert E. Lee Hotel, the most impressive physical object in Colonial Springs. Its cornices and uppermost windows lost now in the darkness but still towering over the modest structures around it, the hotel stood aloof and slightly alien, like a prosperous overnight visitor from New York whose casual glance does not rest on the loafers around the railroad station.

The snow was coming down steadily now. A soft crunchy padding had formed on the sidewalk. The fine flakes were swift and cold against his face. He paused in the snow and the night.

I ask for that most improbable of all miracles: that I be permitted to see clearly....

The Soft Step of the Shawnee

Suddenly Red Boward took his brass knuckles out of his pocket, he slipped them over his fingers, banged his right fist into his left palm and said, "I'll fight any man any time I'm crowded."

Red was a restless fellow. Every so often he would take off his hat and run his hands through his coppery hair.

Nobody asked him who he wanted to fight or why. It was a simple declaration of an attitude.

They were passing the raw moonshine whisky around, drinking out of the jar. They had stopped in the warm night, five young Virginians, up on top of Three-Mile Hill. Ahead of them they could see the stars hanging low in the sky over Colonial Springs. They were silent for a time.

It might have been that they were listening, even then. A majority of the men who have their heritage in that solemn empire of mountains that begin in the western part of the state and extend on into West Virginia, Kentucky and Tennessee are lean and cold-eyed. They have a reputation of violence and unpredictability, of shooting or cutting quickly, without word or reason. But they are a quiet people, a slow-spoken and ordinarily a soft-spoken people, and they have a peculiar trait. A man may be talking to you. Suddenly he will pause and listen curiously; he will cock his head as if to hear a distant sound, as if trying to catch the echo of a lost destiny, before he goes on with what he was saying.

"Just one more little touch," said Ruffin Glendye, and he took the jar and drank again.

The modern highway on which they were parked traversed not only land and space but time and history. Its course had been established by roaming Shawnees, Cherokees and Catawbas. The great hunters, explorers and Indian fighters picked their way westward over it when it was a dim trail. The settlers came. A century passed. The trail became a stage and wagon road. Descendants of the pioneers traveled over it in the ragged armies of Jeb Stuart and General J. E. Johnston.

At the exact spot where they had stopped, their grandfathers and great-uncles had fought a Civil War skirmish under Stonewall Jackson, against a force under General Milroy. The site was now an apple orchard; it was the time of year when young green apples were hanging on the trees. Their headlights shone directly on a state highway marker telling them that their ancestors, although outnumbered nine to one and weary from a long march, had won.

"We done drank enough now," said Tall Bill McManaway, and he screwed the top back on the jar of whisky and put it away.

They started on down toward the city. Through the heavy summer night, passing banks and fences thick with tangled honeysuckle, they clattered along that historic road in Dewey McManaway's fast, red-wheeled, broken-mufflered Ford and threw back their heads and lifted their voices and sang "Red Wing."

> " '... She longed for her brave's
> return—
> Thuh heart of Red Wing yearned...' "

Tall Bill carried the lead. He had a good steady baritone. He was a great, tall, freckle-necked man with wild eyes—a man of dignity and honor. He was wearing an Army tunic that the proprietor of a second-hand store in Colonial Springs had sold him and it was three inches too short in the sleeves. He sat on the back seat, stiff and straight in the short Army tunic, the hair growing long behind his ears, his voice booming out the lead to that old ballad.

All of them except Tall Bill lived in the village of Cherry Glen, out in the foothills. There was a restlessness about all young villagers. They could not loaf around the stores or the porch of the County Bank without scuffling and wrestling. Dewey McManaway would suddenly get a peculiar, faraway look in his eyes and climb in his Ford and race down to the high school and back with his exhaust barking and banging so loud it would wake up half the people in the village. He would drive as fast as the car would go, as if he were trying to make it fly away. He might do that two or three times during the evening without a word of explanation.

They rattled into town, pulled into a free parking lot on Central Avenue and debated what they were going to do.

"Let's go see that Western picture down at the Strand Theayter," said Tall Bill, who was not like the rest of them. He still lived up in a place called Jerkumtight Hollow. Despite the wildness of his eyes he was a calm man. Now and then he worked in a sawmill and sometimes he made a little liquor or worked on a rock crusher. He had made the whisky they were drinking. But most of the time he went around over the slopes of the Shenandoah with a rifle in his hand, hunting squirrels or wild turkey; it takes a good calm man to kill a wild turkey with a rifle. They voted him down on the movie. They knew that calmness of his would keep him sitting through all three shows of the same picture. The rest of them knew what they would eventually do anyway, what they had come to town for. They were just going through the motions of pretending they had a choice.

"Ah'd like to shoot me some pool," said Ruffin Glendye.

They agreed to that and started for Appler's Poolroom. Stores were open for the Saturday-night country trade. They walked along under flashing neon signs. Tall Bill and Ruffin Glendye were walking side by side in front of the others. Tall Bill might have been keeping an eye on Ruffin. Ruffin had that restless undercurrent too, but you had to look sharp to find it. He was a small man. He hardly came up to Tall Bill's shoulders and he weighed less than a hundred and thirty pounds. But he had big bony wrists, and if you ran your fingers over his knuckles it was like feeling the knots on an oak tree. His whole body was bony and hard. He was a fighter and he was unpredictable.

But to talk to him you would not know it. He had a soft, drawling voice. In conversation he would be likely to agree with everything you said and he would be grinning all the time and even as he talked to you so amicably he was holding something back, probably planning an act of revenge. It was an unexplainable thing in his nature, like the way Dewey would silently climb in his Ford and race up and down through the village as if he were trying to attain flight.

Appler's was chock-full of Gatemyers, Lowhatters and Dowdyshells—big clans that populated the mountains and foothills and spread out over the county and even, in drab, bootlegging homes, to the outskirts of the town. They were ill-humored and furtive men, some of them always in jail or at the State Farm or in the penitentiary. They had taken every pool table and more of them were lined up against the walls, waiting for one to be available. The village boys went out of Applers' and walked down to Main Street. They stood around on the corner under the Town Clock over Hoy's Department Store.

The sidewalks of Main Street were jammed with the Saturday-night parade of country folk, people like themselves. There was something raw and beautiful about it. Mountain country has a great somber loneliness. The winters are especially lonely. You live there in country like that. Your neighbors are few. Once in a while, in that great dead winter stillness, you hear a solitary crow cawing and you go to the window and watch its fugitive flight across the dull sky. The snow drifts high in the hollows there. And when the warmth of summer finally does come, you feel the need to go out and be among people.

Now they had come to swarm into the ten-cent stores, the hardware stores and notions stores, the Strand and the Colonial movie houses, to parade along the streets, to look and see, to get a little excited and possibly a little drunk, to give expression to something elemental. They lined up two or three deep in front of the plate-glass store windows, some still wearing their overalls and others changed into their blue serge suits. The sidewalk bulged with people walking on one another's heels. Men yelled at one another: "Hi, Charlie! Whur's ol' Cephus at?" They surged through the main street of the town, up to the foot of Wine Jug Hill, the Negro section, and turned there and came back again, country-mannered, out of place, without urban spit and polish and knowing it and being self-conscious about it.

The boys stood, scuffing their shoes on the pavement or leaning back against the plate glass of Hoy's, descendants of those early explorers and settlers and Confederate soldiers, standing first on heel and then on toe and then flat-footed, restless, shifting about. Red Boward took off his hat and slid his fingers through his coppery hair.

"Let's go out on Jitney Street," he said.

He was referring to a section of cheap houses and cheap women. Red was terrible about women. When he talked about them he got excited. His face became as red as his hair. The rest refused to go. They still pretended they could not decide what to do. There was a kind of vestibule to Hoy's, and all of them except Tall Bill stepped in there and sang a few more verses of "Red Wing," low and just for their own amusement. Tall Bill would have no part of it. He did not think it proper to be singing in town; he was a real gentleman. Even the rest of them soon stopped singing; it didn't sound right.

Tall Bill knew what loneliness was. He lived entirely alone in a shanty on a high shale bank of the Little Bull River, thirty miles from a railroad and five miles from a country store. Now the excitement of all the people and the movement had gone to his head slightly. He stood towering above the others and looking around with great reverence. He had tremendous hands, the biggest hands you ever saw. He could not decide what to do with them. He would put them in his pockets and take them out again. He wanted to pay a tribute to the town, to say something memorable. He probably knew no more than five hundred words and could rarely link a dozen of that number into an understandable sentence, and he must have been slowly forming his words of tribute all the time he was standing there.

"This here," Tall Bill finally said, "is the damnedest crowdedest town I ever been in."

His brother Dewey said, "This's the *only* town you ever been in."

That was smart-alecky and a lie. Dewey did not have that backbone of strength and substance his brother had. They had both been raised in Jerkumtight Hollow. Dewey had come to Cherry Glen and hung around Bruce Kyle's garage until he had become a fair mechanic. But he was neither steady nor dependable. Once he got money enough to buy his car he would not stay on a job. He had driven a taxi in Staunton. He had gone to half a dozen places, staying only a short time. It was almost as if he were following the car in whatever vagrant direction it took him.

Tall Bill had come out of the hollow too. He had gone down to Hopewell and worked for about three months in the Du Pont plant. But he had to come back to Jerkumtight. He missed his rifle. He missed the mountains. He had to get back and see the blue-gray haze of autumn rising above the scattered patches of shocked corn on the hillsides. He had to see the yellow leaves falling off the hickory trees and skittering down the steep shale bank into the cold waters of Little Bull River.

Ruffin Glendye was peering up and down the street, that unnatural, metallic, dangerous grin on his face, watching out for a policeman named Rosy Dunlap.

Rosy Dunlap had arrested Ruffin one Saturday night for hanging around on Main Street. He had come up and asked Ruffin what he was doing. Ruffin had said, "Nothin'." He *was* doing nothing except standing on the sidewalk looking across the street at the luscious society girls in Hoge's Drugstore. He had been standing there for two or three hours with his hands in his pockets. Rosy said Ruffin had better come along with him. Ruffin did not know what he was talking about. He put up a terrific battle before Rosy got him to the police station but he never had a chance because the handcuffs were on him and Rosy had whopped him over the head with his billy a time or two before Ruffin even knew what was going on.

"Aw, hell!" Red Boward said finally. "You all know we're goin' down there and fill our bellies with hamburgers. Let's go!"

So they made their way through the crowd down Main to Pete's Hamburger Stand, directly across the street from Hoge's Drugstore. They stood in Pete's little hole-in-the-wall eating hamburgers.

Hoge's, across the street, was where the young swells of Colonial Springs gathered. That was the very fountainhead of all the beautiful girls in creation—brunettes, girls with auburn hair, girls with chestnut hair, redheads, silver and birch and honey blondes. The town was surrounded by a circle of mansions belonging to millionaires who had come down from the North, and these were their daughters or the daughters of rich townspeople who lived up on Society Hill.

The boys gawked across at these delicious college girls in sweaters and kerchiefs. Every one of the girls had that confident don't-care air of rich society people. There must have been fifteen or twenty of them, spotlighted there in Hoge's like actresses on a stage. Sometimes, during the day, you would see them going into Hoge's in sunsuits and playsuits, legs and shoulders and midriffs bare. Often they were barefooted, coming from some private swimming pool or the pool out at the Robert E. Lee Country Club. It looked wonderful over there. It looked like the most inviting place on earth.

The boys ate six or seven hamburgers apiece, washed down with as many Cokes. They gorged themselves until they were stuffed and the sweat was standing out on their faces.

You might say: "Well, if you boys want to go over there and mingle with that high drugstore society, why don't you go?"

They just couldn't. It was beyond them. How do you suppose it would have been if Tall Bill were to walk over there, him wearing that short-sleeved Army tunic and looking around with those wild eyes. Suppose he approached some girl who had been to Sweet Briar or Vassar and said to her, "Miss, I am a man of honor and these boys are my friends who are likewise men of honor and we just want to make your beautiful acquaintance"?

A part of their natures wanted to hobnob with the swells and go to dances at the country club or at the mansions surrounding the town, but they couldn't even bring themselves to go into the same drugstore. And another part of their natures wanted to go back to the very roots of their heritage, to hear the sounds they were always listening for. So they stood in Pete's crowded little joint, choking down one hamburger after another as if they were trying to spite somebody.

Red Boward was bouncing up and down on his toes and heels, that lascivious flush spread over his face. He could not stand still. Dewey was shoving great bites of bun and hamburger into his mouth and staring across the street with that faraway expression that always came into his eyes immediately before he climbed into his Ford and raced barking and banging through the village.

"It looks to me," Ruffin Glendye drawled, grinning, "like them stinkers got us surrounded agin."

There was something in his eyes that did not go with the grin on his lips—a glitter, a coldness and grimness. He was supposed to be a descendant, on his mother's side, of old Edmund Ruffin, who fired the shots at Fort Sumter that started the Civil War. No doubt he was. Old tintypes of Edmund Ruffin showed a coldly furious and indestructible face, like something made out of granite. There was some of that fanatical and indestructible quality in the lean face of Ruffin Glendye.

They went outside, filled with hamburgers and Cokes poured in on top of moonshine. They stood on the pavement. There were not so many people down that way and they still had a good view of the girls through the plate-glass windows of Hoge's. Ruffin started that looking up and down the street again. Red Boward told him he would help him out against Rosy Dunlap if they could catch sight of him and figure out some way of getting him up into one of the alleys.

Ruffin said he didn't need any help and didn't want any help and didn't figure on tricking Rosy up into any alley.

"Ah ain't said Ah was goin' to fight anybody," Ruffin drawled. "But if Ah do Ah'll fight 'em right out on the street in fair view."

Red took out his brass knuckles and tried to get Ruffin to take them.

"Ah don't need nothin' like them neither," Ruffin said. "Ah got all Ah need right here."

He grinned and doubled up his big bony fist and held it up for Red to look at.

Tall Bill McManaway said he wasn't in favor of fighting of any kind there in Colonial Springs in full view of a lot of nice, dressed-up people. There wasn't any room for it besides. Tall Bill said a man needed plenty of moving-about room when he got to fighting.

They were standing there lined up against the front of a clothing store, reverently watching those girls drinking soft drinks and eating fancy ice-cream concoctions. They had never seen such beautiful girls. Every one of them should have been in the movies. They belonged in another world.

Ruffin suddenly moved away from the others and before they were aware of his purpose he was across the street and down the next block, following after Rosy Dunlap like a grinning bird dog.

Rosy stopped just as Ruffin caught up with him and must have asked him what he wanted, thinking he was just someone who needed information, because he never got on guard. Ruffin let go his rocky right fist and flattened Rosy against the side of a building. They were fighting in the shadows but it was possible to follow their movements. Rosy tried to clout Ruffin with his billy. Ruffin jerked it out of his hand and threw it aside. It clattered as it hit the pavement. Ruffin hit him twice more, in the face both times.

Rosy's head and shoulders were back against the building and he was slumping down gradually, trying to get out his gun as he sank. Ruffin made a lunge for the gun and twisted it out of Rosy's hand and gave it a fling out into the street. He straightened up and rocked back on his heels and then his hard body shot forward and that bony fist plunged into Rosy's face with all the force Ruffin could give it. Rosy crumpled on the sidewalk and lay there, and Ruffin started running. He disappeared around the corner in the direction of the railroad station and Jitney Street.

That was the first time the boys had ever seen a uniformed policeman lying on a sidewalk. It was hard to believe such a thing could happen to anyone like that—a policeman or a judge or the president of a bank or the owner of a million dollars. But there lay Rosy Dunlap on the sidewalk. It gave them all the scary feeling that the wrath of authority might suddenly descend on all of them simply for having been with Ruffin.

People were gathering down there and some were trying to get

Rosy to his feet. The boys started up Main Street in the other direction, walking fast.

Dewey walked in front, almost at a trot. Twice he turned and said, "Come on! Let's get the car and get away from here!"

"No, sir," said Tall Bill. "We're not goin' to run anywhere."

Red was walking with that bouncing motion, just behind Dewey, his face flushed. He wanted them all to go over to Jitney Street and look for Ruffin.

"We're not goin' lookin' for Ruffin either," Tall Bill said. "Ruffin's always gettin' into trouble his own self and he'll have to get out of it his own self."

Tall Bill was calm. His calmness was a thing to rally around. They turned off up Central Avenue to Appler's Poolroom.

The poolroom was still chock-full of Gatemyers, Lowhatters and Dowdyshells shooting nine-ball and French pool, and more of them were lined up against the walls, still waiting for tables. The boys pushed through the crowd. Red was bouncing up and down and taking off his hat and running his hands through his hair. That far-off look had come back into Dewey's eyes; he wanted to get back to his car, the same way a hungry man wants to eat.

Some fellow came in the front door with the news and he had it all wrong. He said three men had jumped on Big Bill Collins, the motorcycle cop, and beaten him up. Men stopped shooting pool to get all the erroneous details. It was understood that the whole police force was out scouring the town for a bunch from one of the hollows in the Blue Ridge.

At a table nearby four Gatemyers laid down their cue sticks to go out and see what they could learn; they thought some of their kin were mixed up in it. Red Boward and Chipmunk Lowhatter jumped for the empty table at the same instant and Red beat him to the light cord and Chipmunk tromped on Red's foot and Red slapped him with his open hand, *kersmack!* Chipmunk's burly brother, Bob, let out a growl and rushed at Red with his head lowered and his stubby arms outstretched. Red had his brass knuckles on by that time and came down on the top of Bob's head and Bob plopped to the floor.

Chipmunk was kicking at Red and cursing at the top of his voice and more of their crowd came pushing up to see what had happened and then the men who worked in the poolroom—Pat Sutton and Roger Bagby and Appler himself—came running back from the front with cue sticks and pool-ball racks in their hands and ordered everybody to break it up and get outside if they wanted to fight.

The boys went, a dozen Lowhatters and Dowdyshells of all sizes and descriptions surging along behind them like a wave. Red Boward and one of the Lowhatters were shoving each other. There was some more shoving going on, more in earnest all the time. It was hard to tell what was going to happen.

Suddenly that towering, dignified Bill McManaway reared back and announced: "I won't fight nobody in this nice town. But come out along the big road and I'll fight the whole crowd!"

One of those cursing Dowdyshells yelled out, "Whur yuh wanta fight at?"

"Out there on Three-Mile Hill where my granddaddy and Stonewall Jackson whupped them damyankees at," said Tall Bill.

And the boys started walking, grouped around Tall Bill, going kitty-cornered across the street toward the parking lot where they had left the car. They all felt fine suddenly, not knowing why, not knowing that every great restless force must find something on which to expend itself.

There was a certain epic quality about that ride out of Colonial Springs and along that historic road. No one spoke a word. They did not even drink any of the whisky. They were headed in the direction of the mountain country where savage fights had taken place between white men and red men. They were traveling exactly the same path the Indians had used as a trail, over which stagecoaches had passed, over which their ancestors had walked in the tattered armies of the Confederacy.

Dewey bent over the wheel of that loud-mufflered Ford, giving it everything it would take on the straightaway and around the turns. Red Boward was sitting beside him, half turned, looking back, his brass knuckles on again now, nervous, alert, ready to meet all comers. Tall Bill was sitting stiff-backed on the rear seat, saying nothing and ignoring the cursing tribe in the three cars that were following.

As they rode along perhaps they had a faint understanding of what young fellows like them from the mountains were always listening for: the old soft step of the Shawnees and Cherokees; listening in a day when their destiny was already over and done, listening for an old lost thing and hearing only the step of those barefooted blondes and brunettes of Colonial Springs—the one as far from them as the other.

Dewey drove as if he were trying to fly out of the present, as if he were answering a deep and unnamable force within him. He went around a sharp turn on two wheels, the car rocking wildly and the tires screeching. The waterworks whizzed past. For a mile or two they were leaving the other cars behind. And then as they started roaring up the long grade of Three-Mile Hill the engine began missing some and they were losing speed and those behind were gaining. Dewey gripped the wheel as if he were impaled upon it.

They whipped on up to the top of the hill and Tall Bill yelled at Dewey, "Hey! Here's where I intend to stop and fight 'em at!"

But instead of stopping, Dewey bounced off the highway in a fast turn that sent the gravel flying and bumped down a lane through the apple orchard that had been a battleground—where Stonewall Jackson's men had defeated General Milroy's men—and then began weaving in and out of rows of apple trees until they reached a hillside clearing behind a mammoth blackberry patch and there Dewey cut off the lights and the motor, a full mile and a half from the highway. The Dowdyshells and Lowhatters could not have found the spot with a compass.

Tall Bill sat there looking in outrage at the back of his brother's head and said, "Damn your cowardly hide anyway!"

Dewey said nothing. He had no words with which to explain that inscrutable quality which, like the quality in each of the others, sought expression in its own way. He simply sat there hunched over in the seat of the car without which he seemed to lack purpose or individuality.

They heard Rib Lowhatter's car, full of his brothers and cousins, and just behind it another car bulging with Dowdyshells, with their pocketknives and rocks and whatever else they had stopped to collect, grinding up a distant hill and racing on down the other side.

"Damn you!" Tall Bill McManaway said again to the back of his silent brother's neck. "I told 'em I'd fight 'em! I give 'em my word!"

That crowd roared a mile or so up the road. Then the noise faded as they must have turned and gone back toward town, bragging and cursing, to shoot more pool.

Tall Bill sat there for a long time studying the back of his brother Dewey's head. Then he reached over and took him by both shoulders with his enormous hands and lifted him and climbed out of the car with him and started threshing him up and down on the ground like somebody beating a rug.

Red piled out and tried to hold on to Tall Bill and tame him down, and he'd stop a minute and shake Red off and then go ahead whopping Dewey up and down on that hallowed soil and, even as he did so, it seemed he would pause and lift his head as if seeking to hear a remote sound—a faint, fragile echo.

↬ A Part of the Town

OLD BERNIE PRICE was alone in the city room of the Colonial Springs *Evening Star*, sitting awkwardly on a high stool before a mechanical wreckage that served him as a typewriter. It was about five o'clock of a raw, blowy Saturday afternoon in November; the office was cold and Bernie had on his threadbare overcoat, with a plaid muffler around his neck. The telephone was jangling persistently and he was trying to ignore it. He had the day's edition of the *Star* spread out on his cluttered desk and was pecking out space-rate obituaries for the Richmond, Charleston and Pittsburgh morning papers.

He finally turned, made a long reach toward the other reporter's desk, got the telephone, and said into the mouthpiece, "*Star*. Price speakin'."

"Bernie!" a voice growled. "This is Diggs Harris."

"On my way up there now!" Bernie babbled. "Just leavin'."

"If you don't pay me that eight dollars," Diggs said solemnly, "I swear, Bernie, I'm goin' to beat hell out of you!"

"See you in five minutes, Diggs!" Bernie chattered. "Wait right there!"

He replaced the telephone and resolved to avoid Diggs until he cooled off. Diggs was a brawny man who worked in the baggage room at the railroad station. Bernie had borrowed the money from him the day the power company cut off his lights the previous winter.

He returned to typing the obituaries. He copied the notices verbatim except for the insertion of such words as "prominent" or "well-known" after the names of each of the deceased, so that when the items appeared in the metropolitan journals an obscure backwoods preacher was identified as "an eminent churchman" and a madam from Jitney Street became "a useful and beloved citizen." Sometimes he even got by with his favorite expression—"noted housewife and mother."

Again the telephone was ringing—long and relentlessly. When Bernie was satisfied that only his wife Agnyss could have that much persistence, he answered it—at the same time grabbing a pencil and a sheet of paper.

Agnyss started rattling off the list of things to bring home almost before he had the receiver to his ear.

She wanted French bread—two loaves.

"Check," said Bernie.

A dozen oranges. Four lemons. Two large bottles of ginger ale. Artichokes.

"Ain't artichokes kinda high?" Bernie protested.

Agnyss said yes but the Drydens were coming for dinner tomorrow and Tiffy was so fond of artichokes with vinegar-and-oil dressing. And two pounds of sweet potatoes. Not yams. Also meat for supper tonight. And—

"Well, great God, Ag!" Bernie said. "Ain't you even got the meat for tonight?"

Agnyss said how could she when he hadn't left her any money.

Well, Bernie said, he didn't have but sixty cents to his name either. Agnyss said he'd just have to get an advance because she wasn't half through. Bernie stopped making the list.

She was still rattling on when he laid down both pencil and telephone and began looking for a cigarette. He reached automatically into his right overcoat pocket. His hand came in contact with a thick wad of crumpled envelopes. No cigarettes. He investigated the left pocket and found only another massive wad of papers. All of his pockets bulged with papers. People would hardly have recognized Bernie if they had seen him without the papers sticking out of his pockets. Some of the more imaginative residents of Colonial Springs theorized that he carried around all kinds of notes on all kinds of low-down doings and that if the papers were examined there would be discovered and exposed a whole bizarre subterranean life of the town. As a matter of simple fact, every one of the papers was an unpaid bill.

Bernie was still searching for a cigarette, leaning down occasionally toward the telephone on the desk to say "Check!" when the intercom connected with the office of Hoyt Walker, the *Star's* publisher and business manager, buzzed. Bernie hopped over to the apparatus. His movement was spry. He always moved spryly when the intercom snapped out its hornet buzz.

"Yes, Boss?" he called down.

"Been tryin' to get you for two hours," Hoyt said with annoyance.

"Out on a special assignment," said Bernie. He had been across the street, since edition time, playing fifteen-cent poker in a lawyer's office.

"Uncle John is givin' a little dinner party at the hotel this evenin'," Hoyt said. "He wants to know if you'll be sure to cover it."

"I'll take care of it, Boss," Bernie said. "You can count on me."

He found a fairly satisfactory snipe in the ash tray on the other desk, lighted it, and picked up the telephone. His wife was still jabbering.

"—Hoy's Department Store said in their ad they had bed sheets on sale. Maybe you better—"

"Gotta go now! Can't make it for supper!" Bernie cried suddenly, and hung up. So much for Ag.

Finishing his work, he took special envelopes from his desk, stuffed his copy into them, and sealed them. Gathering up the envelopes, he trotted out the door and down the stairs, skittered through the alley, and peered around the building to survey the lay of the land down toward Main Street. It looked clear. He set off.

Bernie had developed a technique of walking that no one understood or even remotely appreciated. He had it down to a fine art. His aging legs in his baggy pants went at full tilt in a kind of trot-canter that carried him along at a speed that made it impossible to overtake him and yet, miraculously, left him perfectly balanced to scoot instantly across the street or up an alley, or even whirl all the way around and, without breaking stride, go back in the direction from which he had just come. Occasionally he startled motorists by dashing out into the street and hopping into their moving cars.

Many who witnessed Bernie's elaborate locomotion concluded he was trying to beat a deadline or get to the scene of a disaster. Legs flying, he kept his chin tucked against his collarbone and his head at a peculiar downward slant. His eyes were sharp as a hawk's, and on an ordinary clear day in the level sections of town he could spot a creditor five blocks away.

Creditors sighted from afar presented no problem. It was to escape those who came upon him suddenly—materializing from around corners or springing out of doorways—that he had worked out his unique method of getting from one place to another: spotting an object at the end of the block and then promptly visualizing all of the places in between he could duck into or behind. So, as he now entered the block between the *Star* office and Main, he noted as potential havens a veterinarian's office, four parked cars, one alley, and a pile of empty packing cases left for the trash collector.

He made it to the Tip-Top Cash Grocery without incident. He peered through the misty plate glass to verify an important deduction he had made—that the proprietor, Jim Kilventon, was absent from the store and that the cash register was in the charge of a callow youth already busy with the Saturday country trade. Bernie not only had an uncanny accuracy in gauging the very penny to which he could push his credit, but within the archives of his mind he had filed significant information on the personal habits and idiosyncrasies of every merchant in town, such as the knowledge that at this exact moment Jim Kilventon would be at Dave East's barbershop, getting a fast shave.

He dashed into the bright store, grabbed one of the carts, and scooted through the crowded aisles, snatching packages and cans with less regard for content than for the space of time in which he had to work. A few minutes later, with the inexperienced clerk still bemused by his confident instruction to "mark it down," he came out, laden and triumphant.

Bernie eased through the revolving door into the ornate lobby of the Robert E. Lee Hotel with the bag of groceries in his arms; he left the bag with the cigar-counter girl and put his letters in the mailbox. He was about to take the elevator to the mezzanine when he saw John M. Walker, founder and owner of the *Star*, coming across the lobby with his hand extended in greeting.

"Glad to see you, Bernie," John M. said warmly, with an intimate grip on his forearm. "Glad you could come."

John M. was a lean, white-haired, dignified man who bore few of the marks of his early struggles with the *Star*, when he might pay off an employee with a sack of flour or a bushel of potatoes which had been accepted for a subscription or an ad. It was said around town that John M. today could write a check for four hundred thousand dollars. Always a little scholarly, he had grown mellow since his retirement to his colonial home in the residential section beyond the Fair Grounds.

"Yes, sir, Boss!" Bernie babbled. "Thank you, sir. Thank you."

They started up to the mezzanine, arm in arm. John M. disdained the elevators, choosing to walk up the marble stairs, illustrating the excellent physical shape in which he kept himself with two full eighteen-hole rounds on the country club golf course every day of his life, weather permitting.

Bernie invariably suffered a confusion of mixed emotions in John M.'s presence, compounded primarily of uneasiness and gratitude. The gratitude went all the way back to 1913, the year Bernie quit the *Star* and had his tryout with the morning paper in Washington. In six weeks he was told he could not make the grade in a big city and he had returned to Colonial Springs. That had been the worst period of his life. But John M. had taken him back on the *Star*, with no hard feelings, no cut in salary, right back where he had been and where he knew by then he would always be. And yet he could never quite dismiss from his mind, even now, the notion that John M. might hold it against him for having left the *Star* that time and someday might fire him.

They entered the open French doors of the banquet room. A long banquet table extended down the center of the polished hardwood floor, and standing in groups beneath the portraits of Jefferson and General Lee were Judge Estes, Mayor Fred Baskin, City Attorney Bob Paksett, City Manager Joe Holloway, Police Chief Morrie Cordley, James Aleck Bell of the Chamber of Commerce, and God knows who all.

Bernie was not aware that the dinner had any special significance. He was under the impression it had something to do with Bob Paksett's quiet campaign to become the state's next attorney general.

Colored waiters were passing around trays of bourbon highballs. John M. hung onto Bernie's arm and they joined Mayor Baskin, Paksett and a few others. John M. talked a little golf and Paksett told two of his duller stories.

They were all town boys who had made good. Bernie had known most of them when they were in knee pants. He had watched their progress. He had seen them get a choice piece of real estate, seen them become bank directors, get elected to office, or marry well. And he had seen many of them acquire their money through the simple process of having a relative leave this life, just as some day Hoyt Walker would inherit the *Star*.

Bernie stood uneasily amongst them. Holding his glass, he wanted to put his free hand in one of his pockets, but, because of the profusion of unpaid bills, there was no room. On some he had paid, say, two dollars in January or February of 1936 and a dollar and a quarter in April or October of 1944; some were dated in the 1920's, and one went as far back as 1907. He carried them around with him as a token of good faith, so that if one of his creditors actually collared him on the street he could say: "Got that little matter right here in my pocket! I'll attend to it Tuesday at the latest!"

The soup was brought in. Even when Bernie found himself escorted to a place between John M. and Mayor Fred Baskin at the head of the long table, he still had no idea what the function was all about. He slipped one of the crumpled envelopes out of a pocket and jotted down the names of everyone present except himself, so that he could list them, along with their titles, in the item he would write for the Monday afternoon edition of the *Star*. It was only when John M. stood up—between the fricasseed chicken and the orange sherbet—tapped his water glass with a spoon, and complete silence fell upon the room, and John M. said, "Friends of Bernie Price," that Bernie began to have even a glimmering.

Up to that time, after being sure he had all the names checked, he had been devoting his attention to the fifteen or twenty packages of cigarettes scattered recklessly about the table. He had succeeded in palming a pack of Tareytons and two of Chesterfields and was gauging his chances for some Luckies that were near the edge of Police Chief Morrie Cordley's plate, directly across the table, when John M. began the unexpected speech.

"—I have called you together here," John M. went on, "as a simple token of appreciation to the most loyal employee I ever had—a man who has been with me exactly forty years this month and is now one of the oldest reporters, in point of service, in the state. . . ."

Bernie's face flushed. His Adam's apple suddenly filled his throat. He found it necessary to pick up his water glass and wet his lips. He could not leave his hands on the table. He fingered the sixty cents in his watch pocket with one hand and rubbed his bald patch with the other.

John M. made a fine speech. He reached over and placed his left hand on Bernie's shoulder and let it remain there all the time he was talking. He spoke briefly of some of the major stories Bernie had covered, such as elections, civic campaigns, and the big feed-store fire.

Bernie had never had such a confusion of feelings in his life—embarrassment, gratitude, and a curious nostalgic thing that was like an ache. He wanted to interrupt John M. and remind him that it was not forty years he had been with the *Star*—it was forty-two years. He began with the *Star* in 1909. He was born in 1888 and was twenty-one when he became a reporter. His starting salary had been three dollars a week. John M., with a policy that "you'll grow right along with the paper," had regularly increased his salary a dollar a week every year until it was now forty-five, so that any way you figured it, it came out forty-two years this month.

His mind went back to those early days when he had sped around town on a bicycle—the horse-and-buggy era, before the great wars, a time to which he somehow seemed to have been attuned, before the Northern millionaires came and established their pretentious estates, when only Main Street and Central Avenue were hard-surfaced, when he rode around town on that bicycle, a kind of dashing seriousness to him then, and in his heart a dream of becoming another Pulitzer.

When John M. stopped speaking there was a fine burst of applause and someone shouted, "Yea, Bernie!" Then John M. called on City Manager Joe Holloway. Joe gave Bernie a testimonial to the effect that he knew the City Hall "inside and out," which was not a fortunate reference because it might have included the old boiler down in the basement into which Bernie had once crawled to dodge a process server.

After Joe sat down, Paksett got up and gave his "The Times Are Changing and the South Is Marching Forward" speech. But the keynote of the evening was struck by Fred Baskin, the mayor. In a brief and sincere tribute, Fred said, "Bernie's a part of this town—like the Confederate cannon in front of the courthouse...."

When it came time for Bernie to respond, he rose with a mist before his eyes, and all he could do was swallow his Adam's apple that kept filling his throat. He had it right on the tip of his tongue to remind them he had been with the *Star* forty-two years, but the words just would not come out; he had the notion that to make the correction just then would be an anticlimax, would somehow spoil something for all of them. After a moment, he nervously fingered his wineglass and said:

"I'll be doggoned if I know what to say about all this!"

Again someone shouted "Yea, Bernie!" and every man in the room stood up and drank to Bernie's long life and happiness.

Then, with John M. swinging his hand like a band leader, they sang "For He's a Jolly Good Fellow," fairly lustily, and, while they were still singing, John M. gave a nod to a captain of the waiters.

In a moment the French doors opened again and in came a bus boy with one of the finest sets of matched golf clubs anybody in the room had ever seen.

The fellows crowded around admiring them. John M. had paid real money for those clubs. Lyle Cullin, the manager of the Sport Shop, said to Joe Holloway in a broad stage whisper, "If Bernie ever got in a tight spot, I'd give him a hundred for that set. Cash."

Lyle was probably kidding on the square; he was a man who would take advantage of a good thing when he saw it.

Bernie hardly realized when the party broke up. Soon afterward, and rather abruptly, he heard himself stammering out responses to congratulations and good nights, and then he found himself going down the stairs beside John M., the imposing bag slung awkwardly over his shoulder. For just a moment an unworthy thought plagued him: he had never had a golf club in his hands in his life; the greens fees and the clientele of the Country Club were far too rich for his blood; and if he appeared with an expensive set of clubs among the swarms of his creditors who infested the nine-hole municipal course, he would probably be publicly lynched.

John M. got his hat and coat from the checkroom and Bernie collected his bag of groceries from the cigar-counter girl. They stood out under the marquee together for a minute or two, John M. talking to him in the same sentimental vein that had characterized his speech at the dinner. He wanted Bernie to make use of those clubs. It'd do him a darn' sight of good to get out for a brisk nine holes before going to work.

Again Bernie had it on the tip of his tongue to straighten John M. out as to the year he had begun working for the Star. He knew it was 1909. Somewhere in one of his pockets he had a bill for a bicycle pump, dated July, 1910, from Worthingham's Hardware Store. He had bought the bicycle secondhand from Pete Miller in 1909 and he had so much trouble with flat tires that the following summer he knew he had to have a pump to carry around with him. He wanted to explain all that, but already John M. was shaking hands with him and apologizing for having to run off because of an engagement at the Country Club.

John M. gave him one last pat on the shoulder, bade him a cordial good night, turned up his coat collar, and walked briskly to his Cadillac.

With the golf bag on his shoulder, Bernie set off down Third Street toward Main. A biting drizzle, not quite mist and not quite rain, was coming down from the mountains. He felt the grocery sack getting moist and he knew that every step on the way home he would be afraid that this was the step when it was going to fall apart.

In spite of the weather, a throng of country people crowded Main Street. Bernie made his way along Main to Wine Jug Hill and then headed over to the wooden bridge that crossed the Chesapeake & Ohio railroad tracks. He was in the act of crossing the bridge when there suddenly materialized out of the darkness, not fifteen feet away, the big and brawny form of Diggs Harris.

Bernie moved very fast. He had already sensibly noted that some freight cars stood on the main line directly below him, a drop of only a few feet. With the same desperation with which he had once hopped on a speeding fire truck, he scrambled over the bridge railing. The golf bag went with him automatically. But in the process the sack of groceries disintegrated in his arms and he heard cans and cartons clanking and splattering on the cinders beside the track.

He lighted fairly nimbly on the steel catwalk on top of a freight car. He started gingerly toward the end of the car with the idea of climbing to the ground and taking to his heels down the track. But suddenly the car shuddered and gave a pitching lurch, sending Bernie abruptly to his hands and knees. There was a screeching of steel and an inexorable sense of movement. He crawled to the end of the car, grabbed the iron brake rod and fell flat. The golf bag toppled forward and hung suspended in space between the cars, its strap knifing into his shoulder.

At first all he could do was hold on grimly; in panic he thought fleetingly of Agnyss and the children and grandchildren. He wondered wildly if he were on a manifest freight that might not stop for hundreds of miles, until it got to one of the great cities to the westward—Cincinnati, St. Louis, even San Francisco. He saw lights speeding past. Suddenly an odd but vivid impression seized him: a haunting picture of himself as a young reporter, flying around town on that bicycle, the dream in his heart of becoming another Pulitzer. But it did not seem a memory. It was a bizarre thing, happening all over again in his feelings at this very moment. An unaccountable surge of wild and reckless freedom swept through him and he had an overwhelming impulse to dig great masses of paper from his pockets and let them fly into the wind that whistled past his head, until every pocket was empty to its threadbare lining.

But it was too late. For so long, he knew, it had been too late. A peculiar sound burst from his lips, an involuntary thing, neither moan nor laugh but a little of each.

The sound died away. Already his journey had ended. The train had ground to a halt. Raising his head and looking about dully, he realized he was on a string of cars the switch engine had brought over to the spur track at the furniture factory just outside the city limits. He removed his numbed fingers from the brake rod and climbed shakily down the steel ladder, the golf bag thumping awkwardly behind him. He got his bearings and headed for the lights of a filling station over on the highway beyond the tracks.

Wistfully, he thought of the dinner given in his honor that night. And with a sense of nostalgia and of obstinacy too, he determined he was going to call John M. and remind him that it really had been forty-two years. He walked into the bright glare of lights, and an attendant, lounging in a swivel chair, told him where the phone was. Bernie stood the heavy bag of golf clubs against the wall and got out a nickel before he knew he could not do it after all. John M. was at the Country Club and would be annoyed if he had to come to the phone for so trivial a matter.

He was in the act of picking up the bag again when a thought struck him with a fascinating and pleasant jar: If he were to convert those golf clubs into currency he could have a hundred dollars in cash for the first time in his life. He could go to the bank and get a hundred-dollar bill and carry it in his watch pocket, and if a creditor got him into a really tight spot he could haul out the bill in the absolute certainty that the other would not have change. It would be like having a secret and rather wonderful life preserver that could be used over and over.

He consulted the directory, deposited his nickel, and dialed a number. When a voice answered, he said: "Listen, Lyle. This is Bernie. Don't let this get out, Lyle, but you want to take those clubs off my hands?"

Lyle was jocular and patronizing, but Bernie knew from his tone it was a deal.

"All right, Lyle, but you're goin' to have to give me a hundred and one dollars and fifty cents." He listened a moment. "Well, I'll tell you, Lyle. I've got that hundred earmarked for a special purpose and I need the dollar and a half to settle a bill—for a bicycle pump."

He hung up the receiver, shouldered the clubs, and went out into the biting drizzle. Adjusting the strap for greater comfort, he tucked his chin against his collarbone and set off back toward the town where he wrote mild little items about their births, their appendectomies, their trips, their dented fenders, and their deaths.

✑ Sunday Ice Cream

THE LONG VIRGINIA twilight held on tenuous and indolent and then the heavy boughs of the maples on the Murdocks' hilltop lawn began gathering in the first hues of dusk, like baskets being laden with mellow summer things.

The four of them, the Murdocks and the Goodloes, lounged in big white wooden chairs in the side yard near the outdoor barbecue that still gave off tiny and fitful coils of smoke from fat that had dripped from the steaks.

Cicadas were drumming steadily and now and then a cricket chirped. There was a fragrance of honeysuckle along the stone fence and of early apples fallen in the small and unattended orchard just behind the brick Colonial house that had been built between 1825 and 1830. Below them, the Town Clock stroked off the hour of eight with distinct and cadenced booms and within a few seconds a Sunday evening church bell began tolling; even after it stopped, the notes floated for a while above the streets and rooftops.

"Hunter," Doc Goodloe said, "those steaks were good—veh good. I believe you're gettin' better with steaks all the time."

Doc took a cigar from his breast pocket and bit off the end. He was a big broad-shouldered man who had played halfback for the Cavaliers during his pre-med days at the University. He was still handsome, with an easy and confident manner. Someone had once pointed out his resemblance to the late Edward Stettinius. He wore a brown linen suit that had been tailored in Richmond and even now, away from his practice and with his closest friends, he kept his coat on.

"They certainly were, Hunter," Liz Goodloe said. "They certainly were."

Liz was a supple redhead with arched nostrils and a wide mouth. She wore her hair drawn back tight and knotted and somehow she always looked as if she had a riding horse tethered nearby. She was talkative except when she sat down to play her hard, intensely concentrated game of bridge or, as now, immediately after supper.

"Oh, I don't know," Hunter said, pleased. "If they were it was probably luck. I just happened to have the fire right." He took off his tortoise-shell glasses and wiped them thoroughly with his hand-kerchief. He had a lean, pleasant, sensitive face and iron-gray hair worn short, almost in a crew cut but parted on the left, and he looked more like a jeweler than a lawyer. He had taken off the coat of his Palm Beach suit but still wore a polka-dot bow tie.

"Yes sir," Doc said, almost to himself. "Veh good steaks."

"What would you all like to do?" Mary T asked, her voice effort-less and serene, like her whole manner. She was sitting back, her bare arms as ivory white as the arms of the chair on which they rested: still a striking woman with a lovely and rare complexion and startling eyes so light blue they were sometimes mistaken for gray. Back in her twenties she had had the promise of great beauty, but something had happened—nothing tangible, merely a kind of fixing or determin-ing at a certain point, a refusing to flower beyond that, and then giving over to fleshiness—and she had misssed it. Apparently she knew it, because there was that in her personality, beneath the placidity, that was withdrawn and immovable.

Liz mentioned the dishes.

"Oh, we'll let them go," Mary T said. "Susie'll do them in the mornin'."

"If Susie gets here," Hunter said.

"Does Susie suffer from that Monday mawnin' ailment?" Doc asked.

Mary T smiled, quietly indulgent. "She suffers from *any* mornin' ailment."

"Lord, they *all* do," Liz said.

It was secluded and peaceful, and the dusk was settling down mel-low and impalpable. Hunter and Mary T's place occupied the entire top of the hill, which was the highest in town except for the one, a stone's throw to the west, housing the old Gothic buildings of the Military Academy that had furnished young soldiers for Jubal Early and Jeb Stuart. A driveway wound from the street up through the maples and weeping willows. The property spread over three acres; it was the largest private acreage within the corporate limits and was known as the old General Randolph Holladay place, after Mary T's grandfather. The two-story house, with its high and prominent lo-cation, its six columns and veranda, its polished brass knobs, its green shutters and white trim and, inside, its cherry staircase and original white poplar floors and antique pieces, was well preserved and fairly valuable. Thirty years ago, before the coming of great Northern wealth and the appearance of one mansion after another until there were fifty or sixty in the eastern half of the county, it had been a showplace.

Hunter lit a fresh cigarette from the one he was finishing and spun the old one out onto the lawn. "Do you all feel like television?"

"I'm comf'table to just sit," Doc drawled. He had the peculiarity of speech, common to some Virginians and Marylanders, that gave to all his phrases an odd historical echo, as if not only his tone and inflection but his exact words had been used many times before, on fox hunts and in ballrooms with great sparkling chandeliers.

Liz asked what was on.

"Well there's 'Meet the Press' but I swear I've forgotten the time."

"Oh, it would probably just be some politician," Mary T said tranquilly. "Who wants to go in the house this evenin'? It's so close upstairs."

Doc carefully lit his cigar and waved out the match. "Hunter, you still pitchin' to get that air-conditionin' unit?"

"Still pitchin' but I think I've lost the game. It took me a year to talk her into the TV set. Afraid I'll have to give up on the air conditionin'."

"We like ours fine," Doc said. "It sure he'ps on nights like this."

"I think a modern house should have air conditionin'," Mary T said. "I don't favor it for the older houses."

"Why's that, Mary T?"

"Make fun of me if you want to," Mary T said evenly and quite good-naturedly. "I'll say again I'm sentimental about the graciousness of the old houses as they are."

"This is what we go through all the time," Hunter said. "For my part, the Civil War was over ninety years ago. All the bunk that goes with it, too."

A slight flush overcast the ivory whiteness of Mary T's throat. "I just don't think that's p'ticularly fair."

"All I'm sayin'," Hunter said, "is even if your grandfather did entertain Stonewall Jackson here the confounded old house isn't sacred."

"I don't think of it as a 'confounded old house,'" Mary T said. Though her eyes held a sharp, faintly steely quality, she spoke blandly. "I've simply seen the old families make changes in their homes and then regret it. Somethin' was lost. It's never regained."

"I shouldn't have put it that way," Hunter said, surrendering. "I'm sorry. Anybody feel like a drink? Drink, Doc?"

"Oh, I don't know. I don't 'specially keh for one right now, I don't believe. Relax, man. How many cigarettes you smokin' a day?"

"Too many. A couple of packs."

"I don't preach on the subject but you know chain smokin' don't do you any good."

"I believe I could do with one," Liz said offhandedly.

Hunter turned to her. "Pardon me, Liz? I didn't catch what you were sayin'."

"I said I believe I could stand a small drink about now."

"Yes sir," Doc said with slight mockery, "I spect you could stand one about any time." He laughed lightly and without mirth.

"Sure, Liz." Hunter got up with a lithe movement and went to the portable table that held bourbon, soda water, a pitcher of plain water, ice cubes and sugar. "A little toddy or just fizz water and ice?"

"Just fizz water'll be fine."

Hunter turned to Mary T. "Honey, would you care for one?"

"No, thank you. I wonder why no one drinks juleps any more?"

"Too much trouble to fix, I reckon," Doc said. "I haven't had a julep in years."

"I remember the way father served juleps to his friends," Mary T said. "It seemed like such a nice custom."

"Nobody much keeps up the custom any more," Doc said. "It just died out."

"What did they trade it for?" Mary T asked reasonably. "What did they gain?"

"That I really can't answer," Doc said thoughtfully.

Hunter had poured two drinks and put in ice and charged water. "Sure you won't change your mind, Doc?"

"Not right now," Doc drawled.

Hunter handed one of the drinks to Liz and returned to his chair with the other. He stretched out his legs and crossed his ankles.

"Anything interestin' durin' the week with anybody?" Doc asked.

Hunter shook his head. "Not with me. A few piddlin' cases. I spent three days writin' to the heirs in a hundred-and-fifty-dollar estate. Colored people."

"I'll tell you somethin' interestin' that happened," Liz said, perking up as she sipped her drink. "My husband forbid me to use the telephone. Or is it 'forbade'? I never can remember."

Hunter laughed lightly. "I'll bet that would handicap you right smartly, wouldn't it, Liz?"

"I'm serious," Liz said. "Didn't you, sweetheart?"

"I didn't any such damn' thing," Doc said. "Not that way—and you know it." He too laughed a little.

"What is all this?" Mary T asked, amused.

"He told me I wasn't to answer the telephone."

"All right," Doc said, "you've started it. Now go ahead and tell the rest of it."

"That's all. I'm just not to answer the phone. I'd like to know what's going to happen to my Garden Club and hospital committee work."

"What I told you," Doc said carefully, "was not to answer the phone after you've had a drink before supper."

"It was an order," Liz said. "And I still don't know why."

"Everybody else knows why."

"All right. Why?"

"Because one drink makes you glassy-eyed, that's why."

"I'm glad to know that about myself," Liz said. "I'm *rilly* glad to know that."

"All right, it does," Doc told her flatly. "Take a look at some of those numbers you write down I'm supposed to call. I'll be damned if I'm goin' to have it known all over town that you're an evenin' drunk. You let Edna answer the phone. That's what I pay her for."

"Hunter," Liz said, "do I look glassy-eyed to you?"

"You look charmin' as always," Hunter said. "Charmin'."

"Mary T, am I glassy-eyed?"

"I don't think so," Mary T said placidly. "Doc, you're mistaken."

"All right," Doc said without heat, "I'm mistaken. I still don't want her answerin' the damn' telephone after she's had a drink."

"Well, that's settled." Hunter laughed. Then there was silence, with only the drumming of the cicadas and crickets in the encroaching shadows.

"Would anybody like to have ice cream and peaches?" Mary T asked. "I'd love to have some."

"Sure," Hunter said. "Have we got any?"

"We have peaches in the refrigerator. You'll have to go over and get the ice cream."

"All right. Feel like ridin' downtown, Doc?"

"Sure."

"What kind would you folks like?" Hunter asked.

Doc said any kind would be fine. Liz did not speak.

"Get banana," Mary T said. "They have excellent banana cream at the store this summer." She was referring to the drugstore founded by her father, J. P. Holladay. It was now run by her brother, Stewart.

"I thought I'd just go down to the Tastee Saucer this time," Hunter said. "It's a lot closer."

Two faint vertical lines started to gather on Mary T's white forehead, then disappeared. "Oh, for a minute," she said, "I thought you were serious."

"I am serious. Why? It's hard to park over there on Main, Sunday evenin's."

The slight frown gathered a second time. "I still don't think you're serious. We've never bought ice cream anywhere else. Is he serious, Doc? Sometimes you can tell when I can't."

"I can't see his handsome face," Doc said. "Man, are you serious about gettin' your ice cream anywhere else except The Store?"

"I don't believe I could *eat* any other kind of ice cream after all these years," Mary T said.

Hunter was looking at her with an expression of mingled protest and annoyance.

"Nah!" Doc said, "he's not serious." He got up with a kind of ponderous fluidity.

Hunter's face suddenly became abstracted, as if he did not give a damn where he bought the ice cream. "Of course I wasn't serious," he said quietly. "Doc, I'll meet you around by the garage. I'll have to get my coat."

"Don't stay long," Mary T called after them.

"I never stay long," Hunter said.

A moment or two later Doc and Hunter met on the other side of the house, both of them now wearing coats, the mark of the professional man and gentleman, without which neither would have appeared on Main Street or on any other street of the town.

"Might as well take my car," Doc said. "It's already out." His car was a dark green Cadillac. In the double garage Hunter had a Buick Century sedan and a Plymouth station wagon.

They got in the Cadillac and Doc started it, backed in a half-turn and drifted easily down the driveway.

"I believe," Hunter said musingly, "that Mary T expects to look out the window some day and see the old General come ridin' up this driveway callin', 'Tell all those rich Yankee scalawags to clear out of this country or I'll set the hounds on 'em.'"

"That gal sho holds the fort, don't she?" Doc laughed.

"With cousins when possible," Hunter said, "and all alone when necessary."

"Let's go fishin'," Doc said wryly.

"Right now? I expect I'd better take home the ice cream first."

"Don't forget and take home that Tastee Saucer brand. Mary T'd be put out."

"She'd be remote—*right* and remote. She'd play a hundred games of solitaire without an expression and without a word."

"Liz said Mary T was disappointed over the State Garden Club, or whatever they call it, not includin' your place in the Garden Week Tour."

Hunter nodded. "I tried to make a kind of joke of it and she said, 'Do you know of any *other* house in the county where five Confederate generals were entertained?' And it was important to her, too."

"Randolph and Holladay are a pretty proud family mixture," Doc said. "Relax, man. Stop holdin' your jaw muscles tight. Open your mouth and relax them."

They followed the street around the lower side of the Military Academy grounds and eventually past Court House Square, with its Confederate cannon and the huge equestrian statue of General Lee. Buckeye trees on the lawn had lost most of their blossom. At the Robert E. Lee Hotel, they turned and drove down Lawyers Row, the one- and two-story brick buildings with deep green shutters and small stoops, where Hunter had his own office. Both sides of Main Street were lined with cars and Doc had to double park while Hunter went into Holladay's.

Hunter asked the girl behind the ornate marble fountain to put him up a quart of banana ice cream. Mary T's brother, Stewart, was off for the day; he and his family were at their summer camp in the mountains. There were only three customers. Most of the young people loafed at Hoge's or Saul's Pharmacy. But tonight they would be at one of the air-conditioned movies or out in the park. The revolving fans in the ceiling made a small lulling noise as they limped around. The store had been a loafing place for seventy-five years for professional and business men and a meeting place for country people. Most of those who still came in had known Mary T's father intimately and some remembered the late years of the General as he walked about the town, erect and dignified, with a cane he did not seem to need.

When the carton of ice cream was ready, Hunter paid the girl, said good night and went out. As he stepped in the car he said, "Doc, let's take a little ride."

"Any p'ticular place or just to take a drive?"

"Out to the park or any place."

"Probably a million cars out there this evenin'. We'll drive by and see, anyway."

They followed Main up Wine Jug Hill, the Negro business section, and then through a residential district with frame houses and maple and elm trees. People were sitting out on their porches.

"Man," Doc said, "what's on your mind?"

"You know I'm devoted to Mary T, don't you, Doc?" Hunter said abruptly. "That I'm very fond of her?"

"Veh fond of her, I know."

Hunter was staring fixedly at the dashboard. "Well," he said, "let me see if I can put it this way. I used to enjoy playin' billiards. She never actually said anything but she just somehow let me know she didn't think it was much of a thing to do. A lawyer shouldn't be in a poolroom. I quit it. Doc, you know what I mean?"

Doc nodded. "Lovely, generous girl, but kind of set in her ways."

"We've driven to Richmond a dozen times and for the last five years I've been wantin' to stop at that Farmin'ton Country Club in Charlottesville and have lunch. Every time, she's had some sound reason why it wasn't practical. That fishin' trip last year. I really had a hard time gettin' away. She let on that she wasn't serious about it, but she *was* —Doc, you know what I'm talkin' about?"

"Strong-minded girl," Doc said.

Hunter fell into silence. He lit a cigarette. Just beyond the Confederate Cemetery, Doc turned right and eased down past the park. The Municipal Band was giving a concert on the edge of the artificial lake and the entrance to the park was jammed with cars.

They skirted the park, following the new road that led out of town through the farmland and apple orchards, and came to the crest of Three-Mile Hill, where a state historical marker commemorated the skirmish between Stonewall Jackson's men and a Northern contingent under General Milroy. They had a view of the Alleghenies then, old and rugged and densely blue now with the first shades of night upon them.

"That was a kind of a preface, wasn't it?" Doc asked. "You were leadin' up to somethin', weren't you?" His tone had become serious, concerned, and masculinely affectionate.

"You know my secretary, don't you?"

"That dark-eyed gal, looks like she's got an extry vertebra in her back?"

"I suppose you could describe her—"

"Don't mean she's bad lookin'. Just unusual. Wears sweaters and flat-heeled shoes? What's her name?"

"Dot Sadler," Hunter said.

Doc gave him a quick sidewise glance. "You all ain't in trouble, are you?"

"Not that way. Definitely not."

"Well then, relax. You're all tensed up."

"I didn't know I showed it."

"It ain't as bad as you think. It ain't disastrous."

"It's serious enough, Doc."

"How old is she?"

"Twenty-six. Exactly twenty years younger than I am."

"This has happened before. Don't let your conscience kill you, man." Doc had lit a fresh cigar as they were driving out Main Street. He reached forward and carefully tapped off the ash into the dashboard tray. "How'd it get started, Hunter?"

"God knows." Hunter was staring fixedly at the windshield. "She came to work for me last summer when Miss Annie left. I thought she was a lovely, quick-smilin' girl but I didn't—Who knows how those things get started, Doc? Who knows! I guess it just grew. I know that durin' the fall term of circuit court I got the notion of havin' her come up and take notes when the case wasn't important enough for a regular court stenographer. I told myself I needed the notes to keep in the files and refresh—Doc, I wasn't really thinkin' about that. The girl has always respected me. I saw it in her eyes. Court is my day in the sun and I had to admit I just wanted her there. I just wanted her to be there."

"Made you young, man. Made you young. That's what a fellow our age has to watch."

"It was more than that. One evenin' this past spring Dot came into my private office with some letters she'd typed. I was standin' at my desk thinkin' about somethin', I don't know what. She'd always called me 'Mr. Murdock.' But as she laid the work on my desk she said, 'You'll want to sign these before you go, Hunter.' Then the whole thing just happened. I think it came to both of us in the same second. . . .'' Hunter had been holding the carton of ice cream awkwardly in his right hand. Now he shifted it to the left and laid his right elbow on the ledge of the open window. "I had taken hold of her arms and we were standin' very close, lookin' into each other's eyes. I kept sayin' to myself, 'I've loved this girl for months and months.' It seemed to me that nothin' else had any importance at all—home, town, career, nothin'—just the kind of knowledge that Dot was in love with me, lookin' at me with tenderness, holdin' out an invitation to a whole new life, and I was sayin' to myself over and over, 'I've loved this girl for months and months.' "

Doc had already switched on the headlights. Farm buildings and the low rolling hills were growing indistinct. The heavy smell of warm hayfields drifted in through the car windows.

"Have you been takin' the girl on trips or anything? Takin' her out out of town?"

"I haven't even been seein' her away from the office. There haven't been any complications like that."

"Don't you think it would be better, then, for everybody, if you let her go?"

"No," Hunter said. "No." In a moment he added, quietly, almost under his breath, "I'd rather take poison."

"Man," Doc said in the same understanding and intimate tone, "you're sufferin'. Like I say, don't let your conscience kill you. It's not that serious." He leaned forward and tapped the cigar ash into the tray again. "You know you'd be a good catch for a young woman. I guess you've thought of that."

"A lot. It's not that simple. Dot doesn't think that way."

"Let me ask you somethin'," Doc said. "What were your ambitions when you were a young sprout? Say about the time we were over't the University and you were throwin' that javelin out on old Lambeth Field."

Hunter stared at the windshield. "To do just about what I've done," he said finally,—"to come back here and build up a good practice and fit in. You know, be respected."

"I was just thinkin' of a thing I read somewhere once that's stuck with me. It was somethin' to the effect: 'Beware the ambitions of thy youth. You may achieve them in middle age.' "

They had come to a concrete bridge over a small river. A narrow

dirt road ran up the riverbank. Doc slowed, pulled off onto the side
road and stopped, leaving the motor running.

Hunter had been perspiring lightly. He set the carton of ice cream
on the floor and took off his glasses. He wiped them carefully with
his handkerchief and put them back on. "You know what really bothers
me, Doc?"

"What?"

"I've taken to goin' down to my office a couple nights a week, sometimes more."

"Meetin' her?"

Hunter began shaking his head slowly. "By myself. I don't do a thing
except sit lookin' up toward the old Court House and that mildewed
cannon and the statue of Lee on the lawn. I look at them—and they
don't mean anything to me, don't hold me or impress me—I'm not
sayin' this well, Doc." He kept shaking his head. "I mean I feel free
of things that've been so much a part of my life they're second nature
—landmarks, traditions . . . I'm not makin' much sense, I guess.
Anyway, I sit there like somebody who's decided to go away, seein'
things that way. Sometimes I can get a trace of the perfume Dot's
been wearin' that day. I can still hear her step about the office. I
believe I'm happier there than I've ever been in my life."

"Let me ask you another thing. What's the worst can come of it?"

"That's easy. She wears those flat-heeled shoes because she walks
a good deal. I know: we've talked. She spends her free time readin',
listenin' to records and takin' walks. Unless I make a move, she won't
stay here the rest of her life. This is no place for her. She's young and
realistic. One of these days, a few months, a year or so from now,
she'll make up her mind to go to a city—Washington, New York. And
then some evenin' I'll be sittin' in my office alone, with the years
creepin' up on me. That'll be the thing that's goin' to be hard to stand."

"Well, man," Doc said soberly, "there's only one thing I can tell
you and you know that already. I don't believe you're goin' to do
anything about it. If a man's goin' to do somethin' drastic, he don't
talk it out with anybody. He just does it." He reached over and gave
Hunter's knee a shake. "It would be too complicated, man. Too complicated. We been gettin' ice cream at the store ever since we were
kids. We ain't goin' to change now. It would just be too damn' hard
to explain. By the way, how's our ice cream doin'? "

Hunter felt the package. "Gettin' a little soft. It'll hold out, though.
We'll have to get on back. Is this dashboard clock right?"

"Hell, no," Doc said. "Did you ever see one that was?" He brought his wrist watch up to the light. "Quarter of nine."

He backed the car out onto the highway, turned, and shifted to the forward gear. He pressed the accelerator and the Cadillac lengthened its confident stride and soon they had reentered the town limits.

"Hunter," Doc said just before they started up the winding driveway to the old house, "get out on the golf course whenever you can. Let's really start makin' some plans for that fishin' trip. It just might do you a lot of good. The idea is to get your mind off that whole matter we were talkin' about."

"That's probably the whole idea," Hunter agreed absently.

"Just one more thing I can say to you. There's not any final and absolute woman."

"That's somethin', " Hunter said quietly, "I may always have to wonder about."

They drove on up and parked under the old maples, laden now with the heavy softness of night.

As they walked on around the rear of the house Mary T called out tranquilly, "Well, you *did* get back, didn't you?"

As they approached, Liz asked hoarsely, "Did you all meet a couple of blond nurses and give them a lift to the hospital?"

"No," Doc said, "we didn't meet a couple of blond nurses and give them a lift to the hospital. Did I get a call?"

"I wouldn't know," Liz said. "I'm not allowed to answer the phone."

"There weren't any calls," Mary T said, accepting the carton of ice cream from Hunter. "Doc, I believe Liz really is a little suspicious of you."

"I know nurses," Liz said.

"I know nurses too," Doc said flatly. "They're just like anybody else. Mary T, you don't get these wild ideas about Hunter, do you, every time he steps out of the house?"

Mary T took hold of Hunter's forearm and gave it a light squeeze. "I've never been doubtful of you, have I, dear?"

"No," Hunter said, letting his hand rest on her white shoulder, "I don't think so."

"Veh sensible girl," Doc said. "Veh sensible."

A Happy Story When Seen Backwards

HE MADE HIS WAY through the door and onto the steaming sidewalk. On up the street, through the blistering heat of the afternoon, he walked with his father in his arms. He walked blindly but steadily, making his way among the people coming toward him. Tears glistened in his eyes but his mouth was a straight hard compression of stubbornness and pride. He turned up Nag Alley with his burden, people now stopping to gawk after them, and reached the place where he kept his car parked. With a good deal of effort he managed to get his father onto the back seat. Then he himself got in the front seat and drove away. The tears still flowed, half blinding him, but his mouth remained fixed in that firm stubbornness and pride that was his only refuge. He drove up the street, across Main, on out toward the little house with the locust trees in the yard. He crossed over the city limits just as the Town Clock on Hoy's Department Store boomed the quarter-hour. . . .

It was August, and a blazing hot Saturday. A good many of the townsmen—lawyers, salesmen, clerks, merchants—were wearing seersucker and white linen suits. Country people walked along Main Street in blue serge and gingham with a kind of cautious, reluctant gait and on their faces a disheartened expression as if overcome not primarily by the weather but by a remembrance of everything burdensome that had ever happened to them. Even the traffic seemed to be slower. Filling-station attendants had to be careful not to touch barehanded the hoods of the cars they serviced. The Town Clock slowly intoned noon, each booming stroke riding the hot air for a second or two and then disintegrating into it. A few minutes later Berry Alexander lurched down Central Avenue. He had four or five days' growth of beard and his lips were parched and cracked and his eyes were glazed, as if he could see only a foot or two in front of him. His shirt and pants were dirty and both shoes were untied, the laces flipping along the pavement beside him as he walked.

He turned and stumbled through the double screen doors of Appler's Billiard Parlor and went as straight as he could to one of the chairs against the wall. He sat down, slipping both hands under his legs, sitting on them, and shook his head briskly, almost savagely, several times. On the bridge of his nose was a recent deep cut; before finally clotting, some of the blood had run down over his cheek and dried there.

Games were going on at three of the ten tables. The nearest was a nine-ball game involving a group of six players. Berry's eyes focused on a player named Arch French. He got out of the chair and made it to the table and took Arch by the arm.

"Look, Arch," he said, speaking out of the side of his mouth with a grave, confidential, wheedling huskiness, "I been on one two weeks. You got anything?" His voice sounded like that of a man with chronic laryngitis.

"I swear I ain't got a drop, Berry," Arch said, looking at him. "Wish I did. Man, you're in bad shape!"

"Yeah," Berry said. "Awful!"

Ernie Appler. who ran the place, was an alert, intelligent, rather good-looking Jew who played one of the best games of straight pool in the state and sat around reading good books when business was slow. He was already beside Berry with the palm of one hand in the small of his back urging him toward the door.

"I don't want you in here like this, Berry," he said crisply. "Now go on out." At the same time he quietly pressed a fifty-cent piece into his hand. "Get yourself some soup and get back on your feet."

"Jesus, Ernie, thanks. Much obliged," Berry mumbled, and went out the door.

A nine-ball player shook his head. "That guy's drunk enough booze to float a battleship."

Another said, "I heard he went to give blood one time during the war and when they stuck the needle in him eight pints of pure brandy run out."

A longer story was recalled about his once having persuaded someone with a car to drive him out to old man Hardy Gatemyer's in Jerkumtight Hollow and getting three gallons of moonshine out of Gatemyer by introducing himself as a substantial man from town and then giving him, with elaborate ceremony, a check that was not only worthless to begin with but did not even bear the name of either man since he convinced Gatemyer that a signature was unnecessary as well as being certain evidence to the authorities that they had been dealing in illegal whisky.

"I understand that boy of his won't have nothin' to do with him."

"Has he got a boy?" one of the players asked.

"Sure he's got a boy. Works in Worthingham's Hardware."

"Oh yeah. In the army, wasn't he?"

"Yeah, Korea. Named Frank. Whose shot?"

"My shot. I'm goin' to give the nine a ride." Outside, the Town Clock struck the quarter-hour.

When Berry left the poolroom he went directly down Central to Main Street, gripping the half-dollar in his pants pocket. It wasn't enough at the state A.B.C. store either for the cheapest half-pint of whisky or for the bottle of fortified wine. He had already rejected the thought of buying two bottles of beer or ale; they would be like so much soda pop. He needed something with authority.

" 'Lo, Berry! What's doin'?"

He did not even see who had said it. Rounding the Town Clock corner, he headed down Main. At the Five and Ten he entered and stumbled to the counter of medicines and cure-alls. To the girl he said, "Bottle of that rubbin' fluid, please, ma'am." When the girl looked at him questioningly, he added, gasped, "Sprained back. It's about got me." Without more ado she placed the bottle in a smooth paper bag and accepted the half-dollar and rang it up and gave him a single penny in change.

In the doorway of an abandoned store on Central Place, which was a narrowed extension of Central Avenue after it crossed Main at the Town Clock, he screwed off the cap and drank almost exactly one third of the pint. Immediately there was a volcano in his stomach and he thought it was going to come back up. He hoped to Jesus not. If he lost that he did not know what he was going to do. Standing rigid, clutching the bottle, his elbow against wood, his face suddenly aflame and his mouth open in its fight for breath, he beat it back until he knew it had stuck. Then he screwed the cap on the bottle and put it in his pocket and went on down toward Nag Alley. He was walking better. He went through the Alley to Third Street and started up toward his regular hangout, a little snack place with a beer-and-wine license, called Maggie's Lunch Stand, near the C.&O.

Railway Station. It was run by a hard and determined old bat with a gold-toothed daughter who was a floozy without sense enough to make any money out of it, and a son called Clint, who was always worthless and sometimes mean but who was a good dirty middleweight in the boxing matches held every Saturday night in the Armory.

Berry had been hanging out at Maggie's for a long time and for several good reasons: it was one of the few places where he could sit around in the back room in a stupor without being thrown out; it was always good for a couple of beers or glasses of wine, after hours or not; it was almost directly across the street from an A.B.C. store—from the windows he could spot anyone he knew, either well or slightly, coming out of the liquor store with a bottle; and that section of town, the area around the railway station, had nostalgic memories for him. Sometimes, when Berry was sober enough and steady enough to keep from dropping plates and saucers, Maggie let him wash dishes in payment for a glass of cheap wine. And if she saw that his hands were so jerky his fingers threatened to fly off at the joints, she might give him a drink on the cuff, against the time he would be in condition to sweep and mop the floor.

It was about twelve-thirty when he went into Maggie's. There were some lunch customers on the stools at the counter and Maggie was busy at the grill. She was doing all the work herself. The daughter was off God knows where and Clint had been pressured by somebody into a two- or three-day job unloading a couple of boxcars of gallon crocks. Berry went straight to the soft-drink box and had out a coke and was opening it before Maggie turned, saw what was going on and let out a bleat.

"Just a dope, Maggie," Berry rasped. "I'm perished of thirst."

She gave him a hard scowl. "You're goin' to die," she said, and turned back to the griddle.

He went past the doorway curtain and through a back room containing a round table and several chairs and on into the toilet. He debated briefly whether to pour the coke into the alcohol or use it as a chaser and knew he was too shaky to do any pouring. He set the coke on the tank of the stool and got out the other bottle and unscrewed the cap. He braced himself, drank half of what was left, grabbed the coke and drained it. It worked. He put the cap back on the bottle and stuck it into his pocket and left the toilet. He intended going out front and kidding with Maggie and those customers he knew—clerks and drivers for the retail and wholesale stores around there—but when he reached the table in the back room he knew he could go no farther. He flopped into one of the chairs and let his whiskered face fall on the bare table surface. His mouth was open and his breath was coming in uncertain gasps. . . .

He had come from a little farm near the neat village of Cherry Glen out in the foothills of the old Allegheny Mountains that begin there and sprawl almost endlessly on into West Virginia and Kentucky. His mother, a sturdy and patient country woman, a widow, had an unpainted cottage, slightly better than a shanty, with locust trees and a well in the yard. It perched near the top of a long high hill, adjoining the property of a well-to-do orchardist and farmer named Emerson Madison, a State Senator. Berry had an older brother, a steady and hard worker, who hired himself out to the Madisons and became a right-hand man for the Senator's son, who took over the management of the extensive orchards and fields during his father's later years.

Even as a boy, Berry knew he was no good for farm life. The monotony and emptiness of it made him restless and shiftless. On Sunday, when one was dressed up, there was nothing to do but loaf around the porches of the village stores. At night, from the windows of his room, he could see the concentrated pinkish glow reflected in the sky by the lights from the town and it set up within him unreasonable dreams.

One September day when he was twenty years old he was picking apples with an older man. It was hard work and he was not doing his part. He complained to the other man that the rich people of Colonial Springs "drop more money out of their pockets than you or me'll ever put into ours out here." His brother happened to overhear him; out of patience with him already for his constant talk about townspeople, his brother cursed him, calling him scatterbrained and worthless, and told him to get the hell on into town if he thought it was so wonderful. Berry climbed down the ladder and went to the house and put on his good clothes and did go to Colonial Springs, and stayed.

He got a job as a taxi driver. The first time people ever took notice of the lanky, loose-jointed youth with a spontaneous melting grin he stood with a group of his colleagues at the lower end of the station platform, behind the tall spiked iron fence, yelling at arriving train passengers with a kind of good-natured and ingratiating banter, as if each arrival were not a chance traveler but at the very least a distant relative with considerable money, a small portion of which he was entitled to and would accept with grace. He was a little pushing and impudent. To some fashionable Society Hill matron, returning from Richmond or a visit to a daughter at Sweet Briar, it was not beyond him to bawl, "Aw, come on, Cousin, and ride with ole Berry." But his grin was warm and ingenuous and his whole manner deferential and rather personable. He might not engage the lady as his passenger but he was already establishing himself as a town character.

In his taxi he drove around the town like a prince, like a knight in a chariot delivering noble figures to the Robert E. Lee Hotel or out to the Country Club. He got a heady glimpse of rich fast life. The young set had dances at the Country Club and parties at the hotel or in the mansions around the town. Sometimes his taxi was crowded with lovely girls wearing fur coats and big chrysanthemums, returning from football games at the University or Washington and Lee, perfumed and flushed and chattering and always slightly breathless. The town was an exciting place to be. And soon he learned a way or two of making a fast dollar on the side. Traveling salesmen wanted to know certain things—and college students come to town and grown dry and boastful at three o'clock in the morning. Berry was in his element in those days, a fast-moving, grinning young man who knew what was what.

For several years people saw him that way.

Then he met a girl, Norma Wilson, who clerked in Hoy's Department Store. She had good breasts and very white flesh and red Cupid's-bow lips and auburn hair which she parted in the center and let fall to her shoulders. He used to be waiting in his taxi at the Town Clock corner to take her home when she got off work. He took her to the movies and for drives and now and then to a dance. One day they got married. They rented housekeeping rooms on the second floor of an old house on Locust Avenue and bought furniture on the installment plan. Norma became pregnant during their first year of marriage and bore a son, whom they named Frank.

Berry never thought back over those times very much. They had been good and they had been bad. He was proud of the boy. But it was then that his wife began having a series of major illnesses. Soon after the baby's birth she developed phlebitis and for two or three months was a virtual invalid. When finally she was able to move around she had to wear a very long rubber bandage lapped from thigh to ankle on her left leg. And then she began to lose weight and became so nervous that at the least provocation she would burst out crying and her whole body would tremble. Berry never quite knew when he really started drinking hard. Sometimes, after the state liquor stores had closed, his fares wanted to buy whisky or to be taken to a joint where they could get home brew. At first infrequently, and then more and more often, he began drinking with his customers or by himself.

The doctors found that his wife's trouble came from a thyroid condition, what was called an inward goiter. She had to be in the hospital two weeks before they could build her up sufficiently to operate. But the operation was successful and for a while after that she seemed to be all right. It was hard financial sledding for Berry—hospital bills and doctors' bills piled on top of furniture payments and groceries—and his drinking didn't help the situation any. He admitted that. But somehow he had gotten started and when he had a few drinks in him he could keep his troubles from bothering him. And then, when the boy was three years old, Berry's wife suddenly became gravely ill, something to do with one of her ovarian tubes. Again she was carried to the operating table and the second day after that, about ten o'clock one morning, without arousing from a coma, she died.

Berry's mother, out on the little farm, took the boy to raise. For the next several years Berry still drove a taxi. People would see him with the other drivers along the railway station platform or meeting buses or hauling fares about the city. But something had gone out of him. His grin came back but there was no spontaneity to it; it was as if he grinned because he thought it was expected of him. His movements were jerky and his voice had taken on a chronic huskiness. He had a cheap little room at the foot of Wine Jug Hill and he had made Maggie's place his hangout by now and his companions were the other town ne'er-do-wells—the bums and the police characters. Still he tried, in a sense, to stand up to life. Out in the country his son was growing up. He made it a practice to get out and see him at least every other week. After the boy came of school age, Berry arranged to have him come into town now and then and spend a Saturday night with him. The boy was clean-cut, untalkative, self-possessed and stubborn. Berry would take him to supper at a cheap restaurant and then to a movie and would buy him a couple of comic books. They would walk along Main Street or Third Street while the boy concentrated on things in the store windows. Berry could not carry on much of a conversation with him and never really knew what interested him.

Berry would say, "Frank, you like comin' in here and visitin' your old dad?"

"Sure," the boy would say.

"Would you like to come in here and stay all the time?" Berry asked him once.

"Of course," the boy said, "if you stop drinkin'."

Snapping his fingers as if it had just occurred to him for the first time, Berry said: "Frank, I'm goin' to quit! I'm goin' to make a home for just you and me. How's that?"

"Fine," the boy said, "if you'll just do it."

One Saturday when Frank was nine he came into town and up to his father's room and found him sprawled out on his bed, all his clothes on, two empty wine bottles lying on the floor, unaware of the time or the day or anything else. The boy compressed his lips and walked down the stairs and back along Main Street and out Central Avenue. On past the outskirts of town he walked. Some people from Cherry Glen, on their way home, passed in a car and recognized him. They stopped and called to him and tried to get him to accept a lift. He would not look at them. He would not speak. He did not even shake his head. He simply kept walking, along the side of the road, with that hard proud stubbornness. He walked the full ten miles back to his grandmother's little house with the locust trees in the yard.

In the years that followed, Berry still tried to stand up to life. He did everything: drove a laundry truck and a cleaner's delivery wagon; racked balls in a poolroom; set up duckpins; read water meters; worked in a bakery—countless things. Time and again he went on the wagon, and invariably fell off. He lost one job after another until he was virtually blacklisted from any kind of work that required a semblance of responsibility. He loafed around a run-down hotel on Ethel Street where the town drunks holed up. He cadged drinks. He panhandled college boys for enough money to get a bottle of fortified wine and drank it in a smelly toilet. Sometimes he made his way, at night, to his lonely room so blind drunk that in rounding corners he ran into the hard edges of buildings. He often had a cut cheek, skinned nose or blackened eye. But he did not fall down. He might reel around the streets, but in some tenacious part of his nature it must have seemed of great importance that he not fall prostrate in the town for which he had left his home.

Even at his worst he remembered the boy. "By God, I'm goin' to be sober on Saturday!" he would croak to an alcoholic pal. "That kid of mine's liable to come in here and he ain't goin' to catch me drunk!"

Most of the time, out on the farm and in the village where he went to high school, the boy acted as if he had no father. He never spoke of him. He was untalkative anyway and his stubbornness grew more severe as he matured. A year or so after he finished high school he got a job in Worthingham's Hardware Store. He had acquired a car by then and he drove back and forth every day. He was well thought of by the Worthingham people. Once in a while he met his father on the street, saw him gradually developing into shabbiness and ludicrousness. For a while he tried to get Berry to go back out to the country to live and to give up boozing. Berry made and then promptly violated one promise after another. The boy must have been a little sick, too, in his own quiet stubborn way. Twice Berry came into the hardware store trying to get money from him and Frank gave him an explosive tongue-lashing and swore he would never speak to him again. Another time he ran into Berry down in Nag Alley, drunk and in his stocking feet. He had lost or traded his shoes for wine. The boy got hold of him and literally forced him to his room and locked him in.

Inexplicably, Berry had been cold sober the night Frank left for Camp Lee after being drafted. They had taken a long walk together, out in the direction of the old Fair Grounds, the boy lithe and straight and serious. And the gentle, somnolent evening had held something of importance for each of them.

Afterwards, Berry had sworn, crossing his heart and hoping to drop dead before he reached the next intersection, that he was not going to drink a drop all the time Frank was in the service. And the next night, the boy gone now, straight and courageous and a little scared, but gone anyway, nineteen and accepting his lot, prepared to think of his father with that ray of hope that distance gives, Berry drank again because there was an inevitable time lapse, a gap, between the moment and the indefinite elusive date when certainly he would be able to stop for good—tomorrow, next week, the first of the month, or Christmas Day at the very latest.

During that first winter when the boy Frank was in Korea, Berry went about wearing an absurd black overcoat whose original owner must have been the tallest man in the county because, as tall as Berry himself was, it flapped down around his ankles. In a pocket somewhere beneath the ridiculous garment he carried a wallet, empty except for two pictures of Frank—one taken when he was just a child and the other showing him in uniform. He pressed upon his cronies the pictures and patted the four letters he had received. "To tell you the truth," he said, "I'm just kind of waitin' around. Minute I get word Frank's hit the States again I'm goin' to quit and nobody'll ever get another drop down me as long as I live." And one unfortunate night he lost overcoat, pictures, letters and high resolution all at one time. . . .

The midday local from Covington came into the station at 12:46. Its noise penetrated to the back room at Maggie's and roused Berry enough to go after the bottle in his pocket. Without opening his eyes, he screwed off the cap and put the bottle to his lips. Big globules of sweat were running over his whiskered cheeks in small but unbroken streams. As the liquid went down his throat, he retched once but controlled it and finished the bottle. Immediately his diaphragm began a spasmodic heaving and he slid forward over the table again, lying on one cheek with both arms extended in a half-curve like a man swimming. The heaving in his chest gave his whole upper body a peculiar hopping motion, as if it were trying to jump away from his legs.

Still without opening his eyes, he began vomiting, twice on the surface of the table and then, moving his head a little, three more times on the floor. After that he kept up a steady dry retching with nothing coming up. When Maggie got a chance she went back to see him, to try to rouse him, but she could neither scold nor shake him into consciousness. About a quarter past the hour one of the customers went back to the toilet, looked at Berry in passing, and turned quickly away with an expression of revulsion.

Maggie's boy Clint came in just before the Town Clock struck two. He was a short, stocky, scowling young man, hungry and in a bad humor. He smelled the sour odor almost as soon as he came in.

"Well, Jesus Christ!" he said. "Jesus Christ!"

He knew where it was coming from and who was responsible. He walked on back toward the rear room, flung the curtain aside and stood looking at Berry in disgust.

"All right," he said, "get your ass up out of that chair and clean up that God-damn' mess!"

All the lunch trade had gone now. Maggie was still behind the counter, scrubbing the grill. "Let him alone," she said. "He'll clean it up when he comes to."

"Let him alone hell! The son of a bitch has been layin' around here half his life and now he's done puked all over the place." He went over to Berry and grabbed him by the shoulder. "I said get your ass off that chair and clean up this mess! Hey!"

He shook him. Berry's head wobbled back and forth but he did not open his eyes. His mouth was agape and the convulsive retching went on even while he was being shaken. It should have been obvious even to Maggie's stupid lout that he was ready to die. It was not.

"Let him alone," Maggie said from the door. "He's sick."

"He'll be a God-damn' sight sicker when I get through with him. Hey, you son of a bitch!"

Clint got a grip on Berry's shirt and hauled him up off the chair. "I'll wake the bastard up!" he said.

He was an in-fighter. Holding Berry half erect with his left hand he threw a short ugly punch into his belly with the right. He hit a second time before Maggie caught his arm. Clint let go then and Berry crumpled like a sack, missing the chair and falling heavily to the floor. Clint stood looking at him for a moment, breathing hard, his eyes bright, then sauntered out front and demanded something to eat.

They could still hear Berry retching.

"You go up there and get Frank," Maggie said.

"What for?"

"Just go get him. Get him to take him somewhere."

"The hell with it," Clint said.

"You listen to me. You go get him."

Clint did go out, not saying whether he would go up to Worthingham's or not. He stood in front of the place a minute, in the August heat, and took out a cigarette and lit it and spun the match toward the street. Presently he idled off up Third, in the direction of Worthingham's. He walked slowly past Court House Square, where loafers sat in the shade along the low stone wall, to Main and turned and continued on. When he got to Worthingham's he stood just outside the door looking in. Frank was waiting on a customer, taking some bolts out of a bin and putting them into a bag and weighing them and dropping a couple back into the bin. When Frank was through Clint stepped inside the store and waited until he caught his eye. He jerked his head and Frank came over. He was tall and well-proportioned and rather good-looking. He was clear-eyed and he wore his brown hair in a crew cut.

"Yeah?"

"You better come on down to Mama's place. Your old man's in pretty bad shape."

"He's been that way before," Frank said, his face stubborn and almost disinterested.

"I mean he's in *real* bad shape. Maybe he oughta go to the hospital or something'."

"What do you want me to do? Tell him to stop drinkin'?"

"No kiddin'," Clint said, "you better come on down there."

Frank turned and walked to the back and spoke for a moment to an older clerk. The other nodded and Frank came back to the front, still wearing his white apron. They started down the street together. Frank walked silently along, his face expressionless, but hard.

"I couldn't get him awake," Clint said.

"Yeah?"

"Jesus, I chunked him a time or two. Still couldn't rouse him."

"What do you mean—chunked him?"

"Well, just chunked him a couple tryin' to get him to wake up. I never hit him hard. Honest to Christ I never."

Frank did not answer or even glance at Clint. They walked on to the intersection of Third, turned off and passed Court House Square where the loafers still sat on the low stone wall. When they reached Maggie's place the front part was empty. They went on back. Maggie was bent over, wiping Berry's mouth with a damp cloth.

"He's quit that retchin'," she said, but her face was stiff with fear and she arose and stepped back out of the way, holding the cloth.

Frank looked down at his father with the same studiously controlled, inscrutable expression, his lips a tight thin line. Then he knelt and shoved his hand flat inside Berry's shirt above the heart. He held the hand there for perhaps ten seconds, as if counting to himself, and then it slid on around under Berry's arm. Then he clutched his father convulsively and sank down over him, sobbing out, in a sort of slow, broken agony, "Oh Pop!—Pop!—Pop!"

He was crumpled there for no more than a dozen seconds. Then he stood, bringing Berry up with him, one arm under his father's knees and the other under his shoulders. Berry's head fell back loosely. Frank began walking, not fast but purposefully. Maggie made way for him at the door, looking at him with wide eyes.

"Where you goin', Frank?"

Frank went walking steadily past her toward the door. Without turning, he said: "I'm goin' to take him home. You all've had him long enough."

⊷ Little Woodrow

DURING THE TIME he was on the state convict road gang he must have spent his shackled evenings poring over a library of detective-story magazines dated a quarter-century ago, and from these he apparently selected both his attire and his attitude toward society. Because he came back dressed as a prohibition-era gangster—in a derby, tight double-breasted black overcoat, doeskin gloves and pearl spats, plus a red shirt and yellow necktie that must have been his own inspiration—like a figure in a wax museum suddenly become animate and determined to revive the role of an undersized villain in a threadbare melodrama everybody else had long since forgotten.

His name was Woodrow. And there he was, after an absence of three years and seven months, on the town again. The police did not quite know whether to consider him merely ridiculous or more dangerous than ever. They saw him walking along Main Street in the George Raft clothes, an air of strut and bravado about him, a kind of stiff, stagy smile on his straight lips, and in his peculiar lemon eyes that look of utter deadliness that has nothing to do with human beings at all—that quality seen in the eyes of the jungle cat, not an expression at all, but a baleful glimmer back through the centuries to the primordial chaos. One of the instructors at the military school, standing one day in Wilmer Bros. Drugstore and seeing him go by, expressed it for the town when he remarked, "I can't decide whether they ought to send him to Hollywood or put him under glass."

He had been sentenced originally, by Judge Estes in circuit court, for felonious assault with a deadly weapon. He was twenty-one at the time and he had been hanging around a run-down motel on the Chapman's Switch road, acting as a kind of volunteer bouncer for the man who ran the place, one of the Gatemyers, who sold whisky at five dollars a pint after state-liquor-store hours. One night while Gatemyer was away, the neighborhood constable, a man sixty years old, wandered onto the premises to borrow a jack to change a flat tire on his car. With a pair of brass knuckles, Woodrow broke his jaw and fractured his skull in three places.

When the case came to trial, the lawyer whom Gatemyer hired entered a plea of temporary insanity for Woodrow and tried to establish that since childhood he had been subject to fits. His father, his mother, five of his brothers, and one sister—hard-working, respectable country people all—were there, sitting in the first row of seats behind the railing that divided kinfolk and curious from accusers and accused, watching him with a kind of uniform stoniness as if they were observing not a son and brother but a freakish hereditary mutation involved in a process neither they nor anyone else understood.

It was an act of deference on the part of Judge Estes toward the rawboned, high-cheeked mother that in any way distinguished the trial from the scores of other mountain-hollow shootings and store-porch cuttings with which the court dealt twelve months out of the year. Just before she was called to testify, the judge had whispered to a deputy, who immediately went upstairs to the sheriff's office and returned with one of the tall brass cuspidors and placed it conveniently near the witness chair. She took the stand: stoical, in a clean flowered gingham dress, like any other country mother with a son in trouble, except that pinned on her breast was America's highest decoration—the Congressional Medal of Honor.

She listened to the defense lawyer's desperate leading questions and ignored them. "Never had a fit in his life," she testified with solemn dignity. "He just gets mean and raves. Don't know why. He was the youngest and puniest but that didn't give him cause. I treated 'em all alike. Never had any pets."

Some of the people in the courtroom recalled her. Most of the town had forgotten that Woodrow ever had a mother, possibly preferring to believe that originally he had simply crawled out of an alley or from under a pool table.

Woodrow's own absurd defense, recited with the cocky and theatrical defiance that marked him even then, was that the constable had made improper advances to one of Gatemyer's cousins, and that he, Woodrow, had used only his fists. He had got five years and he was lucky he did not get the electric chair because it was luck, and pure luck, that the constable had not been killed. Woodrow had intended to kill him and, in fact, thought he was dead when he quit beating him.

Later, in his afternoon rummy game at the Colonial Club, Judge

Estes had remarked, "I believe he's the most vicious little punk I ever had in my court."

Woodrow came back in the early part of November, when farmers out in the country were shucking their corn and hauling the big white and yellow ears into cribs and barns; trees stood leafless and stark on the somber mountains and blue shafts of smoke rose from chimneys into the dull gray sky of late fall. The police remembered the time because it was when Sol Dowdyshell, the biggest man in Colonial Springs, was in jail awaiting trial for the attempted murder of his brother, Harve, in a Saturday-night brawl at their home on Jitney Street.

Harve, who weighed two hundred and fifty pounds and was a fireman on the C.&O. yard engine, came home and found Sol, who weighed three hundred pounds and did little of anything, using his, Harve's, shaving brush. Harve called Sol a pot-gutted slob and accused him of having lice. They were up on the second floor of the house. Sol picked Harve up and threw him out of a closed window; glass, sash, frame and Harve all landed down in the yard, Harve with a broken back.

Their father, old man Jasp Dowdyshell, who in his day had been a moonshiner and still was as mean as either of the sons and tight with his money, went down to the neighborhood grocery, where they had a free telephone, and had the grocer call the police. They put Sol in jail, and the next day old man Jasp showed up at the jail and spent the whole visiting hour standing outside Sol's cell reviling him for breaking the window, until Sol got tired of it and told Paine, the jailer, that if he didn't stop the old man from bothering him he was going to pull down the steel door and fix the old man too.

Paine, who was afraid of Sol and believed he might do it, told Jasp he could not come back again, and the old man spent the next week pestering the police, the commonwealth's attorney, and all the lawyers who would give him any free advice, trying to get somebody to let him swear out a warrant against Sol for housebreaking, claiming a house could be broken from the inside out as well as from the outside in. When Woodrow showed up in town again, Sol was lying in a cell bunk in the state of dull, hippopotamus somnolence that passed for consciousness with him.

For the time being the police forgot about Sol Dowdyshell and turned their mild attention to Woodrow, who seemed to want to make sure they did, because one of his first acts, after coming to town, was to strut into the police station and offer to shake hands. The young desk sergeant, new on the force, did not even know him. Otey Thompson, who had been a plain-clothes man for many years, did shake hands and at the same time, laughing a little, frisked him— patted him on both hip pockets and over the breast of the tight overcoat. Woodrow had no gun on him then; he was at least smart enough for that. He gave his brittle smile and departed. The police did not know whether the object of the visit had been to make peace with them, put them on guard, or was merely another episode in the chronicle of senselessness he had been recording since childhood.

Otey Thompson kept a casual eye on him. Woodrow was staying at a dollar-a-night hotel on Ethel Street that was a hangout for the town drunks, and his baggage consisted of a pocket comb, a dirty handkerchief, and a dozen pulp magazines. He paraded up and down Main Street in the preposterous clothes, going once each day to either the Colonial or the Strand movie house, spending a little time in Appler's Poolroom, where, removing his left glove but not the right one or his overcoat, he shot nine-ball with an air of complete disinterest, as if he had outgrown not only the game but his bootlegger cronies of old pool-hustling days.

About two o'clock each afternoon he would enter an Ethel Street hole-in-the-wall café called Guy's Quick Lunch, order two hamburgers, put all his spare nickels in the juke box and listen to "Mona Lisa" over and over again as he sat at the counter consuming his only food of the day, with his derby, overcoat and gloves on, and following with his lemon eyes the movements of an overblown, sullen blond waitress named Rose, to whom he was obviously paying a queer courtship. Before departing he would leave under his plate a fifty-cent tip designed to impress her but wasted because, never having had anything but trouble from them, she saw all males through a kind of gelatinous distrust and could no more imagine herself being embraced by this one than she could imagine herself in a wrestling match with a snake or a midget.

And then in the crisp cool evenings, when other men were sitting around the drugstores or restaurants comparing notes on the hunting of wild turkeys and pheasants, now in open season, Otey Thompson would see him standing in doorways along one of the downtown streets, a cigarette barely clinging to his lips, like a sinister figure come to watch over the town; say, a member of Murder Incorporated come to hold rendezvous with a colleague.

Then for a little less than two days he vanished. Convinced that not a single drunk around his cheap hotel was worth rolling, and now broke, he had gone home.

Home was a grubby hamlet called Chapman's Switch, eight miles west of town on the Chesapeake and Ohio Railway, in a somber and stunted region of little patch-farms, quarries, sawmills, stumps, brush, hounds, persimmons and whippoorwills. It was a harsh and sterile section always, and at this time of the year all the field and hill color dissolved into a dirty brown; it had over it a quality not only of desolation but of decay, as if the earth there and everything on it were quietly undergoing putrefaction.

The Switch itself consisted of Kincaid's flyspecked general store, the railroad station, and four short rows of boxlike, dun-colored "company houses," occupied by a couple of hundred Negroes and whites, on a denuded hillside that once had grown good yellow pine. It was notable for the incredible nauseous smell that still came from the pits of an old tannery that had burned down years before and to which the so-called houses had once belonged. The most exciting community event was the chattering of the crossing bell heralding the big locomotives as they pounded through the string of tunnels through the Allegheny Mountains.

Woodrow's family lived in a house that had been occupied by the superintendent of the tannery, at the end of the second row above the railroad tracks, and was no different from any of the others except that it was two stories high instead of one. His father, a bustling bowlegged man, owned and ran a quarry and rock crusher around the hill from the store, and the limestone dust from this operation turned everybody who came near it, black and white alike, a kind of uniform gray.

It was said later by someone around the store, which, containing the post office, was the neighborhood gathering place, that as Woodrow came up through the yard in his dandy's costume, six or eight hounds sniffing or barking at him, he was greeted at the front door by his mother, one flicker of hope breaking into her stony face, with the question: "Woodrow, did you get converted?"

It was supposed that she so addressed him under the honest misapprehension that his garb was that of a Holiness preacher, an impression corrected in the next instant by his monosyllabic answer.

Perhaps he expected his return to inject some new quality into the household—respect or astonishment or even terror; if he did have such an expectation he must have forgotten something about them: it was a hard country and they were hard people. They were busy in the certain and constant knowledge that only by digging grimly at the sparse land and what it had to offer could they keep money in the bank and afford the cars, the Sears, Roebuck furniture and the radio that kept them a grade above the Negroes who faced them just across the railroad tracks.

As soon as the mother heard his reply to her question, she turned silently and went back into the kitchen, where she and the daughters and two daughters-in-law were rendering lard and canning sausage and tenderloin from the hogs the father and the other sons were butchering behind the house. Their attitude—the attitude of the whole family—was that he had been in the penitentiary and now he was back and if he behaved himself, which was certainly unlikely, he could stay, and if he didn't behave himself, which was expected, he could go away again.

The greeting given him by his father, George, whose two interests in life were quarrying rocks and hunting foxes, was heard by neighbors. The hounds were baying in a loose chorus by then and one of the other sons glanced up from the butchering and said something about Woodrow being back and the father looked up at him, studied him for a moment with the same curious stare with which he had always looked at him, and said, "That ain't no rig to scald hogs in." George had given him up years ago, anyway.

Woodrow had an armload of his favorite literature with him; so, kicking the dogs aside, he went up to one of the bedrooms and lay down and began reading the detective and gangster stories that were to occupy him virtually all of the time he was there.

Woodrow was the youngest of eleven children. The first two boys, who by this time had drifted away from home and been heard from only intermittently for a while and then not at all, were named Henry and Oscar. When it became obvious to the father that two boys would be of only slight use to him in a quarry, he started in on a fresh batch, giving them such names as Stanwood, Linwood and Elwood out of admiration for a county resident named Stanley L. Wood, who had spent thirty years of his life running unsuccessfully on the Republican ticket for every public office from Trial Justice to State Senator and the rest of it writing windy and sometimes incoherent letters to the two Colonial Springs newspapers.

When George began trying to give the girls such names as Woodbine, his wife stepped in and sensibly called them Pearl, Sarah and Belle, but when the last of the whole lot came along and George was sure he had a champion, one who not only would carry on some vague tradition for himself as well as Stanley L. Wood and the late President Wilson (who had been born in an adjoining county and for whom George also had a contradictory admiration), he came up with a real inspiration: Woodrow.

The mountain country began out where Woodrow grew up. On to the west and southwest were the hollows and ridges where the bulk of the population was made up of big clans named Gatemyer, Lowhatter, Dowdyshell and Shimlette, people who never had enough land, enough money, enough education, love, praise or happiness, who never had enough of anything in their entire lives. When World War II came along, more than twenty-five hundred young men (and some of their sisters) left their plows and trucks and loafing places on store porches and joined another fifteen hundred or so from Colonial Springs and went to fight in places most of them never before knew existed. There were eighty of them named Gatemyer and sixty named Lowhatter, fighting together now, whereas most of their lives they had fought one another.

Stanwood, Linwood and Elwood all went off to war when Woodrow was fourteen. Stanwood and Linwood were in the Navy. Elwood was in an Army infantry outfit. After some two years in camp, during which his immediate superiors tried without success to make a corporal of him, he was sent to England and took part in the D-Day invasion of Omaha Beach.

Elwood's outfit had to make its way across the sand and the shingle under the raking fire of Nazi machine gunners whom the naval bombardment had failed to dislodge from caves and dugouts in the steep cliffs behind the water. They tried three times to make an advance up the vertical heights, and each time they lost men. They were simply pinned there at the foot of the cliff. Elwood, remembering childhood rock battles on the crags around Chapman's Switch, stuck four grenades in his pockets and took his rifle and started up the cliff alone, worming along on his belly when he could and literally hauling himself up by his hands when he had to.

He finally flopped into a kind of ditch that cut across the face of the cliff to the first machine-gun nest and there he let a grenade go. He killed six Germans and captured three and then made those three precede him along the ditch. Then he let his second grenade go.

When he came back down the cliff he had forty-two prisoners, and neither he nor anybody else ever knew exactly how many dead he had left up there. It was not quite as notable as Alvin York's deed, but that was only because there simply weren't that many Germans around.

Shortly thereafter, at the very climax, so to speak, of humanity's most violent paroxysm, Elwood sat down on a crate somewhere near the French coast and wrote a V-mail letter home that began, "Nothing special to write about."

Elsewhere in the letter he did concede that "our bunch had some trouble getting up a kind of a clift and I finally made Corporal." He wrote only one more letter home, a brief one saying it looked like he was going to get to see Germany, which he did. They fought through the hedgerows of France and then on into Germany and there he was shot squarely through the heart as he started with his squad across a river he never knew the name of.

Woodrow got into the Army too, in the early summer of 1945. He went as far as Fort Meade, Maryland. In the language of the loafers around Kincaid's store: "One day they come around and give Woodie a uniform and they says, 'Put it on!' Next day they come around agin and they says, 'Take it off! War's over!' "

Now he sprawled on the bed, reading with enigmatic eyes the literature that gave him the only importance and the only role and niche he had ever found for himself. The family did not tell him he could not stay. They did not tell him anything. One of them yelled at him when it was mealtime and he wandered down to the crowded table. It must have been almost the same as it had been in childhood—the boxlike company house shaking with the passage of each train, the noise of the rock crusher, the dust from the crusher on everything and in everything, the constant odor from the tanbark pits, the busy older brothers not exactly ignoring him but certainly paying no attention to him. Of his childhood he had little memory beyond a vague, jumbled recollection of hounds licking at his face or perhaps biting him, and of being under the front porch as his father and brothers and visiting kinsmen spat tobacco juice down through the knotholes while they talked of fox hunting or quarrying.

At the age of eleven he had taken a crowbar and pried loose the derail from the old spur track running up to the burned-down tannery and placed it on the main line of the railroad for the specific purpose of wrecking the next through passenger train, which it would have done had not one of the brakemen on a freight train taking the sidetrack discovered and removed it. It was through no fault of his own that he had not become a neighborhood and possibly a national celebrity.

So perhaps his memory occasionally wandered from the blood-thirsty glories of the gangster magazines on back into a dim blur of hounds, cornbread, his own outbursts and his attacks on whoever happened to be convenient, and then returned to himself lying on the bed with things in no way different except that when he looked up on top of the dresser he saw photographs of all the brothers in their uniforms, the most prominent being one of Elwood, taken before he went over to a place called France and climbed a cliff and had his brief fling as a corporal until a bullet from the gun of some unknown German killed him.

It was in September, 1945, that the Congressional Medal of Honor was awarded posthumously to Elwood. The presentation was made in the banquet room of the Robert E. Lee Hotel in Colonial Springs before the chairman of the County Board of Supervisors, Mayor Fred Baskin, Judge Estes and a dozen other notables, by a Brigadier General who had come, with his decorations, all the way from the Pentagon in Washington. The whole family was there with the exception of Woodrow, who was in jail serving concurrently three sixty-day terms for illegal possession of and illegal sale of ardent spirits, to wit, a fifth of blended whisky which he had bought at the state liquor store, and for assault upon his after-hours customer who had protested, not that Woodrow was charging him exactly three times what he had paid for the whisky, but that he had diluted one bottle into four.

"A glorious chapter of Old Dominion history," said the Brigadier General to Elwood's mother, "was engraved upon the sea cliffs of France by your heroic son. His valiant deed will dwell forever in the hearts of his grateful fellow citizens and his indomitable spirit will march on in the imperishable company of those great heroes of the world."

The mother was standing before the Brigadier General, her stoical face swelling oddly, the long cheeks puffing out, and then she had out her handkerchief and was holding it over her mouth. Judge Estes, noticing her discomfort, asked one of the town ladies, immediately after the General's speech, to take her to the rest room; and there the town lady, patting her on the shoulder, told her just to go ahead and cry as much as she felt like.

"Cried once about Elwood," was the reply, after she had found what served as a cuspidor. "Cried hard. Not cryin' now. It's my snuff. Had to spit."

Now, not Elwood but Woodrow was back home, lying around reading, getting up only to go to the table and to walk down to Kincaid's store for cigarettes and to plan how best to rob it.

The second night he was home, Saturday, he did rob it. Early in the evening, sauntering into the store, he slipped under his double-breasted overcoat a small steel wrecking bar which the old merchant used to open packing boxes and which made an excellent jimmy. He returned just before closing time and stood waiting in the dark at the back of the railroad station, again like a member of Murder Incorporated and this time the real thing because, across the road, only a decrepit eighty-two-year-old man stood between him and what he wanted and was certain to acquire.

It was a clear crisp night with the stars bright overhead and a skim of frost already beginning to form; in the distance to the south a pack of hounds was running along the slopes of Bull Mountain. He saw the last customers and loafers wander away from the store and watched Kincaid put his receipts in a drawer in a cubbyhole office at the rear of the store, cut off the lights and start out the back door.

Anyone less savage would simply have waited another minute or two until Kincaid finished locking the door and went on down the path along the hill, and then pried off the lock hasp with the jimmy. Not Woodrow; such a comparatively civilized method would not have answered that deep and inscrutable compulsion that had guided him for as long as he had walked by himself. Kincaid was still fumbling with the lock when Woodrow hit him over the head with the wrecking bar. He left Kincaid for dead and, not wanting to bother searching through the old man's pockets for keys, stepped over his slumped and silent form (had he groaned a second time Woodrow would have smashed his skull) and entered the store, pried open the drawer, stuck the ninety-odd dollars in his pocket, went out, stepping over old Kincaid again, and strolled on back home.

That was when he had his first outburst since his return. He walked in on them in the dining room, that served them also as a living room, crowded with the substantial Montgomery Ward and

Sears, Roebuck furniture and decorated with gimcrack trophies from the county fair. He stopped just inside the doorway, watching them with his flat lemon eyes. In warmer weather all of them would have been in Colonial Springs parading up and down Main Street and swarming through the dime and notions stores.

But they were at home, listening to one radio program after another—Stanwood and Linwood and their wives playing poker for matches with two of the girls and two young men who had come calling on them, the father reading the paper, the mother darning socks from a pile on the floor beside her chair, the grandchildren playing some kind of game that kept them scampering under the dining table—nobody excited, nobody doing anything out of the ordinary or expecting anything out of the ordinary, simply spending an evening at home, with that acceptance that had marked most of their lives. Woodrow looked at them and gave a jeering yell: "Just one great big damn' happy family! What the hell you think you're waitin' on?"

They would not even let him pick a quarrel; most of them paid no attention to him. The father glanced up once with that speculative, puzzled look but said nothing and returned to his newspaper. And the mother said only, "Woodrow, if you don't like it here you don't have to stay."

He had not stayed. He went on upstairs and got the keys to Stanwood's new sedan and came back down again and went out. They roused themselves when they heard Stanwood's car starting, but he was gone before they could get out there.

"He's done done somethin' again," the mother said quietly.

The boys got a flashlight and went down toward the station and the store and finally found old man Kincaid still lying beside the back door, groaning now. One of the girls went upstairs to the room Woodrow had been occupying and found nothing amiss except that across the face of Elwood's picture there was savagely scrawled in pencil: *Just Luck—you Jurk.*

He showed up in town the next day, driving Stanwood's car. By then Stanwood and Linwood were scouring the town looking for him. They walked in on him in Guy's Quick Lunch, where he was just beginning his first hamburger and listening to the second playing of "Mona Lisa" while preparing to invite the waitress, Rose, to run away with him to Baltimore.

Linwood walked up behind him and without a word yanked him

off the counter stool, pinned his arms behind him and held him while Stanwood went through his pockets until he found the car keys.

They would certainly have beaten him up had not Stanwood had a sudden and better idea. He pulled off Woodrow's derby, picked up a ketchup bottle from the counter, shook it empty into the derby and then returned the hat to Woodrow's head, jamming it down so hard the brim came off in his hands and was left hanging around Woodrow's neck like a lavaliere. Then Linwood gave him a cracking kick in the rear end and the two of them walked out of the place.

Rose at first thought of running next door and calling the police and would have done so had she not become fascinated by Woodrow's raging struggle to get the brim of the derby from around his neck. He had already lifted off the remainder of the hat and was standing there cursing, ketchup dripping out of his hair and down around his ears. As he tore at the stubborn brim, Rose began to laugh.

She was standing back at the end of the counter, shaking with great torrents of laughter that came and went and came again like gusts of rain in a downpour. Woodrow finally ripped the derby's brim from around his throat and then simply stood, wiping the ketchup from his neck, forehead, ears and eyes, gazing at her with utter ferocity and hatred.

When he had finished wiping himself off, he sat down on a stool and removed his right shoe and took from it the money he had stolen from the store. Then he, too, left. He walked a block and a half down the street and into Worthingham's Hardware Store and bought himself a .32-caliber Smith & Wesson revolver and six shells and paid and went out and started back up the street.

The clerk who had sold him the gun, a man named Lester Omodundro, immediately called the police and told them about the sale.

Woodrow was already shooting when he opened the door of the Quick Lunch. By then Rose had stopped laughing; she had picked up a cloth and was swiping at the counter, her habitual sullen expression back on her face. Woodrow had no expression on his face at all. But when he fired the second time, after she had screamed and was still transfixed at the counter, he had the brittle smile on his lips. She ran into the kitchen, the screams now coming in the same kind of torrents as the laughter had a few moments before, and was trying hysterically to get the back door open when Woodrow appeared in the curtained doorway leading into the kitchen and fired the other four shots as he stood there, the last two after she had fallen.

As he turned and walked on back along the rear of the counter, toward the front, he stopped at the place where he had been eating, hauled a fifty-cent piece out of his pocket and, in imitation of something he had seen in a gangster picture, scudded the coin under his plate as a tip.

At the cash register he changed a quarter into five nickels; then he went over to the juke box and inserted them. He was sitting there, rigid and motionless, listening to "Mona Lisa," when the police car lurched to a stop outside.

So, for the third time in his life, he had left a human being for dead as a result of violence at his hands. He still believed her dead, apparently, when they took him to the jail and put him in the cell with Sol Dowdyshell, who lay in his bunk, looking at him in dull dislike as Woodrow walked stiffly about the cell in the preposterous clothes, telling Sol: "I bumped a couple of 'em off out there. The paper'll be full of it."

They delivered two copies of the *Evening Star* at the jail for those inmates who could read; and Sol Dowdyshell, the most important prisoner in the place at the time, got one of the copies first. Paine, the jailer, shoved it through the opening of the door, and Sol heaved his three hundred pounds of bulk out of the bunk and walked over and got it and went back and lay down again. Woodrow stopped pacing and came across to read the headlines as Sol lay in the bunk. Sol reached out with one hand and slammed him against the opposite wall. Woodrow leaped up and started to make the last in the series of disastrous mistakes he had been making all of his life, but he was prevented from it when Sol tossed the paper at him and growled, "Screwball!"

Woodrow grabbed the paper, glanced hungrily at the headlines on national and world affairs and kept searching until he found near the bottom of the page the three-paragraph item under a two-column caption:

WILD-SHOOTING EX-CONVICT
WOUNDS WAITRESS IN ELBOW

Sol apparently had become fascinated with the word "screwball," and he repeated it four or five times, even as Woodrow, his face white and wild now, ripped the paper to shreds and then started on the plumbing. He succeeded in yanking the washbasin from the wall and slammed that on the floor and then got his hands around the pipe and, doing what no man twice his size could have done, snapped a section of that off and turned to face Sol, who again growled the single word "screwball." Woodrow advanced across the floor with the pipe drawn back, and Sol grunted, "Know where you'll wind up? In the booby hatch."

He said it without venom, without much interest even, only as a simple statement of fact, and he would have let it go at that if Woodrow had not brought the pipe down and knocked out four of his teeth.

Sol had to get up then, to spit out the teeth and the blood, and since he was up anyway, he decided he might as well take care of Woodrow then and there, because he knew he would have to do it sooner or later. He grabbed Woodrow and threw him to the floor, and then let his whole three hundred pounds drop on Woodrow's narrow chest, promptly crushing almost every rib in it.

The jail was in an uproar. Other prisoners were yelling and Paine raced in with two deputies and several trusties and, in not too long a time, an ambulance and a doctor from the hospital arrived. By then Sol was back in his bunk, spitting over the side from time to time and muttering "screwball" to himself, still without venom but without any amusement either, and they were lifting Woodrow onto a stretcher.

The doctor, accustomed to dealing with misfits who did violent and unaccountable things, wondered briefly what motivated this one. Then for the first time he noticed the fixed, primordial deadliness in the stare meeting his own and wondered if there was any use even wondering.

✑ Snowfall on Fourth Street

J. LLEWELLYN NEWCOMB sat at the bay window of his furnished room over Bosserman's Meat Locker watching the people and automobiles that moved about in the gray cloud of snow falling upon Fourth Street.

He had a cold, shredded remnant of cigar between his teeth; without touching it, using tongue and lips, he slowly rolled it back and forth across his mouth, from one corner to the other. His face was lean and finely veined, the skin drawn tight over prominent cheekbones, expressionless as a mask save for a trace of dignity still there, a faded touch of aristocracy yet, the tenuous thing once known never entirely lost. He was bald except for a musty diadem of graying hair that grew in tiny tight ringlets above his ears and on around the back of his head.

It was a capricious January snow. During its first half-hour it had flirted with the light wind, gay and playful, but in the last few minutes it had acquired the special slanting drive and concentration that usually goes with fine flakes; it was already forming a skim on the street and the parked cars. Women were carrying umbrellas and some of the younger ones wore red or white galoshes. Though Mr. Newcomb could not see the sidewalk immediately below, he could hear customers stamping their feet before entering the Meat Locker, which was the fancy new name for the old butcher shop. Across the street, men going into the Elite Pool Parlor were pausing and kicking their shoes sidewise against the single step at the door. Those wearing overcoats, lumberjacks or flight jackets would unbutton them, grip the lapels and give a hard upward and backward shake to get rid of the snow on their shoulders.

Even before Mr. Newcomb heard the quick nervous knocking on his door, thrice repeated and insistent in its very lightness, he could tell from the creak of the banister and the torment of the treads that his visitor was McPherson Arnold, whom everyone called Fatty.

He carefully took the fragmented cigar out of his mouth, holding it delicately between thumb and forefinger of his left hand, leaned

75

and let an accumulation of saliva and tobacco juice flow into a squat brass cuspidor on the linoleum beside his chair; then he got up, crossed the room and admitted his caller.

Immediately, his face that had been as devoid of expression as a section of granite as he sat alone, took on an animation of hospitality and pleasure.

"Howda do, McPherson," he said with warm cordiality. "Howda do. Glad to see you. Come in. Come in."

"Just got a minute or two, sir," Fatty panted, taking off his hat and entering the room with his labored walk-waddle that required the use of even his shoulders to propel his bulk. He was winded from climbing the stairs and there were big unnatural spots of color in both cheeks of his round moon face. He was wearing a grayish-green topcoat he had shaken free of snow at the street door.

"How've you been, Mr. Newcomb?"

"Pretty tolerable," Mr. Newcomb said. "Pretty tolerable. Sit down, McPherson, sit down." He stepped back and indicated his own chair.

"I just have a minute or two," Fatty said again and gave a nervous chuckle that was utterly without meaning. His chest was heaving, his breath came in gasps, and he twisted the whole top half of his body first right and then left. Fine beads of sweat stood out on his forehead. He took a handkerchief from his topcoat pocket and dabbed at his brow and then wiped his palms. Even standing, he had to keep some, any, part of his body moving—hands, feet, lips, eyebrows.

"You had a splendid Christmas, I hope?"

"Pretty fair, sir. I spent it with Mother," Fatty said, chuckling, and a series of expressions like tiny clowns chased one another across his eyes: jocularity, solemnity, mirth, concern, and finally something stricken, haunted, pursued. "Did you have a nice one?"

"Yes sir, I did," Mr. Newcomb said. "Very pleasant. I went up to the Firehouse both Christmas Eve and Christmas Day and we had quite a few games of checkers. One of the boys had a bottle, too, and that added to the cheer." His voice turned amused and confidential. "Wasn't supposed to have it, I believe— Sit down, McPherson."

Fatty went over and lowered himself onto the edge of the davenport that made up into a bed. He sat twisted around on one hip, kneading his hat. The fine sweat had gathered on his brow again and he blotted it a second time. All trace of the high, unnatural color had left his cheeks, leaving in its place a hothouse pallor; his hands had the bleached whiteness of ivory.

"You didn't get out home this year?" he asked. His gasps had become short sighs and the fast parade of very tiny sad or laughing or cynical clowns came popping out of the pupils of his eyes, slid down across his irises, hung for a second to his eyelids and tumbled off into space and disintegration.

"No sir, I declare I didn't," Mr. Newcomb said. "I didn't make it this year, McPherson." He had not in fact been inside the old brick house on Lee Avenue for eight years. "My wife's been delicate, you know, and Dr. Goodloe advised her against seein' anybody— By the way, my son, Llewellyn Junior, made me a present of this suit."

"It's certainly a nice suit, sir," Fatty said, mopping again at his brow.

Mr. Newcomb crooked his left arm and held out the sleeve, feeling the material. It was a salt-and-pepper tweed that had come from Weinstock Bros., Clothiers, where his son was a clerk. With the salt-and-pepper, Mr. Newcomb wore an old-fashioned batwing collar and a black string bow tie. On his feet were a pair of ankle-high grandfather slippers with wide strips of felt down each side.

"I'm goin' to have to step by Weinstock's soon and thank the boy," Mr. Newcomb said. "I didn't get to see him Christmas. He was all tied up with his own family doin's and I missed him entirely— I'd offer you a cigar, McPherson, but I declare this is the very last one I have. I've been intendin' all day to step down to Hoge's or Wilmer's and pick up a supply but I just haven't got around to it."

"That's all right, sir," Fatty said. "I just seldom ever smoke one." His gasps had become both sighs and chuckles running indistinguishably through his words.

"Well, could I fix you a cup of tea? That's about the best I can offer you in that line today."

Mr. Newcomb had a hot plate in a corner. His son had a standing arrangement for him to take three meals a day with the Duncans, who owned the flat, but sometimes he brewed tea for himself in the afternoons spent looking down onto Fourth Street or made a cup of hot chocolate before going to bed.

"Now I hope you're not goin' to be offended, sir," Fatty said suddenly, getting up as quickly as his bulk would allow, "but I brought a little bottle along. I just thought you might like a taste, it bein' the holiday season, or soon after. I hope—"

He took a pint bottle of bourbon whisky, sheathed in a paper sack, from his left topcoat pocket.

"Why, no, *sir*, McPherson!" Mr. Newcomb said, his eyes sparkling. "I'm not offended a-tall. Not-a-*tall*, sir. I like a touch now and then but I can't seem to remember to keep any on hand. I thank you most kindly."

Mr. Newcomb returned the cigar stub to his teeth, took the bottle from its sack, admired the label a moment and then peeled off the stamp and foil and unscrewed the cap.

"After you, McPherson." Mr. Newcomb took the cigar from his mouth.

Fatty quickly held up a hand in protest. "Oh, no, thanks. I don't care for any."

"Oh, that's right," Mr. Newcomb said. "You never touch it, do you? I declare I'd forgotten that. Well, I expect you're better off. I expect a man's better off without it entirely. Still, I've had a mighty lot of pleasure from it. Well, here's to your health and prosperity, sir." He tilted the bottle and took a sedate pull. "I'm sorry you won't join me," he said, touching a knuckle lightly to his lips.

"Oh, that's all right, sir." Fatty put a hand on his stomach and fought back an expression of pain.

"You're feelin' all right, aren't you, McPherson?" Mr. Newcomb said kindly. "You've been well, of course?"

"Well, no sir," Fatty said, panting slightly. "I've been in the hospital again."

Concern came to Mr. Newcomb's face. "I'm real sorry to hear that, McPherson. I certainly am. Your liver again, was it?"

"Well, it's the trouble in there somewhere." He was pressing his stomach hard now; sweat beaded his forehead again.

"I do wish they could locate your trouble and do somethin' for you. You've been in the hospital several times, haven't you?"

Fatty let out a short gust of low, nervous laughter. "Twenty-six times. They claim the X-rays don't show anything. I don't believe they'll ever find it."

"Is there anything I can do for you?" Mr. Newcomb asked, still very kindly and concerned.

Fatty was shaking his head, holding his stomach, his face contorted as if he were trying to outwait a spasm. "Well, now there might just be," he said in a moment, looking at Mr. Newcomb as if the idea had just struck him. "There's a medicine that helps me a little.

Would it be too much to ask you to walk down to the drugstore and get me four ounces of paregoric?"

"Why, gladly, sir," Mr. Newcomb said. "Gladly. I'll go right away, McPherson. I believe I'll just have another little taste of this before I get out in the cold and then I'll step right down there for you." He took another drink and set the bottle on top of the bureau. Then he opened the door of the closet, leaned down and brought out a pair of rubbers and went over to his chair and put them on over the grandfather slippers.

"Which store would you like me to patronize, McPherson—Hoge's?"

"No, I don't think so," Fatty said with a quick, meaningless chuckle. "I expect you'd better try Saul's."

"All right, sir. I'll patronize Saul."

Mr. Newcomb returned to the closet and took out his derby and fitted it on his head, and then brought out a very old black overcoat with a fur collar and made his way into that.

Fatty had a five-dollar bill out. He had folded it into a ribbon and was nervously threading it through the fingers of his left hand. He handed it to Mr. Newcomb.

"I wish you'd buy yourself a half a dozen cigars," Fatty said.

"Well, now that's not necessary, McPherson," Mr. Newcomb protested halfheartedly. "Not necessary a-tall."

"I wish you would, sir," Fatty said earnestly.

"Well, all right, McPherson, I'll get a few cigars, if you insist on it. I'll be right back. You just go ahead and make yourself at home."

Fatty had already started the heavy pacing across the room that he would keep up until Mr. Newcomb returned.

Mr. Newcomb went out the door and on down the stairs.

The snowfall had changed again, the flakes larger now and less insistent; they had a buoyant and spumescent quality. The skim on the sidewalk and the parked cars had become a substantial coating. It was mounting on window ledges.

Mr. Newcomb was now out on the street, abroad in the town where he had once been the second or third richest man—respected, bowed to—owner of the furniture factory, a director of the leading bank, a member of the city council, consulted on municipal affairs—all this before he had squandered a quarter of a million dollars on a dream: a huge unfinished resort hotel in one of the valleys of the Alleghenies. It was an absurdity as a hotel—a great sprawling old-fashioned place with sweeping verandas, ballrooms, trellised walks and cottages—a place, actually, that resembled someone's attempt to recreate everything ante-bellum—standing out there now empty and pelted by snow, wondered at or laughed at by everyone who rode by—an unrealized dream not only because the money gave out and J. Llewellyn Newcomb's wife and son stepped in and salvaged what they could, a tenth of the resources perhaps, and sensibly tied it up in court, but because the concept behind it was a flagrant and romantic impossibility. . . .

Mr. Newcomb's face returned to the utter absence of expression that had marked it as he sat alone before the bay window of his room. He walked with his hands clasped behind him, chewing on the shred of cigar. He did not even blink as the snowflakes pelted his face. At the intersection, just as he turned down Main, he tossed the butt away.

Nearly every afternoon and evening there was a stud-poker game in a large room over Saul's Drugstore down at the corner of Main and Second. The game had not started yet and two of the card players were sitting in the rear booth facing each other, waiting for the others to arrive, talking to Saul, who was working at the prescription counter. As Mr. Newcomb entered, Saul left them and came forward to greet him. Saul was a pleasant, accommodating, swarthy man who looked more Greek than Jewish. He had prospered and in recent years had become important in local politics.

"Yes sir, Mr. Newcomb," Saul said politely. "What can I do for you?"

"Just some cigars, Saul, if you please."

Saul stepped behind the tobacco counter and brought out a box of Mr. Newcomb's favorites. Mr. Newcomb removed a half-dozen.

"Now, anything else?" Saul asked, accepting the five-dollar bill.

"No, I don't believe so," Mr. Newcomb said. "Oh yes, there is too. I'd like to have a little paregoric."

"Yes sir. How much?"

"I'll need about four ounces, if you please."

Saul thought very quickly, considered, nodded and went on back to the prescription department. Before long he returned with the bottle and the drug book. He took his pen from his breast pocket and had Mr. Newcomb sign the book. Then he wrapped the bottle and made the change at the cash register.

As Saul was counting out the change he gave Mr. Newcomb a

candid look. He had large, shrewd brown eyes. In an undertone he said: "Tell Fatty that's all for another month. Absolutely. Will you tell him that?"

Mr. Newcomb nodded gravely. "I'll be glad to convey that message to McPherson," he said blandly. He carefully lit one of the new cigars and then strolled out.

Still gazing after Mr. Newcomb, Saul walked back toward the rear booth, shaking his head.

One of the poker players said, "The old man ain't got a dime, has he?"

"Him and that Fatty Arnold," the other poker player said, "they make a pair. Yes sir, a pair to draw to."

"Sometimes you wonder why," Saul said, still shaking his head soberly and reflectively, "it's always the kindest-hearted people that wind up with the shortest end of the stick."

The first poker player asked if they had ever heard about the time Fatty had to hitchhike all the way back from Norfolk with his bull fiddle. He had traveled to seven cities throughout the state by bus, taking the bass fiddle along to sell or trade or pawn for a supply. . . .

Mr. Newcomb ambled on up the street, the fresh cigar between his teeth, his hands clasped behind him, indifferent to the snow that was driving hard now, drawing a curtain between himself and the town in which he had been born and spent all his days and in which he had known success and honor and failure and sufferance.

Fatty was waiting at the top of the stairway, out in the hall, dabbing at his forehead, shifting his feet about. When he realized that Mr. Newcomb had the paregoric, relaxation passed through the enormous folds of his body like a wave; the tragic little clowns popping out of the stricken depths of his eyes suddenly began tumbling and somersaulting with whoops of joy.

"I s'pose," Mr. Newcomb said, "you were kept busy durin' the holidays playin' at the various functions here and there?"

"Well, yes sir," Fatty said. "Fairly so. We played two dances at the hotel and one out at the community house in the park."

They were both seated before the bay window. Fatty was easier now; he still sighed occasionally as he spoke but the meaningless chuckles had subsided. He had drunk two ounces of the paregoric; a little later he had eaten six heaping teaspoons of granulated sugar from the supply that Mr. Newcomb kept for his tea. He hoped that he would not have to take the other two ounces until fairly late in the evening; that would see him through the night. He would take a warm bath to go with it.

"I s'pose there'd be more work in your line, McPherson, if you went to a larger town, some place like Richmond or Washington, wouldn't there?"

"Oh, yes sir," Fatty agreed quickly. "If I could leave Mother I'm pretty sure I could play regularly with a band in one of the big hotels."

"That's true," Mr. Newcomb mused. "You wouldn't want to leave your mother. She's gettin' a little age on her." He inhaled on the cigar that was smoked far down now. "Do you s'pose, sir, the Dixie Theater will ever revive the orchestra you fellows had there?"

Fatty chuckled again and shifted about in his chair. "No, I don't think there's a great deal of chance of that. The talkin' pictures pretty well finished theater orchestras except in a few places in the big cities. And now of course they've got all this Cinemascope and that stuff—"

"That's too bad," Mr. Newcomb said. "You young men had a very fine orchestra there at the Dixie, I always thought. A very fine orchestra."

"Thank you, sir."

"I used to go there every once in a while. Enjoyed your all's playin' mightily. Spent some enjoyable evenin's there. Very enjoyable."

"Even if they did," Fatty said, "we wouldn't have the same group. You know Hal and Charlie are both dead."

"Oh, yes," Mr. Newcomb said, "they did pass on, didn't they? I had forgotten about that. By the way, McPherson, if it's all the same to you, I'm goin' to fix myself another toddy."

"Oh, yes sir," Fatty said, "help yourself. It's all yours."

Mr. Newcomb's third and fourth drinks had been toddies, and now he got up and went over to the recess containing the hot plate and his few glasses, cups and saucers, and prepared another. When he returned he saluted Fatty's health and prosperity and sat down with the toddy in one hand and the cigar in the other. His face shone with benignity and philosophy.

"McPherson," he said in a moment, "I was just thinkin'. You know, I haven't completely given up on my project."

"No," Fatty said. "I wouldn't think so. That stands you quite an investment, don't it?"

"Yes, sir," Mr. Newcomb said. "I have considerable tied up in it and that's the main difficulty as things stand now—financin'."

"Yes, sir," Fatty agreed. Fatty was beginning to shift and squirm a little in his chair now, considering taking the other two ounces around eight or nine o'clock instead of later. It was not holding him down too well. When it did not hold him down he felt as if every corpuscle of his body was trying to separate and fly apart from all the others.

"I think I'll step down to the bank in the next day or two and have a talk with young George Worthingham. His father and I were associates for years, you know."

"Yes, sir," Fatty said. "I know you and Mr. Worthingham were close."

"Yes," Mr. Newcomb said, "I'll probably step down there and have a talk— Our trouble, McPherson, was two things: the golf course and the lack of mineral springs. I'm convinced there's mineral water on the property and if we put down another well or two we'll find it."

"I expect it's there all right," Fatty said.

"The golf course was what threw us off stride," Mr. Newcomb said. "I don't think any of us in the project realized what it was goin' to cost. Golf was fairly new around here in those days— Well, sir, McPherson, what I have in mind is a question I'd like to put to you. I'd appreciate your advice on a little matter."

"What's that, sir?" Fatty said.

"Most of the leadin' hotels have some kind of music in their dinin' rooms, don't they, McPherson? Like the Greenbrier and the Hot?"

"They usually have a string trio or quartet, places like that."

"That's what I thought," Mr. Newcomb said. "Well, I don't say as a certainty that we can open next summer or fall, but, in case we can, could you form a little musical company of that kind for us?"

"Well, yes, I'm sure I could."

"And then a larger company for the ballroom? That is, for the formal gatherin's?"

"Yes, sir, I could get enough fellows together. Certainly."

"Well, it's somethin' for us to keep in mind," Mr. Newcomb said. "But we won't talk any more business now. You just keep it in mind. —How would you feel about a game of checkers now?"

"All right, sir, I'll have time for a game or two. If you don't mind, though, I'm goin' to take the rest of this medicine."

"Certainly, McPherson," said Mr. Newcomb, getting up to get the checkerboard from the top bureau drawer. "That medicine's helped you some, hasn't it? I'm glad you ran onto that. You ought to remember to keep some on hand. It seems to ease you."

"Yes, sir," Fatty said. "I expect I should. Tomorrow do you suppose you could get me some up at Holladay's or Wilmer Bros.?"

"Why, I should think so," Mr. Newcomb said, bringing the board over and getting ready to set it up between them. He waited while Fatty tilted the paregoric bottle and drained it. "You know, McPherson," he said then, "I'd mightily enjoy seein' the ballroom filled with couples dancin' the Virginia Reel and the other gracious old dances." He was gazing out into the snow now, his eyes mellow and benign. "Yes sir, that would be a most pleasin' sight. I believe that's the thing I thought about more than anything else all the time I was pushin' that project—people dancin' the gracious old dances and enjoyin' themselves."

Fatty sat down in front of Mr. Newcomb and they spread out the board on their knees and located the men and began playing, two polite, considerate and gracious gentlemen themselves.

Outside, the character of the snow had changed for the third or fourth time. Now great fluffy flakes, the size of silver dollars, were softly falling. Before tomorrow's slush, the snow tonight would lie white upon the streets and sidewalks and yards. It would lie white upon the rooftops. It would cling to the branches of the barren trees. It would lie white and gentle upon all the town.

Incident at Chapman's Switch

"WHICH ONE OF the sheriff's boys was it?" Mr. Nelson asked, leaning forward.

"That God-damn' Clyde," I said. "He—"

Mr. Nelson got up abruptly and closed the window, though there was hardly any noise coming up from the street: only undistinguishable scraps of conversation and footfalls on the sidewalk as people walked up toward Court House Square.

Mr. Nelson came back and sat down and picked up his cigarette from the big amber ash tray on the ledge of his typewriter desk. He was a dignified man with a distinguished head of silver-white hair parted on the left side. His cheekbones were high and his skin had a thin, delicate look.

We sat face-to-face, close together, our knees almost touching.

"Look," I said, "why don't I just go ahead and write it now, while it's so fresh in my mind?"

Mr. Nelson said, "No." He cleared his throat with a prolonged *hach-huch-ah*. He laid the half finished cigarette on the broad amber ash tray and then took another from the package lying within the glare of the desk lamp and lit it. The first one was still going.

"You tell me about this thing," he said. He peered at me across the typewriter in which he had a partially finished editorial supporting the proposed new park near the Fair Grounds.

"All right," I said. I found myself running my hand around over the back of my neck and up into my hair, as if I could marshal my words that way. "You know about that business out there this evening?"

"Out where?" Mr. Nelson asked.

"Out there at Chapman's Switch, where it started."

"I want whatever you've got on it," Mr. Nelson said, very professional.

And I thought: I wish I could somehow say this whole thing without using words. I don't know exactly what I mean but, as sure as I put it into words, somebody's going to twist them. "That's where the whole thing started," I said. "Out there at Chapman's Switch. Daniels was out there horsing around looking for some moonshiner. Somebody's been peddling shine to the colored people out there and Daniels—God-damn it!" I broke off, "That's all any of them do: horse around looking for stills. Why don't—?"

"What about the store?" Mr. Nelson interrupted. "What happened at the store?"

"Well, as near as I can make out, what happened was this. That family lives out there—these Johnsons. There was this Johnson woman and one of her boys that lived at home. Maybe she's got more boys that live at home—I don't know about that. But there was this one. And then there was this other one named Ragland that's been working up in Washington. He was home too. He's got some kind of job up in Washington, a waiter or running an elevator or something, and once in a while he gets home—"

"The store," Mr. Nelson said. "What happened at the *store?*"

"All right," I said. "They went down there to the store to get a pair of shoes for the woman."

"The woman and *both* men went down to the store?"

"Yes, I guess so. They must have. Well, they got to the store and the storekeeper, Kincaid—"

"The old man?"

"No. His nephew. They call him Jack. I think his initials are J. L. I've got them here—"

"Never mind," Mr. Nelson said. "Go on."

"Kincaid was busy or something and must not have waited on them right away. Something like that—I don't know exactly what. Anyway, the Johnson woman started to give the storekeeper some sass and he told her to shut up."

"Had she been drinkin'?"

"Some, I guess. When I saw her she looked like she'd been drinking some, but not too much. . . . Anyway, Daniels was over across the road at the railroad depot and somebody went over there and got him— Look, Mr. Nelson, can't I go in now and just write down what happened here at the courthouse? I want to get the whole thing down now while it's clear in my mind. This is the first big thing like this I ever—"

"You give it to me first from the beginnin'," Mr. Nelson said with mild, careful importance, "just like you're doin'. We'll take care of the story end of it later. Did Daniels go over there to the store?"

"Sure he went over to the store. But he didn't see the first part of it. According to what Kincaid and some of the niggers around there told Daniels, Kincaid told the Johnson woman to get the hell out of his store. He told her to get the hell out of there and stay out. All right, she slapped his face and he knocked hell out of her. Then this Ragland, the one that has the job up in Washington, he hit Kincaid."

"Did Daniels see that?"

"I don't know. I couldn't get that part straight. Daniels is so damn' changeable in what he says. I guess he saw most of it."

"Did the other Johnson nigger take any part in it?"

"I don't think so. Daniels didn't say he did and he didn't say anybody else told him he did. He—"

"That doesn't hold together to me," Mr. Nelson said. "You mean to say this other one was just standin' around while—"

"I don't mean to say anything, Mr. Nelson. I'm just trying to tell you how I think it was—or how it must've been. It wasn't much of a fight anyhow because Daniels was over there at the store by that time, I know. It was just kind of a scuffle. This Johnson woman slapped Kincaid and Kincaid knocked hell out of her, and then her boy Ragland took a swing or two at Kincaid and Kincaid took a swing or two at Ragland and then Daniels got there and arrested Ragland and the woman."

"What'd Daniels charge them with?"

"Assault and battery and disturbing the peace."

"He brought the two of them into town, did he? He didn't bring the other one?"

"No. The other one didn't have anything to do with it, I guess. Daniels—"

There was a rapid, peremptory tattoo of knuckles on the door from Mr. Nelson's private office into the darkened little city room. Mr. Nelson called, "Come in." Sidney Tallmert, the composing-room foreman, who had been setting up some ads, pushed the door open. He was wearing his greasy apron and his green eyeshade and had a cigarette stuck into the eyeshade strap over his right ear like a pencil. He came a step or two in and then sensed what was going on and merely said, "You all got all that up at the courthouse, didn't you? Bishop just come down by there and said—"

"We got it, Sid," Mr. Nelson said.

"Lot of people up there, Bishop said. Just thought I'd be sure you got it."

Tallmert knew we had it; he just wanted to be in on it himself and talk about it some.

"It's okay, Sid," Mr. Nelson said. Tallmert started to withdraw and Mr. Nelson said, "Oh, Sid! See the alley door's locked, will you?"

"Yeah, you bet," Tallmert said, and closed the door respectfully. In a moment we heard him going down the stairs to see about the alley door.

This is going to get twisted up, I know, I thought. I can feel it. It's going to be like that time Mrs. Peterfish hung herself out on the old Fair Grounds and was there four days and we just carried a regular obit because her husband—because none of them want the words to suit the deed; they want them to suit the community. And that's not all. It's got to conform to some kind of tradition that never was very true in the first place or at least never was true in the way it's claimed. . . .

"Go ahead," Mr. Nelson said.

"Daniels brought them on into town and locked them up. Then that bastard Clyde—I don't know what he—"

"Never mind that," Mr. Nelson said. "Just be factual, son."

I did not know why, but at the moment I resented Mr. Nelson's use of the word "son." It put me under some kind of obligation to him—of accepting the judgment and wisdom not only of an older man as an individual but as a representative of something which I knew myself to be still too young to define with any real understanding.

"All right," I said. "Daniels handcuffed the two of them together and put them in the back seat and brought 'em on in here and locked them up. Then Clyde got the bright idea of questioning them. Clyde thinks he's a kind of a prosecuting attorney or supreme court judge, I guess. He was too dumb to get through law school but he's got to blow everything up big. There just wasn't much to the case. I don't know whether it'd even been worth carrying a story about, otherwise. They just had this assault-and-disturbing-the-peace charge against these niggers and they'd have come up in Warren's magistrate court

Friday. But Clyde, he gets the bright idea of questioning them, what the hell for *I* don't know—"

"Never mind all that," Mr. Nelson said again. "I want you to tell me exactly what happened there in the sheriff's office."

"It didn't happen in the sheriff's office. It happened out there in the magistrate's courtroom."

"Well, wherever it was—"

The telephone rang, sharp, high and jangling. Mr. Nelson reached over across his desk, put the receiver against his ear and brought the mouthpiece close to his mouth and said, "Yes? Hello." He felt around on the desk for his cigarettes, found the package and shook one out and held it in his hand unlighted. "Yes, Major," he said. "We've got it." For some time he was silent, listening, holding the cigarette unlighted. I could hear the rasping voice in the receiver. The Colonial Club, which ran everything politically in the town and in the county, was having its say. "Yes, I understand that," Mr. Nelson said. "Yes, he's right here with me. We're talkin' about it. . . . I'll see that he gets it straight. . . . You want to look at it?" His voice rose and then abruptly fell. "Well, I don't know about that. . . . You represent the sheriff? . . . Sure he can make a statement. I *want* him to make a statement. What? When did they find that? . . . Well, why didn't Daniels find it? Is Daniels blind? . . . He never *thought* about it! . . . All right, we'll get together on it, Major. You come by here first thing in the morning. . . . All right, Major . . ."

He replaced the receiver and pushed the telephone away and lit the cigarette.

I said, "You're not going to let them see the story?" and I knew my voice was suddenly high and not quite steady.

"I didn't promise him he could see the story, son," Mr. Nelson said. "I don't make a practice of lettin' people see stories before they go in the paper. I run this newspaper and I try to be fair to all sides. Now, what happened there in the courtroom?"

I hesitated, and when I went on I began studying his face carefully. "I was up there hanging around the sheriff's office," I said, "when Daniels came up from the jail. The sheriff was there and that bastard Clyde was there and I was there. We were just sitting there in the office. I like the old sheriff. I like to go in there and gas with him. We were just sitting there gassing. Clyde was reading some kind of textbook in some phony correspondence law-school course he's been taking. Daniels comes in and tells us about it and Clyde starts

going into his prosecuting-attorney routine. I mean that way of half
opening his mouth and just looking at you with that important,
mocking ... That's why they kicked him off the State Highway Pa-
trol—stopping people and leaning in their cars with that damn' superior buck-toothed—"

"All right now, get back to—"

"Well, that's the way it started. Clyde got out the blotter and told
Daniels to give him their names and ages and so forth. Daniels said,
'I ain't got 'em.' Clyde looked at him with his mouth half open and
says, 'What do you mean, you ain't got 'em?' 'They wouldn't give
'em,' Daniels said. 'They wouldn't talk.' Clyde just looked at him.
Then he said, 'You go back down there and get 'em and bring 'em
up here and let me take hold of 'em for an interrogation.' Now what
in hell did *that* mean? I swear to God I almost believe he started
the whole thing just to show he could use that word 'interrogation.' "

"All right," Mr. Nelson said. "Did Daniels search them when he
locked them up?"

"I don't know whether Daniels searched them or not," I said. "I
guess he searched them. They're supposed to search everybody when
they take 'em in."

"All right," Mr. Nelson said. "So Daniels went down and got them
and brought them on up there?"

"On up to the courtroom. The sheriff and Clyde and Daniels and
I all went in there. The sheriff was sitting up in the magistrate's chair
with his feet propped up, not much interested in it. I was sitting up
there beside him in the clerk's chair. I didn't see anything to it either.
Clyde had the blotter and a pencil in his hand and he was asking
them things like their names and ages and where they live and what
they do. The two prisoners were sitting there on one of the benches,
not far apart. The woman was sitting up very straight and had her
hand over her mouth. The young one, that Ragland, was all dressed
up in a check suit and was sort of leaning forward over the back of
the next bench. Neither one of them would look at Clyde. The
woman would answer him but wouldn't look at him, and this Ragland wouldn't look at him or answer him either. Daniels was sprawled
out on a bench right across the aisle from the prisoners. And so help
me God, this is what happened and *all* that happened—"

"Go ahead, son," Mr. Nelson said.

"We were sitting there and Clyde was 'interrogating' them like a
Gestapo agent or something—I don't know what. There wasn't any-

thing to get out of them, there'd just been this little ruckus in a country store, but you'd think Clyde was questioning two people who'd tried to assassinate the President. I mean he has that damn' superior, persistent way. . . . Well, I heard the telephone in the sheriff's office ring. Daniels got up off the bench and went to answer it. In a minute or so he came to the door and called the sheriff to the phone and the sheriff stepped down out of the magistrate's chair and went on in there too. Suddenly this Ragland, still without looking at Clyde, said: 'I want a lawyer. I've got a right to a lawyer and bail. I know my rights.' Now I think that's what got Clyde going and I *know* it got him going when Ragland opened that knife—"

"You saw the knife?" Mr. Nelson asked.

"It was just a little silver knife he had on his watch chain," I said. "A kind of trinket. He was wearing it openly. The blade wasn't more than an inch, inch-and-a-quarter long. He opened it and started cleaning his fingernails. That was when I wanted to get out of there. If he just hadn't done that, hadn't sat there cleaning his fingernails and not answering . . .

"Then Clyde says, 'Nigger, when I ask you a question I expect an answer.' He said it very quietly, watching that Ragland cleaning his fingernails, and I never saw eyes any colder—"

"All right," Mr. Nelson said. "What then?"

"By now this Ragland was leaning forward over the back of the next bench with his lips moving like he was cussing under his breath. He wasn't looking at Clyde and he wasn't cussing at Clyde. He was just sitting there leaning over, working at his fingernails and cussing to himself, like he was just cussing things—"

Mr. Nelson shifted his knees under the typewriter and took another cigarette and lit it.

"Well, this Ragland is sitting there moving his lips, not looking at Clyde and then finally he does look up. He looks straight at Clyde and says: 'You can keep me here a year but you still ain't goin' to force any respect out of me. Get me a lawyer!' Clyde's face was white and he was actually trembling, his upper lip twitching over those buckteeth, and he said, 'I'll lawyer you, you mother—' Well, I don't like to repeat it, and this Ragland said, 'White man, don't you nor nobody else talk to me that way!' He was a mean-lookin' nigger, I'll say that, but he wasn't actually *doing* anything."

"What about the knife?"

"*Knife!* It wasn't any kind of a knife! He never even thought about it. Now, this may not sound reasonable, but this is exactly what happened: Ragland started to get up. He got part way up from the bench and Clyde said, still very quiet: 'You're lookin' for trouble, nigger. Well, I got your kind of trouble right here on me!' And he reached toward his holster.

"This Ragland looked him right in the eye and said: 'Let's have it! You ain't got the guts!' And Clyde got the gun out and shot him deader'n hell. And that was the first one."

Mr. Nelson squirmed around and got his handkerchief from his pocket and patted his forehead and then returned the handkerchief and said evenly, "All right, what happened next?"

"Well, then he killed the woman."

"How?"

"I don't know—exactly. She was screaming and making some kind of scramble."

"What do you mean by 'some kind of scramble'?"

"I don't know, Mr. Nelson," I said with what must have been a note of helplessness. "Jesus! If you never saw one of those things you don't know. . . . Well, she was either scrambling to get to her son, or else scrambling to get past him so she could get to Clyde, I don't know which. It happened so quick. Anyway, he shot her at the end of the bench."

"At the end of the bench?" Mr. Nelson said. "If she was at the end of the bench, then she must have already been past the boy and tryin' to attack Clyde. That begins to look like mitigatin'— Well, you were right there and you're not even very coherent about it—"

"Yes, but good God— That bastard Clyde—"

Mr. Nelson got up very abruptly. He swung around and opened the top drawer of his metal filing cabinet in which he kept filed copies of his editorials. I found myself watching his every movement. There was something very precise and stiff, an exaggerated formality about him, even a careful control of the facial muscles. He took out a fifth of whisky and two glasses and said: "Son, I'm goin' to do somethin' I've never done before. I'm goin' to invite you to have a drink of whisky with me. And then I want to say somethin' to you."

Mr. Nelson poured a generous slug into each glass and handed one to me and sat down. "You have already done your duty," he said then. "You saw a story and you reported it fully to your editor. I don't want you to write that story tonight. You're too upset. I want you to wait till mornin' and then we'll talk it over."

I raised my glass and drank a little of the whisky and listened and had the feeling that I was experiencing some kind of initiation. I thought: *I knew it would get twisted. He's not going to use my story at all. He'll use the straight A.P. Even if he wanted to, the publisher wouldn't let him. And something bigger than the publisher wouldn't let him. I just wish there were some way of telling these things without having to use words.*

"You and I," Mr. Nelson was saying, "are not goin' to be the ones to try Clyde. He will be tried by a jury of his peers and they'll fix his sentence. I can't say what the sentence will be but there *will* be a sentence. The defense is goin' to make somethin' out of that knife and the fact that the woman was drinkin' and that they were sullen and tryin' to obstruct justice. These things are never clear-cut—"

"It's always clear-cut when it's the other way around," I said. "It was clear-cut enough when they sent seven niggers to the chair for that one rape."

Mr. Nelson put a hand on my knee. "Son," he said quietly, "I don't like these things any better than you do and I thank God they don't happen very often. The day will come..."

I listened and I felt I was listening to an ancient refrain . . . the anthem of the unseen nation of ancestors and fathers and sons and brothers and cousins and old friends and those to whom allegiance was owed. . . . "We are movin' slowly and gradually to improve things and no matter how much you would like to you just can't do it all at once."

I listened and I thought: *I am a part of it. . . . I was born into it and raised by it. . . . It is my native land and I love it, but there are times when I hate it. They've made me talk like them and look like them and even act like them. . . . But they can no longer make me think like them. . . .*

❧ Part 2

The Village Bells

The Summer of the Insistent
Voices

I COULD HEAR my mother and grandmother talking down on the front veranda. My mother had been deaf since childhood and Grandmother was speaking in a special clear decisive tone which Mother was always able to hear. Grandmother was giving the official family version of the battle of Monocacy Junction, in the War Between the States, which had been related by her uncle, who had played a part in the battle as a brigadier general of cavalry.

Grandmother spoke in the decisive, irreconcilable tone.

"—I don't say Jubal Early wasn't a great general who brought credit to the Confederacy but I do say there was some reason he would never give Uncle Harrison a free hand. When Uncle led his men across the river there—"

They sat side by side in the rose-back rockers, knitting in unison, the needles clicking faintly, a barely perceptible squeak in the runners of both chairs. As the twilight faded and the evening wore on they would draw their shawls about them and talk of other deeds of my ancestors—some witnessed, some guessed at, all exaggerated now to proportions of nobility. It seemed to me that the conversation about ancestors was as much a part of the old Colonial-type house as the white two-story columns or the wide double verandas. It went through our lives like an echo in reverse, which, instead of growing fainter and fainter, thrived on and grew stronger with each repetition until at length it was the echo and not the original deed that had form and reality. Often it was strangely disturbing; sometimes listening to it filled me with such acute restlessness I had to get up and walk away from the sight of the house, which itself, at those times, seemed a relic of a lost era.

I was in my room, before the mirror of the dark cherry dresser that had been in fashion a half-century ago, putting on a clean white shirt and whistling softly to myself. It was toward the very end of summer. In the last twilight I could see splashes of yellow and here and there a premature touch of crimson on the leaves of the old maple tree outside the window in the broad yard. Within a few weeks I was supposed to enter the Colonial Springs Business College and learn to be a bookkeeper. A four-year education for me at Cavalier University was just beyond my mother's means.

I continued whistling softly. When you are young—I had just turned seventeen—certain songs have a way of fastening themselves upon your mind and your heart. They come to you gently . . . like the fragrance of honeysuckle or the old climbing rose which spread over most of the west wall of the house.

Such a song had come to me that summer. It was called "Tender Is My Love" and I thought it a beautiful song. It was a gentle thing—to be whistled or sung by those in love. I had gone about the village humming or whistling the tune. Sometimes I went down along the creek under the sycamores or wandered around alone over the hills whistling, as if I had no connection—or sought to have no connection—with the rest of life.

It had been a peculiar summer. Boyhood ending, manhood trying to begin, neither being done graciously—I had become aware of great nebulous wants and contradictions. There had been the attempts at dreamy detachment when, perhaps sitting in the cool parlor with a book in my hand, I was conscious of a deep affection for the house itself and of the peculiar intimate call of ancestry; at these times I viewed the irony of living on the verge of indigence in the oldest and largest house in the village not with anger but with a strange fierce pride. And then again I often had a quick alarming impression of the house as a frail protective shell against the crush of present-day life and of myself as a crippled and bewildered being floundering within the shell first in this direction and then in that. And there were the terrible wants. Sometimes at night in bed I lay flat on my back, my body in rigid extension, arms doubled back and fingers clutching the metal rods of the headpiece in throbbing resistance of the demands that welled up from the unexplored depths of my being like the entreaties of a thousand infants deserted in the bowels of a cavern. . . .

Standing before the mirror, I heard Aletha open the door of the room which she and her mother rented from us. She came down the long musty hallway with her strange, disturbing, infant-like step. She always walked as if she were a poor-relation child come to visit and enjoy the sound of her own step in the manor house.

Abruptly I quit whistling. She paused just outside the open door of my room. A quick tightening went through my body. I would not look at her. She would be standing there like an ugly plaintive midget, her curious frustrated eyes fastened on my face. She must have been twenty-five years old and was little more than four feet tall. Her face was diminutive, her teeth crooked, her feet and hands the pitiful feet and hands of a doll.

"Are you goin' somewhere?" Aletha asked.

Her voice was like that of a child who would experiment desperately with coquetry before discarding it once for all, knowing it was no help—knowing that there was no help.

"Nowhere special," I said.

I knew the lie was obvious. I was getting ready to go down the road to see Mary Frances. I had been whistling in quiet adoration of Mary Frances. When I thought of the beauty of her deep blue eyes and the delicate whiteness of her flesh above the low line of her dress I found it hard to talk. In her presence, and there only, there was no duality in my nature; I felt myself in accord with a destiny. It was something Aletha could know nothing about, would know nothing about as long as she lived.

"What've you got on your good suit for?" Aletha persisted. Her lips were drawn in a feeble, reproachful grin against the crooked teeth.

"I just felt like dressin' up," I said.

I had to control my face to keep it from twisting in impatience and my voice to keep it from bursting out in annoyance.

She hung there upon the heavy banisters—her eyes scrutinizing my face—while I finished brushing my hair and put on my tie and carefully tied it.

"I've got a surprise for you," she said coyly.

"Yeah?" I asked absently. "What kind of a surprise?"

"Just a surprise," she said. "You come down into the parlor and I'll let you hear it."

"I haven't got time for any surprise—I'm goin' somewhere."

"I thought you said you weren't goin' anywhere."

"I've changed my mind," I said impatiently.

"All right, I'll keep it until you come back," Aletha said.

She went down the stairs and into the parlor and to the upright piano. She began playing and singing "La Paloma." Her little midget fingers stumbled over the keys and she sang in a thin, quavery voice.

I closed the door of my room. I could not stand her playing and singing.

I shined my shoes with a handkerchief, slipped on my coat and went down the stairs and out of the house.

"—I never trusted that woman," my grandmother was saying to my mother. "I warned your Cousin Josie at the time, when he first brought that woman into the house as a nurse for the children. A nurse! Hah!"

They had moved on for the time being to another generation.

I went out through the yard and started down the road. Aletha stopped playing "La Paloma" and I knew she was standing at the window watching after me in the twilight. I passed the nondescript clapboard house in which Aletha had formerly lived with her father and mother. I used to walk past their house on my way to and from school. The blinds were always drawn. The family—the old man, who was of normal size and worked as a field hand for Miss Addie Gordon, and the dwarfed mother and daughter—lived in the house behind drawn blinds. I used to hear an organ being played as I went by—Aletha playing hymns and trying to sing them in her pitiful quavery voice.

I would be walking down the road and as I neared the house I would hear Aletha pumping the frightful organ and singing "Rock of Ages" or "In the Garden." Then one day as I approached the house I saw the movement of a window shade and realized that Aletha was peering at me and I suddenly knew that she peered at me each time I walked up or down the road and that she ran to the organ to play and sing just as I came along in front of the house.

One of the hideous memories of my life concerned a morning of the winter before when snow was on the ground. I awoke that morning and heard screaming. I lay in bed for some moments listening to the screaming. I got up and went out on the small upper porch that was next to my room. Aletha and her mother were out in their yard in their white nightgowns. The mother was jumping up and down in the snow shrieking. Aletha was screaming, too, but she stood still; her fists were clenched and outheld and her arms were jumping up and down convulsively as if she were clutching some electric shaking device. Mr. Rohrer, the garageman, came hurrying down the road.

"Papa's dead! Papa's dead!" they kept shrieking.

There was a sort of extra-terrible quality to their grief, as if they were afraid people would think they had sat in their kitchen and devised some macabre game and were now out in the snow in their absurd nightgowns playing it. It almost seemed to me that they were shrieking: "We are not ugly little dolls! We feel and suffer! You must come into our world and respect and understand our grief!"

Mr. Rohrer tried to get them back into their house. They would not go. I watched them come across the road to my house. My mother had them come in. Then I could hear them in the parlor crying and moaning. Once in a while one of them shrieked wildly.

The women could not bear to go back to the empty home even after the funeral. My mother let them have one of the upstairs front rooms and a cookstove was placed in it and they stayed on there for months while an effort was made to sell their home. And my mother, though she would not have admitted it, found the money from the rent very convenient.

I never saw or thought of Aletha without a feeling of utter wretchedness. I resented her intrusion into my home. She brought into my life the constant reminder of ugliness and deformity and the memory of death and grief. Did I hate *her*? Could I hate anyone so harmless and defenseless? Could I be so base? Did I hate her for a still deeper reason—a reason so ugly I could not begin to examine it? I did not want to hate her. I did not want to hate anyone. But I did hate the presence of deformity and grief. I wanted, at times—at least I *supposed* I wanted—to study to become a bookkeeper and eventually to rise to the presidency of a large corporation. At other times I wanted merely to go through life whistling a tender song in quiet detachment. It was the summer when I heard for the first time—incredulously and sometimes with a peculiar fear—the desperately insistent voices. . . .

"It's like I'm a lot of people at one time," I said, speaking with great earnestness, groping after a remote thing. "I don't know exactly how I feel. When I'm around you I feel, well—pure."

Mary Frances gave a brief, faintly chiding laugh.

"Don't laugh about it," I said with the same imploring earnestness. "I mean I guess I could go ahead and be a bookkeeper and keep on till I got to be the head of a pretty big corporation or something like that. But a lot of the time I don't want to be that at all. I think I'd like to be a poet."

Once, indeed, I had written a poem. "Gentle people should walk down the ages together" was the only line I could now remember from it and I was not sure what that meant.

We sat in the porch swing in the shadow behind the honeysuckle vine. It was a fairly warm evening without a breeze to stir the poplar leaves in the yard. There were still blossoms on the honeysuckle vine and they gave off a fragrance that merged with a delicate perfume Mary Frances was wearing. The old brick house itself, sitting back in a yard almost as large as our own, seemed to extravasate a certain mellowness into the night.

I went on talking with a kind of inchoate fluency, losing as always my natural restraint in her presence. I was at the same time elated and composed. For the moment it was as if I were in the place I should like to remain for the rest of my life; but no matter where I might have to go in the world I would hereafter be competent to any situation that might arise because the situation would be on a lofty scale and would draw out a nobility that lay somewhere within me.

The moon came up from behind the Baylor hill to the east of the village as we sat in the swing. A fringe of oak trees on the crest of the hill stood momentarily illuminated in a molten glow, as if about to burst into flame against the hot orange globe, and near me, for me to study in adulation (before the moon turned gradually to a pale yellow as it climbed solemnly up and over the village), was the sharp silhouette of Mary Frances' profile with the mass of soft light hair, the rather large brow, the slightly upturned nose and the full rich lips.

Mary Frances permitted herself to be drawn close against me. I touched her hair with my lips. I began softly kissing her white throat. I could hear her breath coming and going in a low musical murmur. She was soft, yielding and vibrant.

Mary Frances was nineteen. She was a student at the girls' college in Colonial Springs. In her presence, I felt honestly and deeply as if I were fulfilling a destiny, as if the two of us, descendants of the two oldest families in the community, must join hands and walk down the ages together, mystically reuniting a near-lost thing. She would lean back with lips parted and eyes closed as I read love sonnets from the volume of *The World's Best Poetry* in the parlor. Or she would listen in apparent full sympathy and understanding as I tried to speak of my slowly forming and contradictory longings. And then there were times when she seemed to be struggling with contradictions of her own; after permitting a caress behind the honeysuckle, she might suddenly and rather meanly taunt me with the name of a movie star or All-American football player she had never met and would never meet or a radio crooner or a pilot for whom she was and would forever remain equally distant, as if she hated within my nature a certain something almost impossible to define ... a gentleness verging on effeminacy perhaps—a thin and fading vestige that grows soft and destructive unless now and then it is able to replenish and strengthen itself in the test of such great events as war.

Now a tremendous gentleness swept over me; it was as if I had gained maturity in an instant. All life had a subtle glory to it that I was aware of for the first time at that moment. There was a peculiar nobility about everything—nature, the quiet obscure village in the moonlight, men, women, Life—that only poetry could capture. A thing of inexpressible grandeur was about to begin.

All the contradictions, I believed, had resolved themselves as if by magic; my thoughts took on order and a startling lucidity. It seemed to me, as I held Mary Frances in the spell of the evening, that I saw with astonishing clarity that beauty and truth and nobility of feeling were an inseparable trinity and could be expressed only in terms of poetry or great music. I knew I would be not a bookkeeper but a poet or a composer.

"You shouldn't kiss me that way," Mary Frances murmured at last. She said it quite without conviction, as if in obedience to a faint necessity to repeat something of the kind one last time before yielding herself completely.

"Mary Frances," I said, "I want to marry you. I want to write songs about you."

I was aware then that a car had drawn up at the front gate and that someone was gently tapping the horn. Mary Frances straightened herself with quick decorum and in a high, unnatural voice called out, "Oh, there's Max! Come on in, Max!"

It was a fellow named Max Adams. He lived up in the village. His father was a lawyer who drove back and forth to Colonial Springs every day. Max was in his late twenties and was an instructor of physical education in a small college in the Shenandoah Valley. He was home for the summer and soon would be going back to the college. He was a big blond with a good-natured smile. He was not in love with Mary Frances; he had merely dropped by as he might have called on any other girl in the village.

Max sauntered up the flagstone walk under the tall Lombardy poplar and sat down on the porch with his legs draped down the steps. He had been playing tennis earlier and still wore a sweatshirt and sneakers.

The rays of the moon fell upon the porch as before but the enchantment had ended.

All at once I wanted to be alone. I did not know why; I just felt it necessary to be alone to find out why I wanted to be alone. I abruptly excused myself and went through the house to the kitchen and drew a glass of water. I stood for a few moments at the kitchen window with the glass in my hand looking out toward, and barely seeing, a double row of aspen trees winding up a lane in front of a neighboring house. "Mary Frances," I said desperately under my breath, "don't let's forget times like that! Please, let's never forget!"

I went back out on the porch. Max was sitting in the swing now with Mary Frances. His left arm was lying across the back of the seat.

"Mind if an old man sits next to your girl?" he said.

I sat down on the porch where Max had been sitting. I had a feeling that something was happening. I did not know what it was. Max and Mary Frances had begun a silly chattering banter that excluded me and was hateful to me. A deep perverseness and a blazing hatred of Max Adams ran through me. I hated Max Adams because he was twenty-seven years old, because he was not a Virginian, not even a Southerner. His people had come from Ohio. I hated his pleasantness and casualness that spread like marmalade over everything. I hated him because his casual intrusion was the signal and reminder that all things—all feelings, all passions—must eventually and inevitably return to the commonplace, as if following a geometrical chart and pattern; and every affirmation have its denial.

The excluding banter went on and on. Mary Frances' voice rose shrilly. She told Max how good-looking he was ... how much he looked like a certain movie star ... how irresistible to all the girls. And I knew her words were directed partly at me—at that certain indefinable quality I lacked.

"Why, Mary Frances," Max said with mock chiding, "you know you're the only girl in my life. Will you marry me, Mary Frances?"

Her laughter was sudden, nervous. unreal. "—The second proposal in one evening," she pealed out. "Tucker wants me to marry him too—he wants to write songs about me—don't you, Tucker? Would you write songs about me, Max?"

I sat leaning against the pillar, sickness and outrage welling within me. I was hearing her words and was thinking, "Just a few moments ago there was a fineness about it. I thought people like us should walk down the ages together."

I had wanted to shout the words to the world so they would never be lost. I felt now that one was never allowed to love fully and directly. One must never live deeply. It must be a secret and devious thing, a thing to be ashamed of, and if ever indulged in must immediately be denied.

I arose, trying weakly to smile. Max turned toward me then and soberly asked if I had ever thought about going to Old Dominion College or Cavalier University. I shook my head, the feeble smile still there; I felt inane, sick.

It is not a crime to be seventeen, I thought. It is not a crime to love with all your being. It is not a crime to be confused. It is not a crime to be the descendant of a fading aristocracy. It is not a crime to need.

"I'd like to see you go," Max said. "I'd like to talk it over with you. Maybe I could help you get a scholarship that would take care of some of the expense."

I could only shake my head mutely. I wanted nothing from him. My chest was tight, my throat closed. I wanted to do wild, desperate things—drink, take dope, jump from airplanes, rob a bank, go off to a foreign country and disappear.

"Do you feel all right, Tucker?" Mary Frances asked with a note of concern.

"Kinda got a sick headache," I said. "I'm goin' home."

I have committed only the crime of being seventeen, I thought—only the crime of exposing myself to betrayal and not knowing how to conduct myself after the act. I have committed only the crime of being defenseless.

Without a word I went down the steps and started toward the gate.

"Don't you want some aspirin, Tucker?" Mary Frances called out.

"No thanks," I said.

"Hey, Tucker!" Max called. "Wait, I'll take you home." .

"No thanks," I said again.

After that there was complete silence on the porch. I knew they would discuss me. Max would think I was leaving because of jealousy. Mary Frances would say I was just peculiar that way at times. Perhaps she was right. I did not know. It seemed to me I knew nothing. I felt without a shred of dignity.

I went on up the moonlit road, past the school, past Aletha's home, to my own yard.

My mother and grandmother were still sitting on the veranda. I did not stop. I went into the house and into the parlor. I lay down on the divan.

I lay with my eyes open for a while. I was looking at a big dark red rose in a small blue vase on a table across the room. I closed my eyes. I put my forearm across my brow. I did not want to look at anything.

The odor of honeysuckle from the vine on the side porch came to me. It was sweetish and sickening.

My grandmother was telling my mother of an incident that happened in the life of her father, my great-grandfather, before the War Between the States—the only war that was ever discussed with any interest in our house. There was always this talk of people who had lived their lives out long ago and by that mere fact had achieved greatness. It seemed they were speaking of people who from childhood had found their place in life and had known and done what they wanted to do or were supposed to do. I did not want to hear it. I wished that I could not hear a human voice. Here I was at seventeen and I did not know what I wanted to do—or how one even went about living.

I heard footsteps in the room. I did not open my eyes. I knew it was Aletha. I heard her cross the room. I heard her crazy little voice.

"Keep your eyes shut," she said coyly. "I've got a surprise for you."

I heard her go to the upright piano and twist the seat of the stool up as far as it would go. I heard her climb onto the stool and place a piece of sheet music on the rack. I heard her open the lid of the piano. I heard her clear her throat a little. I had the picture of her sitting there on the piano stool, her ineffective hands poised, ready to play, the sheet of music open before her. I knew her little eyes would be shining.

She started singing. I heard her thin quavering voice:

" '—Tend-er is my love—so tend-er is my love for you—' "

I opened my eyes and looked at her. She was glancing first at the sheet of music and then at me.

"Alike!" I thought. "Oh God! Like twins! The way she looks and the way I am!"

A book was open on the table near the head of the divan. I grabbed it without a full realization that it was my grandmother's Bible. I drew back my arm and threw it at her as hard as I could throw. It hit her on the side of her neck.

"Damn you!" I shouted. "Damn your awful ugly little face!"

I had no control over my words. They hardly seemed to be my own. I could not hold them back.

"I wish you were in hell!" I cried.

Her little eyes batted at me in shock for a moment and then she threw her hands to her face and began to cry. She slipped down off the stool and started to run from the room. Then she turned and went back to the piano and snatched up the piece of sheet music and tore it savagely to shreds. She spun around and faced me, her face twisted, her fists clenched, her arms jerking up and down and her whole upper body shaking in convulsion. And my own body became rigid and I knew that if she came closer or uttered a single word I would kick her in the stomach with all the viciousness within me.

She ran from the room, her arms still shaking convulsively, and I was left alone.

I heard my grandmother say from the porch, "Tucker! You come out here!"

I jumped up from the divan and slipped out through the kitchen, the yard, the garden, Stuart's cornfield, and finally climbed the far fence of the cornfield and went on up the hill to the top. There I stood in violent, sick trembling. A light was on up at the Presbyterian manse. There were also lights in the homes of Dr. Gilbert and Viceroy Baines, the undertaker, and in other homes in the neat trim little village lying below me on the floor of the quiet valley. I wanted so badly to hold someone in my arms and I wondered now who it should be; I wanted so badly to embrace a belief and I wondered now what it might be.

The Man Who Looked Like a Bird

EVERYONE IN CHERRY GLEN remembers the day the highway froze over. I am not speaking of the patched macadam road that ran beside Whisky Creek past the Jordan place and the new cemetery and on up to Chapman's Switch. (That froze over too.) I mean the Main Highway to Colonial Springs. We remember it because of the strange thing it did to Antietam Blankenship, not because its freezing over was unusual in itself.

What got into Antietam none of us can say. Maybe he had a trace of the pixie in him all along and we didn't recognize it. You would never have known it to look at him. He was a scrawny, wilted little man, so badly henpecked by his wife, Sarah, the village postmistress, that he was a kind of standing joke—a perennial horrible example to the loafers around the stores.

He wore a high stiff collar four sizes too big and his Adam's apple jumped pitifully up and down within the collar as he quavered a good morning. He had a little pointed suggestion of chin, a beaked nose, a nearly bald head and big solemn brown eyes that looked out at the world with astonishment and apprehension.

We would go into the post office in the mornings and see him sitting behind the gilded grill window through which the mail was passed and almost invariably we thought: Well, by God, Antietam *does* look like a bird sure enough!

We thought of him as being caged there. We tried to recall what kind of bird it was that he looked like. It wasn't a robin or a swallow or any other bird familiar to us. His face didn't even have the dignity of gauntness that many birds have; he just looked bedraggled and forlorn. He looked faintly like a young buzzard that had fallen out of its nest and been rained on.

As we came to think about it later, we realized we didn't know much about Antietam although he and Sarah lived right across the

107

highway from the Piggly Wiggly store. He never sat around arguing politics and he took no other part in the life of the village aside from handing out the mail when Sarah was busy at something else. Occasionally we saw him scratching around in the garden back of his house and on summer evenings he and Sarah would come out on their front porch behind the thick honeysuckle. She was a loud, lusty woman and as she shouted to passers-by Antietam would sit beside her, meek and wilted. Whatever greeting he might have attempted was drowned out by Sarah and we suspected that if his voice could have been heard at all it would not have been a word but a cheep.

Once in a while Sarah sent him over to the Piggly Wiggly to get a loaf of bread or a package of salt and his crossing of the highway was a pathetic spectacle. He would come shuffling down through the yard under the two Lombardy poplar trees and stand at the front gate craning his neck and peering up and down the highway. He could see a good half-mile in both directions. If a car was in sight, he'd wait until it passed. Sometimes he would stand at the gate for three or four minutes before ducking his head and scooting across the road like a chicken. Then some boy might yell, "Watch out, 'Tietam, here comes one!" and he'd turn and run panic-stricken back to the gate and have to go through the whole process again.

The highway froze over during that bad winter when snow or sleet or slush was on the ground practically all the time from November until late April and the wind howled and battered the village and tore off the big tin Coca-Cola sign in front of Willard's store. None of us did much except loaf around the Piggly Wiggly or Willard's or Cliff Updike's barbershop. In the mornings we went over and got our copies of the Colonial Springs *News-Leader* and then sat around cussing the politicians and looked out the frosted windows and wondered if spring would ever come.

When we awoke that particular morning the village had turned into an ice fairyland under a two-inch fall of sleet during the night. The yards were frozen over. Long icicles hung from the eaves. The fields were frozen over. The hills beyond were frozen over. The trees were encased in ice. The Main Highway to Colonial Springs was an icy mirror. There was a stillness over the ice-bound village. No traffic ventured upon the highway. It became a kind of unofficial holiday. Children went out with their sleds and coasted on the surface of the road. Young couples put on their skates and skated up and down through the village. We sat in the Piggly Wiggly and watched them flashing by. It was somehow unreal, almost as if we were watching a stage and as if the children and young couples were the chorus going through the preliminaries before the dazzling appearance of a star performer.

What got into Antietam we cannot say. We only know that he came slipping down through his yard with a pair of old-fashioned skates in his hand. He was wearing his old black overcoat and had a scarf tied around his scrawny neck. We left the stove and crowded up to the window to watch. We thought it was going to be one of the funniest things we had ever seen.

Antietam sat down by his front gate and clamped on his skates and kicked the back of the blades against the sleeted ground. He arose wobbling, holding onto the gate. We wondered where Sarah was. We almost hoped she would see him and make him go back into the house before he fell and broke an arm or a leg. We thought maybe there would be a farcical scene there in the icy yard—Antietam wanting to try to skate and Sarah insisting he get back into the house and both of them ending up sprawled in a heap.

Antietam stood up. He seemed much taller than the extra couple of inches of height the blades gave him. He let go of the gate. He quit being wobbly. He had a fierce expression on his face. He took a few tentative steps forward. Suddenly he streaked out to the middle of the highway and did a half-dozen electrifying spins.

We blinked.

Antietam stopped spinning with a suddenness that was dizzying. Then he cut loose and went flying down the road. We forgot about the cold and ran out on the porch to watch him. Back up the road he swooped, his scarf like a banner in the breeze. The younger skaters got out of his way. He changed his pace from time to time, now furiously fast, now sinuously flowing. He skated up the road until he reached Wilson's house. Then he spun suddenly and came sailing back down the road through the village that had always snickered at him. The fierce expression had gone from his face; it was now just quiet and triumphant.

Antietam still looked like a bird, but a noble one—perhaps a great golden eagle—as he flew along the highway he had always been terrified to cross. He soared up and down the road for an hour like a majestic bird in flight. He halted once in front of the store and executed a number of graceful and highly involved figures. He did

a whole series of Figure Eights down past Willard's and the poolroom.

We never saw anything like it.

Some of the more imaginative among us insisted later that at one
point he actually left the ground and soared through the air for almost fifty feet. Finally he sailed up before the Piggly Wiggly, did a
series of whirlwind spins, slowed, lifted his right foot and gave the
ice one final tap with the toe of his blade as if to punctuate his stun-
ning performance.

He slowly removed his skates and walked into the store and said
in a clear resonant voice to Pete Boyer:

"Pete, I'll have a cigar. I don't want any cheap two-fer. I want a
good nickel cigar."

It started raining within the hour. The ice vanished from the
highway and Sarah came over to the store with an umbrella and
summoned Antietam home. But until then we stood around him
very respectfully. We felt crippled and earthbound.

৺ Last Blast of the Trumpet

THOSE OF US who had known him—perhaps as many as two hundred of us in all—stood in the slushy March snow, back a little from the fresh and open grave, in the windy cemetery a mile out of the village. The pallbearers lifted on the broad heavy cloth straps and the undertaker quickly removed the three pieces of planking athwart the grave, and the casket was gently lowered. He was quietly gone now.

The preacher Talley, of course, was there with his outrageous trumpet. Jake Timmons looked on with solemn and thoughtful countenance. A few glanced in compassion at the gentle woman who was his widow, Miss Lou Ellen, supported on each side by a female neighbor, and saw only the black satin mourning dress and the thick veil guarding whatever expression her face held....

In his later years he looked like the pictures of Mark Twain, and the village called him Colonel. We saw him as a harsh figure with a cackling laugh, sporting the ragged white mustache, a corncob pipe stuck in his mouth, wearing a Panama hat in summer and, in winter, an old fur cap that must have come back from the West with him, and walking with the odd rolling bowlegged gait cowboys are supposed to have—a man with that hard inner core that makes intransigents.

Only the very oldest ones knew anything about him as a young man or remembered the actual beginning of the strange courtship, with its curious aspect of contest, that continued for almost exactly forty years. It went on before our very eyes but I doubt that any of us understood what must have been the true strength and depth of it.

All of us, of course, knew Miss Lou Ellen. We saw her a time or two each week, dressed in her velvet or satin, a touch of lace at collar and cuff, a cameo at the throat, her feet encased in the high-button shoes, coming from her fine but decaying Colonial home down to the stores for scanty and necessary purchases, a kind person, stop-

111

ping along the way to exchange greetings with a neighbor or a child. We thought of her not as an old lady but as an old-fashioned lady. She must have been lovely as a girl; even at the age of sixty-five her cheeks still held traces of a peach-blossom complexion and her eyes were clear gray and rather beautiful. We had not, of course, seen her as a young gentlewoman; we remembered her face only after it had become fixed and overcast with a mild but constant expression of care, a certain habitual creasing of the brow and between the eyes, as if her heart were troubled by a pain of which she never spoke.

She lived alone in a twelve-room house with high white columns and double verandas, wide halls, a sweeping stairway of solid cherry, walnut panelings and poplar floors, a showplace that had been built by her maternal grandfather. It was situated in a vast yard filled with white oaks and was approached by a lane bordered with old maples. Our parents, who had seen its interior, remembered the tester beds, the walnut and mahogany highboys and lowboys, the gate-leg tables, the rose-back rockers and the Governor Winthrops, the settees with their needlepoint, the Seth Thomas clocks and the corner whatnots. It held for the village one of our few reminders of the ante-bellum days.

Miss Lou Ellen played the organ each Sunday at the Baptist Church. We all knew she had dedicated a great part of her life to her older sister, Miss Jessie Claire. Their maternal grandfather had been a landowner, a squire, a man of means, and their father had been a preacher. He died when Miss Lou Ellen was in her late twenties, and a year or two later his wife followed him. Miss Jessie Claire was paralyzed at the age of forty-five, when Miss Lou Ellen was in her thirties, and did not again leave her canopied bed until she died at the age of seventy. All that time Miss Lou Ellen took care of her, quietly selling off one exquisite piece of furniture after another to support them. Her devotion to her sister became almost as much a village legend as the prolonged courtship which we of the present generation observed only in its later stages and which had that odd undercurrent, that peculiar conflict of wills or spiritual strengths. For all those years Miss Lou Ellen was an old maid and yet hardly ever did we speak of her or even think of her as such. And that is strange.

The Colonel had a Negro handyman, a lanky, shiftless mulatto named Karo, with whom he sometimes engaged in profane and blustering quarrels which seemed to be without consequence because the Colonel never fired Karo and Karo never left of his own free will. They remained together for at least three decades in a kind of testy and snappish relationship that ended only when Karo, who sometimes worked on the side for Viceroy Baines, the undertaker, helped George Mustard dig the Colonel's grave and a few days later simply got up and sullenly walked out of Willard's store when Viceroy tried to pay him for it.

They went about the countryside in a spring-wagon—the walrus-mustached white man and the disagreeable-looking brown man—buying things at auction sales, coming back with the wagon body filled: expeditions that eventually crowded all the spare rooms in the Colonel's house and two big sheds as well with faded pictures, vases, silver pieces, musical instruments and every imaginable odd and end, some of which society matrons from Colonial Springs came out to buy, but concerning which Karo would mutter, "What the hell he wan' with I doan know."

But he probably did know. And certainly the Colonel knew. Because, along with the gimcracks which he must have bought for the specific purpose of taking up all the storage space about his own place, he acquired a number of fine antiques. He had seen, over the years, the lovely old furniture going piece by piece from the old house up the road until it was virtually barren. And so he kept on buying at the sales until, as Karo expressed it, "He ain't got no damn' place to put no more." Then he must have persuaded Miss Lou Ellen to accept the furniture—not as a gift, for her pride and decorum would have balked at that—but simply to allow him storage space in her house. So the one time we saw the interior of the place, when her sister died, it was comfortably and respectably furnished again.

We saw the solitary and contemplative side of the Colonel against a background of quiet night. He lived a bachelor's life in a red brick cottage, just above the post office, with a small front porch and a green front door and heavy green shutters at every window. In his yard was the only magnolia tree in the village and sometimes the spent white blossoms and the waxen leaves dropped upon the sidewalk beyond the fence and were trampled under the feet of passers-by. We saw him at all hours, at any hour, even when one of us might be coming back late from an evening in Colonial Springs. He would be sitting in the double-seater swing under a maple in his yard or

standing at his front gate, under the magnolia, leaning over the white
wooden pickets at the gate, possibly tapping out the corncob pipe
with crimson and amber sparks falling to the pavement like a cas-
cade of distant stars. And he would demand to know, in his harsh
rasping voice, what we were doing astir at that time of night.

Each Sunday evening we saw him dressed in a neat black suit and
string-bow tie, freshly shaved and a trace of talcum here and there
on his face. The corncob pipe exchanged for a meerschaum now,
he would set out up the road with the self-conscious, courtly and
courting air of an elderly gallant.

Down the road through the Sabbath twilight we would see the
Colonel escorting Miss Lou Ellen to the evening church services.
She would take her place at the organ in front of the choir and he
would sit on the very last bench in the church—an aging and im-
passive man.

And then we would see him squiring Miss Lou Ellen to the oyster
suppers given in autumn in the old Town Hall building and to the
lawn parties under the great white-oak trees in one of the church-
yards. We did not think of him as being a harsh man then. There
was in his expression an unmistakable radiance. He was still gruff
perhaps; but through his gruffness shone a kindliness and an obvious
love for the woman of his choice.

The physical character of our village was shaped around its
churches. There were four—Presbyterian, Methodist, Baptist and
Lutheran—as opposed to three stores . . . as if those who lived there
drew their sustenance less from bread and meat than from that brilliant promise that has, in one way or another and in one degree or
another, sustained so many so long. When we walked up on one
of the old rounded nearby hills and looked back toward the village—
the clustered roofs and the elm and maple and poplar and sycamore
trees—we saw those slender spires tapering toward the vast and open
sky. On heavy Sabbath evenings of summer we heard the ringing of
the steeple bells, the air alive with their sound. We would hear the
slow tolling of one of the bells and then a moment or two later
another—and another—and still another—until the whole dusk was
filled with solemn and stately clangor.

The people of our village were in the main a quiet and devout
people, held together by the traditional conventions. But here in
their midst was this peculiar relationship, this odd thing; not a sudden, explosive, violent thing like murder, but its very opposite—a

thing whose very essence seemed to be of deliberation and quietness, of time and ambivalence.

What the Colonel had done in the five years he had spent in the then turbulent West—in California and in the Nevada silver country about the turn of the century—no one (with the possible and likely exception of Miss Lou Ellen) could with certainty say. Occasionally, appropriate to some discussion on a store porch or in the nightly nickel-ante poker game in Cliff Updike's barbershop, he mentioned having seen thousands of dollars at once on gaming tables. So some inferred, of course, that he had been a gambler. Another version was that he had been a magician with a small-time troupe or medicine show traveling about the mining towns; he had been interested in legerdemain since youth and even in his later years, although his fingers were stiffened, he would once in a while do tricks with cards or haul absurd objects from some embarrassed onlooker's pocket and as promptly make them disappear. It is doubtful that either version was true.

There was still another.

Like many men who went West at that period and came back, he returned with hint and rumor of scandal hanging over his head. He had obviously made money, and had done so in less time than is ordinarily required to make it in a customary and acceptable manner; and so it was whispered upon occasion that his dealings had been dark indeed—darker than outright and comparatively honest wagering for huge sums. The origin of this story we were never able to trace with any satisfaction whatever.

Often, as we sat on the porches of the stores, we speculated upon the relationship between the Colonel and Miss Lou Ellen. The oldest of us remembered having seen her, as a girl, riding along in a surrey drawn by the finest of pacers. It must have been with considerable resolution and daring that she, a genteel young woman of a devout and conventional and then well-to-do family, accepted as a suitor the Colonel, who even then would have been harsh, uncombed and defiant. Obviously there had been a remarkably strong tie between them for as far back as desire went. She was known never to have had another swain and he, certainly for forty years, never cast his eyes at another woman.

Then why, we asked ourselves, had they not married when they were in their twenties and settled down to the same ordinary life as had our grandfathers and grandmothers? We decided Miss Lou El-

len's family had doubtless objected, that her father had probably
forbidden it—or that she had had some presentiment that she would
have to dedicate a large part of her life to her invalid sister—or simply
that he wanted to go West and make his fortune. But none of these
seemed quite the answer.

And then, in later years, there was that rumor about his having
made his money if not actually at gun-point, then still in a manner
that would be sanctioned by neither law nor Almighty. It could have
been that we of the village invented that as a kind of proof to ourselves that those who break with tradition and convention are neces-
sarily nefarious. And it could equally have been that the story was
true, that the Colonel had confessed it to Miss Lou Ellen on one
of his Sunday-night calls many years ago; and perhaps she, distressed,
her very house furnished by ill-gotten gains, seeking spiritual advice,
had repeated it to her pastor, old Dr. Shumate, who had been a friend
and colleague of her father's, and he in turn might have consulted
his friend, old Dr. Blaine, and the latter, in his mental aberrations,
could have mentioned it to someone else without realizing he had
done so, until it had gradually spread out like the onyx fan Miss Lou
Ellen carried with her to church and held before her gentle, care-
worn face. There was a gossips' tale, lasting a while, that one day
Miss Lou Ellen had Karo move every piece of the Colonel's furniture out of her house and that it stayed in the yard overnight before
she relented and had the harassed and muttering Karo return it the
next day; others said it was merely spring housecleaning.

It was perhaps Jake Timmons, the scholarly clerk in Willard's
store, who came nearest to being a confidant of the Colonel. Jake
Timmons himself was a man apart from most of us. Quiet, reflec-
tive, in his forties, he read Freud, Dostoevski, Proust, the Greek
classics and had some learning in science and the arts. He was a
graduate of the University and it was vaguely known he had spent
a number of years in commerce. Somewhere along the line he had
lost heart. He told a story of standing one night (in what period of
his career this took place we did not know) before a microphone
in a radio station, holding in his hand an advertising commercial,
and suddenly developing an absolute conviction that if he read to his
thousands of listeners those preposterous words he might be placed
in an insane asylum.

He said he came to the village and took a job as a clerk in a store
because it was the least obnoxious thing he could think of. Perhaps

there was no truth to his story; we did not know. Anyway, he re-
garded himself as a failure. He used to walk about at night a good
deal and sometimes he stopped by the Colonel's gate and they talked.
He told us about one time, one warm Sabbath dusk, when he was
leaning across the fence in one direction and the Colonel was leaning across it in the other, both silent with their different thoughts.
They stood so, under the magnolia tree, both hearing the insistent
peal of the church bells, all chiming together at the moment, so that
a remark the Colonel had made was lost.

"What?" Jake Timmons said.

The Colonel raised his rasping voice, almost shouting, to make
himself heard above the bells.

"I said it's a shame it's only a fairy tale."

Jake Timmons pondered a moment and replied carefully. "Well,
science says that nothing is ever lost. Maybe that life force—biologi-
cal instinct, something—picks up again somewhere in some kind of
form, just as mass can suddenly become energy—"

"Jakie," the Colonel said, "I won't be here too much longer." He
tapped a finger against his chest. Then he tilted his head, resignedly
or sadly or defiantly, looking up into the night. And then he said,
"Cold, black, endless space, Jakie—endless black inhospitable space,
and here and there a star."

Then Jake felt he understood something of the tremendous force
of the issue between the two old people. There was Miss Lou Ellen,
the gentle and steadfast church worker who doubtless said her pray-
ers every night of her life, devoted to and courted by and loved by
the Colonel, the obdurate Unbeliever.

Jake had a sudden vision of them sitting in her parlor each Sunday evening for all those years, even after so many normal desires
must have been lost to them . . . he believing in a brief existence here
and now, and she believing in it forever hereafter. Jake thought of
the patent devotion between them—that had kept each of them from
joining their lives with another—and of the terrible strength of the
thing that had kept them from the final consummation of marriage
between themselves.

"It is incredible," Jake said to us later. "No, not incredible. But
fantastic."

And then we saw the arrival of the Baptist preacher named Talley.
He came from a remote and mountainous part of the county—an

overgrown man with a grim mouth and fanatical hazel eyes and run-
over heels and in need of a haircut.

He was not like our other ministers. We wondered how the board
of deacons had come to extend an invitation to him. We wondered
if he had even been ordained out there in those backward hills. Anyway, he came and was the assistant to the aging Dr. Shumate. He
lived up on the Chapman's Switch Road with an overgrown wife
and three overgrown daughters, all with that same fanatical accusing
stare—lived in a house with the shutters always tightly closed, as if
to keep at bay the mortal sin they found in their new surroundings.
We heard hymns being played on a wheezing pump organ, and lusty
family singing, and we heard another sound—less music, we believed,
than a strident, raucous call to salvation and redemption.

In time we saw the trumpet.

We saw the preacher Talley bustling about the village, his furious
gaze peering into hearts and eating its way through walls, ferreting
out our small sins wherever they attempted to hide. We saw him
denounce the loafers on the store porches. And the drinkers and the
pool players and the nickel-ante poker players. We even saw him stop
children in the road and ask them if they had been baptized.

Jake Timmons saw him buttonhole the Colonel in the doorway
of Willard's store and stare down into the Colonel's astonished face,
heard him demand, "Have you been cleansed of your sins?"

The Colonel recovered and scowled and made a brief speech that
was, for our devout village, historic. He stood looking at Talley eye
to eye.

"Parson," he said in even harshness, "I haven't got a damn' one.
Man doesn't commit sin. He commits crimes. And his greatest one
was when he invented that word 'sin' to scare himself with."

Jake Timmons watched the Colonel disengage the preacher Talley's hand and return the pipe to his mouth and stride away with
unruffled dignity.

It was inevitable that a preacher like Talley should conduct a pro-
tracted revival meeting. On the first night we stood under the great
white-oak trees in the churchyard, all of us wearing neckties and our
best suits and saved-new shoes with a polish being lost in the dust,
waiting for the first uncertain strains to be drawn by Miss Lou Ellen
from the organ, to be followed a moment later by the irresolute
voices of the choir. We stood solemnly in the gathering dusk, tram-

pling acorns under our feet, a restlessness upon us, unable to dismiss from our minds thoughts of death and eternity.

There among us was the Colonel, having escorted Miss Lou Ellen up the road to the services. We must have realized that by now he was a gnarled old man, almost seventy, puffing impassively on the meerschaum until at length he knocked its contents out against a tree to send the tiny star-sparks cascading down to the hardpacked ground at his feet. When one of the ushers came to the door and halfway down the steps and stood motioning to us, we filed inside to join our women. The Colonel came along and sat on the farthest bench from the pulpit, the one nearest the door.

We were assaulted by the shouted sermon. In the gloom of the old church, beneath the smoking, flickering reflector-lamps high on the walls, the horrors of brimstone and damnation were thundered at us. The hulking hillbilly preacher extended his long arms toward us and flung them about. His coat-sleeves were too short. Then he lowered them and gripped the lectern and glared at us with his fierce hazel eyes and quoted that inevitable injunction from St. Mark to be baptized or be damned. . . .

But virtually all in the church—we could bring to mind a sole exception—had long ago been duly baptized by their regular pastor. Out of the corners of our eyes we glanced at the Colonel. There he sat on the last bench, an aged man, alone, unmoved, not even adamant but simply unreachable. Not only did he not believe in the preacher Talley's exorcism; he did not even believe in the thing Talley was trying to exorcise.

We seemed to sense that the old quiet duel of wills had, in a fashion, been brought out into public. From time to time our eyes sought out Miss Lou Ellen; having slipped away from the organ stool, she sat now with the rest of the choir, limp hands in lap, a frail aging lady, and weary.

Then the preacher Talley was saying, "And now we will have a solo." We turned expectant eyes toward Miss Annie Sprouse, the choir's soprano, but Miss Annie did not arise. Talley himself had knelt behind the lectern and had arisen with the gleaming trumpet at his lips and was already blaring the opening strains of "Rock of Ages," a chawbacon Gabriel determined to deafen us one way or another.

We sat and listened as the raw notes beat against the ancient walls and made the windows rattle. We had no choice. We shifted in

discomfort under the uncouth torrent of sound and shifted again as
he hauled the mouthpiece from his lips for one instant and wiped it
with a sleeve before charging us once more. We heard him through.
And before the service was over we heard him through twice more.

We vowed that never again would we return. We said so in public,
at the stores—that neither heaven nor hell placed such demands upon
us—and later we said we would have stuck to our vows had it not
been for our women. But we knew what we said was untrue, that
we were being drawn back by something we could not define, perhaps by a trace of superstition that we were hearing a symbol, a
brash last call to redemption.

And so for a week we returned dutifully each evening. We saw
and heard Talley in the pulpit gesturing with his lengthy arms and
denouncing sin. We stole glances at Miss Lou Ellen sitting quietly
in her regular place with the choir. We were aware of the Colonel
there on the last bench, as unmoved as one of the upright marble
tablets in the old cemetery behind the church.

On the last night of that first week Talley had just finished the
first part of his sermon and was in the act of stooping behind the lectern for the trumpet when, for no reason that was apparent to us at
the time, the Colonel quietly arose from his seat on the last bench.
There was a stir in the church, a turning and craning of heads, and
whispers. The Colonel walked stolidly down the aisle with the trace
of the rolling cowboy gait he still retained.

He stood silently before the pulpit, head slightly lowered, in the
attitude of a penitent finally ready for the act of conversion. The
preacher Talley turned and stared at him with even more astonishment than we all felt. For a moment he simply looked incredulously
at the figure below him; then he leaned over and extended his big
beefy hand and shook that of the Colonel and said, "Bless you,
brother! Bless you!"

Miss Lou Ellen gave no indication of her emotion beyond bringing out a lace handkerchief and dabbing once or twice at her eyes.

The Colonel stood before the pulpit as a brief prayer was said and
then we followed him with our gaze as he moved up the aisle to the
place he had occupied each evening for a week and we heard
the preacher Talley say, "And now we will have a solo." We saw
Talley kneel behind the lectern. We imagined later we saw his body
stiffen. Puzzlingly, he got down on all fours. We saw him crawl all

the way around the lectern. He did that twice. Finally he arose empty-handed.

His face at first looked pale and empty, like the moon, and then into it rushed a kind of glaring, gangrenous outrage. We heard him announce in a hoarse and quavering bellow:

"We'll pray again! This time for all the lost—especially the hypocrites and the thieves!"

We heard the preacher Talley through to the end of the revival meeting. We were buffeted by his maledictions; and for that last week there was a new fury in him we did not understand. But we were spared the trumpet. Not once did we hear it again. And we did not then understand that either. Nor did we understand why the Colonel was never baptized; we merely heard that the preacher Talley refused to go through with the ceremony, saying he would have no hand in mockery and blasphemy.

Some three months after the revival the Colonel and Miss Lou Ellen were quietly married in Colonial Springs. That evening we burst into the big yard of her old home rattling bells and beating with hammers on circular saws. We did not cease the din until they appeared on the veranda ... these two gray, aged people, but looking somehow young and radiant that evening, fluttering as any bride and groom ... and we noisily wished them long life and happiness.

The Colonel had a little more than a year of life left to him. We saw him about the village as before, setting off in the spring wagon with Karo and returning with a roseback rocker or a grandfather clock, unchanged except for a little stoop, a laboring of the breath now, a tendency to fall asleep on a store bench, an uncertainty of step now and then, those marks left on all by the insatiable monster among us.

On summer evenings he walked about under the white oaks in the big yard and strolled down the lane under the maples—puffing his pipe, keeping his own counsel and noting whatever there is to note in the way of men. Sometimes he and Jake Timmons talked together and one day, a bright autumn afternoon when crimson and yellow leaves were dropping into the water, they strolled down the bank of the creek that wandered through the village behind Willard's store and the Town Hall.

Beside a pool where the leaves gathered and tarried before being carried on to the riffles below, the Colonel took Jake's arm and gestured. Jake's eyes followed the direction of the gesture and saw, at the bottom of the pool, still bright, catching and reflecting a fragment of sunlight, the almost forgotten shining object; and the Colonel started cackling, standing there on the creekbank with his friend, his cackle rising higher and higher until it became a sustained and rather bizarre defiance—final and absolute—of man's whole doom.

Two small boys, fishing for white suckers early the next spring, found it. They got most of the rust off it with cleansing oil and one of them was trying to play it when his mother recognized it and made him return it to its owner.

The Colonel died of a heart attack as he and Karo were returning home from an auction sale. We were saddened when we saw Karo driving into the village with the Colonel's body in the wagon bed. In the stores that evening we talked about the Colonel and about Miss Lou Ellen. A few of us tried to philosophize about it. We could not believe that Miss Lou Ellen knew nothing about the Colonel making off with the preacher Talley's outrageous trumpet. So why had she married him then? We could not decide whose will had finally prevailed. Someone asked Jake Timmons how he summed it up, what moral he drew from it.

"Well," he said, "I don't know. Never forget Miss Lou Ellen's quiet goodness and faith. The truest Christian among us, maybe. Her marriage to the old fellow after he was given up as lost—well, wasn't that an act of Christian faith and compassion? I don't think there ever was a question of triumph, of who would win over the other. It's as if, well, as if at the very beginning of time man set, or was set, upon an endless path. And woman must have been beside him even then ... divided, much of her love and care centered upon him as he was and as she probably knew he would be on down through the ages, and another part of her believing in or glimpsing or longing for—I don't know—a kind of vision of what he could be ... a vision of light at the end of the path. I don't know. It's so hard to say about such things."

And now the preacher Talley took the trumpet from beneath his coat and lifted it to his lips and the notes of "The Old Rugged Cross" flung themselves wild and free into the March wind. Talley blew furiously, not like one triumphant but like one cheated and enraged, and we remembered the Colonel as we had last seen him at the end, placid and unreachable. We stood and heard him out and then all of us—Miss Lou Ellen, supported by the neighbor women, the veil concealing her face—walked down to the gate and got into our cars and slowly drove in a loose procession back to the village where we lived. And behind us the cemetery was still again, still except for the wind slicing across the snow above those who remained.

All the Petals of All the
Roses in the World

SOMETHING OUT OF the ordinary, something haunting, takes place in the autumn of the year. Some kind of magic occurs in the month of October. It is not a thing to talk about before sophisticated people who have no belief in magic. I think there are too many people everywhere who have no belief in magic. Sometimes I get an impression of a civilization peering through microscopes, telescopes, fluoroscopes and, by now I suppose, radarscopes and psyche-scopes—all to the purpose of denying that there is any such thing as magic.

All I can do is deny their denial. I do not like clinical, probing, know-it-all people. I feel no kinship with them. I cannot feel that human flesh is only beef and human spirit id. I dislike the outrage clinicians have worked with words and the ugliness of their phrases. When I hear them talk I think of decayed teeth and old shoes with holes in the bottoms. Neither truth nor the absence of truth can be expressed in scientific terms. Rarely can it be expressed at all; it is felt only in the heart. And each tree and each life has old, deep, dark roots that have long ago reached down and entwined themselves in magic.

I, for instance, have a private world all my own in which all the wishes of my heart are immediately gratified and in which there is no pain and no death and no sorrow and no unkindness and which I shall retain and defend until the day that I die. I do not admit even my dearest friends to this private world; I admit only their better natures. As for the people I resent—well, I resent them not so much for what they are as for the danger they could bring to this private world of mine.

The magic of autumn had come upon me that year in the village that was our home. I had already built my private world by then. I went about alone a good deal. I felt withdrawn and detached.

It was a warm autumn—sunny, almost balmy. Frost was holding off. We had many trees and their leaves were turning: yellow and crimson and all the hues and tints between. The world had a golden floor. It seemed to me that everywhere I looked that year I saw beauty.

Not only the leaves and the bright colors against the blue sky, but a sad beauty in everything I saw . . . in every familiar and commonplace thing. I saw the creek flowing quietly along through the village under a double row of sycamores, and the somnolent flow of the water was beautiful. I would walk out to the surrounding hills and look back over the village itself and wander through the woods and come upon a vine heavy with wild grapes. And it seemed that all of this belonged to me—that I had ordered it to be. It was as I said: the magic of October was upon me.

I had trouble getting along with people who did not have a place in that private world of mine—my older brother, the boys I was going to school with. Some of them made fun of me—of my dreaminess, or what my brother called my laziness. I hated them, and I feared them. They did not understand the things that happened in that world of mine, did not realize that actually I was very busy. Things were going on in my heart I could tell no one about. I think the year when you are fifteen is the loneliest year of your life. I am not certain of that. I have had years since so lonely and bitter I did not care whether I survived them or not. But this was not that kind of loneliness. A lonely year is bitter only when a terrible violence has been done to your private world and you fear you will never be able to rebuild it—when you fear there may be no magic left.

I had started liking poetry that year. I had come across Emily Dickinson's poem that begins:

> "Beauty is not caused,—it is.
> Chase it and it ceases,
> Chase it not and it abides. . . ."

I fell in love with that poem. I thought it had some kind of special meaning for me.

The loneliness and retreat into the self at the edge of fifteen come, I think, because you do not see the same things other people see, nor hear the things they hear. Instead you are looking and listening for other things. You are waiting for something that is always just about to happen. You are not sure what it is. You see the corn shocks standing in the fields around the village. You watch strangers speeding along the highway toward mysterious destinations. Now and then you see a thin shaft of smoke rising from a chimney, indicating an early fire. You see the cawing crows and the screeching killdees in the brown meadows. You go to the nearby town and a girl of surpassing loveliness passes you on the street. You see and hear these things and you are waiting for—you know not what. . . . But the essence of all of it is caught in a few words of a poem.

You are in high school and suddenly you hear footsteps that are unlike all the other footsteps you have ever heard and you look up and see a face that is unlike all the other faces you have ever seen. And Miss Merryweather is there.

I am not sure where she came from. I heard someone say from Colonial Springs. Or perhaps it was Staunton or Charlottesville. I am not certain. I did not like to think of her as coming from any particular place. It seemed to me that I had been reading that poem of Emily Dickinson's and lifted my eyes and there she was in that world of mine. This enchantment unfolded as Miss Merryweather sat at her desk and taught us American Literature.

What is the use of my trying to tell you what Miss Merryweather was like? It is impossible. One cannot describe an enchantment. Her gray eyes and her slenderness. The soft white curve of her throat. The way she lifted her hand to brush back a strand of dark hair that had fallen across her forehead. The thoughtful hesitancy in her voice before she found the phrase she wanted. I can say that these things were, but I can say nothing about them.

All that sunny, magical autumn I was in love with Miss Merryweather. She was twenty-five.

We lived near the high school, just on the other side of a broad empty lot. In the afternoon, when school was over, I used to go to my room. I did not feel like playing baseball. My heart was too bruised and too full. I had my whole nature to contend with.

I used to lie in my room, on my bed, looking out the window down toward the high school. I did not study. I did not practice the violin. I just lay there on my bed, creating fantasies.

Miss Merryweather would still be down at the high school as I lay on my bed. By and by I would see her come out of the schoolhouse onto the wide porch and down the steps and down the concrete walk and through the open gate. She had a quick, light step that I thought rhapsodic. It may sound silly to speak of a rhapsodic step, but in the mere tap of her heels upon the concrete walk and then on the asphalt of the road I heard notes of glorious music. I lay there watching Miss Merryweather go up the road past our house, and when I could no longer see her from the window of my room I would get up and go along the hallway to a front room and watch her from there until she was out of sight.

It was a terrible way to be, at fifteen in the autumn. Some day somebody should write a whole book about a boy of fifteen, honest and unashamed. It should be made plain how he wants every desirable woman he sees, how terribly he wants some of them, and how ludicrously far he is from having them. It should show how that private world of his own keeps getting mixed up with the world other people live in. How he has to suffer without protest all kinds of jealousies and indignities and rages. The secret storms of his heart, so much greater than hurricanes! The terrible longing and the pain, unmanageable and unanswerable!

My family had an automobile. Once in a while, on those sunny autumn afternoons when I came home from school sick with love for Miss Merryweather, I would think up some excuse to get the car out. I would drive it from the shed and park it in front of the house. Then I would go back up to my room and watch for Miss Merryweather to emerge from the schoolhouse.

Delbert Collins, the cashier of the bank, sometimes came down and met her and I would see them drive off together. I would lie there on the bed sick with rage and grief. I would think of turning bank bandit and getting a revolver and putting a mask over my face and walking into the bank and killing Delbert.

But usually Miss Merryweather came up the road alone. I would wait until she got alongside our house. Then I would go out and pretend I was just on my way up to the stores. I would offer to drive her to the place where she boarded, up on the other side of the village, on the Chapman's Switch road.

I have often wondered if Miss Merryweather sensed the violence that was going on within me. Her presence beside me in the car filled me with an excitement I have rarely known since. My heart pounded in my chest and I felt weak, hardly able to drive. I stammered when she asked me some question. I had a fervent hope that something beyond imagining would take place on one of those rides —a thing impossibly romantic and sensual: that she would suddenly suggest we ride on together out into the yellow and crimson mountains and spend the rest of the day making love or even that we should run away and get married. Those fierce, sensual fantasies I could confess to no one else on earth. I imagined taking her home, that no one would be there, that she would invite me in and suddenly get out of her clothes and open her arms to me.

What I wanted was for Miss Merryweather to recognize that private world of mine in which the love of a fifteen-year-old boy for an older woman was reasonable and natural and worthy of fulfillment.

Down in our front yard, at a corner of the house, was a bush of white rambler roses. They grew all up the side of the house. I used to come home and look at that rosebush as I went by. I made its beauty a part of that sick, sad, distorted life of mine. In my desperate emptiness, filled only with fantasies more real to me than the world around me, I never went by that rosebush those autumn days without, in a sense, making love to it.

I assume that I was sick. I think any normal, practical person would say my behavior was neurotic. No doubt the rosebush had some twisted, hidden significance. To be in love with a woman ten years my senior was bad enough, but to be in love with a rosebush!

One day after school I was walking down the road with two other boys. We were talking about school and about the teachers. One of them mentioned Miss Merryweather and where her home was. Without thinking I said, "She came from beauty."

Both boys hooted with laughter and I turned pale. When we got to our house I went into our yard without a word. They were still laughing at me.

I went on up to my room and lay on my bed with an ache all through my body. After a while I got up and walked back downstairs. I don't believe I knew quite what I was doing.

I went around to the corner of the house and stood before the rambler rose bush. Aloud I whispered: "You thing of beauty, you and Miss Merryweather are the same. You are a part of my life and I love you. I can tell you, because you understand. I can never tell anyone else, but it is true all the same."

I picked one of the white blossoms. I went through the gate and started down the road toward the school. I stuck the blossom in my pocket. I was ashamed to carry it openly in my hand.

I went into the school yard and into the building and climbed the stairs. Miss Merryweather was sitting at her desk correcting papers. As I entered she glanced at me and smiled. I pretended I was there to get something out of my desk. I felt very weak and I know I was pale.

As I passed her I took out the rose and stammered, "Here's somethin' I had in my pocket."

I laid the rose on her desk. I went on to my own desk and got the tablet I pretended I had come for. Then I simply stood there, unable to move. It was warm in the room and the windows were up. The odor of chalk dust hung in the air.

Miss Merryweather had picked up the rose and was gazing at it. She must have known how I loved her. I know she did. I could tell by the careful expression that came over her face after one quick flush.

The rose had become crushed in my pocket and one of the petals had come loose. It fell and lay alone on the desk. Even as I looked at it a little breeze from the window caught it and slid it over the edge of the desk. For an instant we both watched it spiraling down and then Miss Merryweather reached out and caught it. She brought it back in the palm of her hand. . . .

Even now I can see the calm, compassionate, understanding expression on Miss Merryweather's face as she looked at the crushed petal. She did not at first say a word. Then her eyes met mine with that utter candor of which many women and a few men are capable. In a moment she lifted her hand abstractedly to her face and held the rose petal against her cheek.

I could only stand there, weak and pale and sick.

Then I heard her murmur, almost to herself, "All the petals of all the roses in the world . . ."

Maybe that was not what she actually said. I don't know. I can't be sure. But whatever the actual words may have been, their rhythm —their *intention*—combined with the words of that Emily Dickinson poem . . . "Beauty is not caused,—it is" . . . and together they made a refrain that has sung in my mind and my heart ever since. Though never quite so strongly, never quite so purely, as that magic-filled autumn when I was fifteen.

✑ The Little Bailey Girl

THIS IS ABOUT the little Bailey girl. It is a very brief story. It can be no longer because there are certain people about whom only brief stories can be written.

The Bailey family were quiet, amiable people who moved to the village from Bath County and lived in an old but small brick house on the hill about a quarter of a mile back of the high school.

Mrs. Bailey, in middle age, was still a rather pretty woman; she had a lovely light complexion, an easy natural smile and a general daintiness, as if she respected and liked to take care of her body. In her twenties and thirties she must have been an extremely attractive woman.

Mr. Bailey was a quiet-spoken, agreeable man who had a mild chronic asthma that made him breathe with some difficulty. He had been a cattle dealer out in Bath County. He must have saved up a little money because when he came to the village in 1939 he bought the two-hundred-acre farm that went with the brick house and was able to send his son, Bennett, to Cavalier University for two years. He used to spend an hour or two at one of the stores nearly every evening, sitting on a counter and taking a mild part in the conversations about politics and the state of the world.

The time came when he could, if he wished, have talked about his son being in the war. Bennett had wanted desperately to become a doctor. The expense of sending him to the University was heavy, and it meant a considerable sacrifice on his father's part. In the fall semester of 1941 he was waiting on tables in the University's cafeteria and getting excellent grades. Two weeks after Pearl Harbor he enlisted in the Marines. At Iwo Jima he took a full burst from a Japanese submachine gun in his left arm from shoulder to elbow. After the war he lost all heart about trying to do much of anything. One-armed men, even if they have money, have a hard time becoming doctors.

It is doubtful if a dozen people knew the little Bailey girl's first name. Her father called her Jannie. It might have been an affectionate

130

diminutive of either Janice or Janet. When people spoke of her it was always as "the little Bailey girl." They thought of her that way, as a person with only half an identity. She had had poliomyelitis in 1938, when she was nine. She was wearing braces and walking with that jerky, twisted, violent hurling of the body when her family moved to the village.

People used to see her at the Presbyterian Church with her parents, or making her way alone up and down the long hill between her home and the school. In winter, when snow was on the lane, she moved with extraordinary effort, slapping her heels down and heaving herself along like one climbing up an icy incline with the aid of shoe-spikes.

She was a shy girl, probably made all the more so by her affliction and the interminable year she had spent in bed. She could not, of course, take part in the rough-and-tumble schoolyard games of tag or prisoner's base or whatever the other children were playing. She stood by and watched. In some respects she resembled her mother. The smile was the same, and like her mother she looked as if she enjoyed such delicate feminine things as colognes and bath salts.

On one side of the lane up the hill was an apple orchard. In spring for two or three weeks the apple trees would be in bloom. Jake Timmons met her in the lane one day in spring and from time to time long afterwards he remembered the scene—the crippled girl moving along with great effort, her braces making a curious squeaking noise, her face set but fragile looking, against the background of the white-and-pink apple blossoms. Jake once said the picture made him think of all womankind trying with quiet and supreme effort to climb toward some high, vague, doubtful destiny.

She never had a date with a boy in her life. She never went coasting or skating or dancing or swimming. There is so little to tell about her.

She was a good student in school. The year she had to stay at home, she kept up with her studies. She spent much of her time with her school books: history, geography, arithmetic, grammar and, after she entered high school, geometry, Latin, French, physics and so on. She was fond of her brother and was happy when he came home from the war even though he, like herself, was now crippled.

There would be more to tell if her brother had been able to finish his medical courses and become a skilled surgeon and had performed a dramatic operation returning to her the full use of her limbs. But it did not happen that way. It would be fine to say that all the while—all the months and years she sat in the old brick house on the hill while the other young people of the village were exercising their right to be young—she was quietly practicing the piano and eventually became a famous concert pianist . . . something of that kind. It would even be good to be able to say that some young man came along and fell in love with her and she with him, and that later they were married and would doubtless live a long and happy life despite the cruel thing that had happened to her. But not even that was so.

She finished high school at the age of seventeen. She was the class historian. With the others in the graduating class she stood on the stage of the old Town Hall and received her diploma. With her sweet, timid smile she made her labored way to the front of the stage and accepted the scroll from Miss Cromwell.

That was in the early part of June, 1946. In the latter part of August, suddenly one afternoon, just as she arose from a chair on the front porch, an embolus that had been in her bloodstream made its way up to her brain and she collapsed in the doorway. She was dead within an hour.

So little can honestly be written about the little Bailey girl. You wonder—again and again—what her hopes and feelings and dreams were. You remember her only as a kind of half-identity. You think of her, as Jake Timmons did, trudging up a hill with painful effort against a background of apple blossoms, a beauty and bounty which, like the girl herself, nature had brought to the earth.

That is all there is to the story. Except that afterwards Mr. and Mrs. Bailey went on living in the old brick house back of the high school. If you are people like these, in circumstances like this, what do you do? What do you feel? You have to believe there is a just God who knows better than we what is best and wise for us. In all the time afterwards you have to believe it with all the strength in your heart. You have to believe it—believe it—believe it.

Mr. Sampsell's Thirty-Pound Diamond

ONE NOVEMBER DAY in his fifty-eighth year—out of a clear sky, so to speak—an extraordinary notion seized upon J. K. Sampsell, who had been the mail carrier on R.F.D. #7 out of Cherry Glen for almost exactly half of the years of his life.

He had drawn his old car up to the lane of a young farmer named Chuck Roudabush and was preparing to place a circular in the mailbox when he noticed Chuck's two little girls hanging to the yard fence across the pasture. He lifted from the seat beside him a metalcapped cane, stuck it out the window and playfully waggled it at them. Ordinarily the older girl waved back timidly but today neither of them paid any attention to him; they were looking at something in the sky.

As he leaned out to place the circular in the box he heard the high drone of an airplane overhead. Peering upward, he saw a large passenger liner making its steady way toward the Allegheny Mountains to the west. Faintly stung because the child had not waved, he watched for a moment the plane's silver flight against the open blue sky. Suddenly he found himself wondering how he must look to someone in the airplane gazing down.

Thoughtfully he took from a pocket of his shiny blue serge suit a package of little brown cigars the size of cigarettes, selected one and carefully lit it. Then he eased out his clutch and drove on with no immediate answer to his fanciful speculation. But the shadow of an answer had already fallen across the perimeter of his thoughts. Farmers were shucking their corn. From time to time, as he drove along, Mr. Sampsell threw up his hand and called, "Mornin', Roberto! —How're you, Juliano?" For some reason he invariably addressed his familiars not as Cliff, John or Bill but as Clifford, Jonathan or Wilhelm.

Everyone about the countryside knew Mr. Sampsell. Of undistinguished height and build, his hair gray and thin, he was an elder in the Presbyterian Church, a Past Grand Master of the Odd Fellows and the father of six uniformly unattractive daughters, none of whom was married. He had a vocabulary of expletive "botherations!" and "faddles!" locally famous for their paleness, and the most acrimonious remark he was ever heard to utter about any of his fellows was that "Clarence Elliott ought to catch the very old Harry." He was, in short, a man of thoroughgoing good will desperately engaged in the struggle to make both ends meet. On village occasions he carried the metal-capped cane with a halfhearted flourish, as if trying belatedly to give his life a little dash, but the gesture was pathetic because he never quite managed to rise above a kind of limp seediness. He had worn the same stained linen suit for many summers and the same shiny blue serge for a number of winters and into his eyes there had crept a set expression of nervous and shielded concern, as if he saw ghosts in his sleep.

Mr. Sampsell knew the road thoroughly—each turn, each culvert and grade—and he drove as automatically as he laced his shoes. Much of the time he sat in the middle of the seat and drove with one hand, making it easier to reach out the right window. Constantly at the back of his mind, as he made his round, was his nagging worry about money. Aside from the skimpy mail contract he had no other source of income except a few dollars contributed to the family budget by his two eldest daughters out of their salaries as country schoolteachers, and it was a rare and wonderful time when he did not owe bills at all three village stores, as well as Kyle's garage, and did not have a promissory note in the Valley County Bank. Even when he concentrated on other matters these vultures of worry sat waiting just beyond his immediate thoughts.

And now that irrelevant reflection of how he might look to anyone in an airplane was plaguing him.

Route #7 wound northward out of Cherry Glen, and eventually back again, in an irregular twenty-eight-mile circle through a monotonous jack-pine region of eroded hills with great raw gullies. With the exception of a four-and-a-quarter-mile stretch south of Amsterdam Hill, the road was unpaved. In winter his car fought ruts and mud puddles every foot of the journey, and in summer his progress could be followed by farmers' wives and children as far as a mile away by means of the cloud of dust funneling out behind him. Almost within the shadow of the solemn mountains just westward, the hillsides and limestone bottoms were over-worked, the farm-houses drab and shapeless, and the barns neglected. Here and there was a peach or apple orchard but these were few; it was not quite hound-and-buzzard country, but it was thistle-and-persimmon country. And at this time of year the crimson and scarlet and golden glory of woods and fields was fading into bleakness.

He was just passing Aubrey Beck's stable when the sweat broke out above his collar and drew a cold rim around his neck. Every day that he made his round, Mr. Sampsell noticed certain small landmarks. This stable was one of them. A piece of guttering had broken loose at a corner of the eaves and was hanging free; invariably he would glance at it to see if it had come all the way loose or if Aubrey had fixed it. Today, at the same instant, he was mechanically searching through his pouch for the circular for Box #536. It was when he realized he was using both hands for this purpose that the sweat suddenly rimmed his neck. He had neither hand on the steering wheel. He was not even looking at the road. The car was going along, its wheels in the deep ruts, just as well as if he had been steering.

He clutched the wheel. Almost immediately he had to fight a strong temptation to let go of it again. A strange image had suddenly framed itself in his mind. "I have known it for years," he said to himself, "—just like a mechanical beetle on the end of a string!"

He wanted to take both hands off the steering wheel again and see just how far the car would go without leaving the road, but he did not dare, not because he feared a wreck but because he feared just the opposite—that the car would keep safely to the road all by itself, completing its rounds and uncannily finding its own way back to its starting point like a wound-up infinitesimal automaton.

By the time Mr. Sampsell returned home, just after noon, he had a headache and his body quivered with the chill that often precedes illness. He lived down near the end of the village in what was commonly called the old Temple house—a two-story affair with gables and bay windows of the 1890's—now badly in need of paint which he could not afford.

Ordinarily, upon completing his route, Mr. Sampsell ate his midday dinner and lay down on the couch in the parlor for a nap. Later he read the Colonial Springs *News-Leader* and perhaps looked through the *Pathfinder* or *Farm Journal* and had fantasies about the neat orchard-farm he often dreamed of owning. In spring and summer he spent much of his free time working in his garden or grape arbor. And sometimes as he hoed away among his vegetables, with his sleeves rolled up and his collar detached, he could almost forget his bills and the fact that the very shirt he was wearing had been given him by his wife's cousin, Delbert Collins the bank cashier.

This day he took only a glass of milk for his dinner. Then, instead of lying down at once for his nap, he put on his patched black sweater and went out on the back porch and sat in an old rocker looking down over the spent garden and tangled back lot toward the row of sycamores along the creek. . . .

Mr. Sampsell's wife and two of their daughters were canning late pears in the kitchen. The strong odor of spices and cooking fruit drifted out to him and he found it unpleasant.

Anxiety held him taut. He unraveled a loose piece of yarn in the sleeve of the old sweater several inches and wadded it up in his palm before he realized what he was doing. Had he failed to apply for extension of the note at the bank? Lost registered mail or neglected church or lodge duties?

A dull late autumn brownness—a kind of ugly decrepitude—had taken hold of that part of the earth he could see and that he felt today to include himself. The tomato vines in the garden were dead, the weeds in the lot were sere, and the leaves had fallen from the sycamore branches now standing stark against a sky that soon would turn gray and cold. His neighbor's aged bony roan horse, stiff-jointed and useless, stumbled about in an adjoining field.

There was something of utmost importance on the edge of his thoughts he could not quite capture. Other things kept intruding. What had happened to his dream of a tidy farm owned mortgage-free? It had perished not only as a possible reality but even as a dream. Simply because the thing called time passed with such quiet inexorability. The image of the deep ruts of Route #7, which he had followed for so many years, kept coming before his eyes. He saw them separately; each assumed the immensity of one of the great raw gullies scarring the landscape so familiar to him, in which he had floundered as time passed like an unnoticed golden cloud until the rut or gully became the exact size and shape of the grave that one day would be dug for him in the cemetery on the long hill back of the village.

He was very confused. His mind would not come into focus. He groped now not for something he might have forgotten but for something he deserved and had never received.

He arose from the chair. Nothing looked right or felt right. The most familiar object on the porch—the old cupboard with its tin doors—seemed, oddly, as if it belonged on another planet. He felt so rattled, so strange to himself, that he went through the hallway and entered the parlor, where the shades were drawn, and lay down on the horsehair couch with an old laprobe over him. Later he was never able to say whether he slept or not. He did not think so. He closed his eyes but he felt almost certain that he did not even doze. He lay there for perhaps a quarter of an hour.

At the end of that time he appeared at the door leading from the pantry into the kitchen. He was holding to the doorjamb as if otherwise he might fall. He was so pale and there was such a peculiar cast to his features that the girl Florence asked in quick alarm, "Papa, are you sick?"

Ignoring his daughter, Mr. Sampsell addressed his wife. Speaking slowly, very distinctly and with great emotion he said, "Clara, I have a conviction!"

Mrs. Sampsell was carefully wiping the rim of a filled jar with a dishcloth. The kitchen was sultry with steam. She was hot and very tired. She turned her perspiring face toward her husband.

"What on earth are you talking about?" she asked wearily.

"I have a conviction," Mr. Sampsell repeated with the gravity of a mystic, "that—there—is—a—diamond—worth—millions—of—dollars—in—this—house!"

Mrs. Sampsell, an extremely gentle and patient person, did not know what to say or do, so she began laughing with great low heavy swells that made her whole frame heave like a sea. When she finally stopped laughing she wiped her eyes with her apron and asked Mr. Sampsell where he had ever got such a notion.

"It came to me. As a conviction," he said in the same imposing tone.

Mrs. Sampsell made a disparaging sound in her throat.

"You dreamed it," she scoffed gently.

The younger daughter, Dora, asked her father if he had had a vision. She had read a historical-religious novel in which not a few of the characters had experienced visions of fascinating natures.

Mr. Sampsell denied that he had had either a dream or a vision. He said it was purely an overwhelming *conviction*. He could explain it in no other terms. It had simply come to him while he was lying on the sofa that there was, in or about the house, a diamond of immense size and inestimable value. Its origin he could not account for. Perhaps old Mrs. Temple had once owned it and it had been there ever since her passing. On that point he was not clear. But he had the feeling, he added, that the diamond was under the front steps and he now proposed to go out and look for it.

When Mrs. Sampsell saw that her husband was in deadly earnest she could do no more than stare at him. As he turned from the doorway she and both girls followed him through the house.

With his wife and daughters watching him in mute anxiety, he got down on his hands and knees and poked around under the steps and the porch. He found nothing except leaves and the usual debris that collects under porches, and finally he emerged with his hands and the knees of his trousers dirty.

"Well, are you satisfied?" Mrs. Sampsell wanted to know.

Mr. Sampsell stood on the lower step thoughtfully scratching the back of his neck.

"No, to tell the truth I'm not," he said gravely. "There's a diamond around here somewhere and I'm going to find it if it takes me all day."

Mrs. Sampsell implored her husband to go back into the parlor and lie down until he felt better. He said that he felt all right—quite calm. He admitted that he knew this must seem unusual and he wished that she and the girls would go on back into the kitchen and leave him alone. He was so firm about it that they retreated into the house.

In a moment Mr. Sampsell himself went into the house and stood in the front hallway trying to plan a systematic search. A heavy excitement was upon him now. His hands shook, his heart was pounding and perspiration trickled from his armpits. He went to the pantry and snatched up a handful of matches and started hunting through the closets. He was under the impression that the diamond was to be found in a silver-plated jewel box that was just small enough to be held in the hand, had curving ornamental legs and when opened would have a velvet lining. He knew these things because he had seen the box. He was not certain precisely what he meant by this except that he could picture the box with such tremendous vividness that it was startlingly clear in his mind. He thought it might be in a corner of one of the closets, simply overlooked there in the many years of their residence.

He went through each of the three closets on the first floor and then bounded up the stairs with a sort of youthful sprint.

On a dresser in the bedroom of his two youngest daughters, the twins Eula and Constance, he spied a box roughly resembling the one he had in mind. It was of bronze, about four inches square, with a Chinese pagoda embossed on the lid. He grabbed it up and yanked it open only to discover it contained nothing more consequential than a small string of cheap coral beads, an English two-shilling piece, a French franc, a large black button, a small white button and a roll of Kodak film. He recalled then that one of the twins had been given the receptacle by a village youth who had joined the army and traveled in foreign lands. He had seen it a thousand times.

Mr. Sampsell's delusion left him as quickly as it had come. He went over to the bed and sat down, trembling, shaken by the strength of the hallucination. After a few moments he was aware that his wife was standing at his side and he looked up, his face white and haggard.

"Clara," he said, "I've had a spell of some kind. Do you think I'm going out of my mind?"

Quietly, Mrs. Sampsell sat down beside him. Very easily and naturally she began rubbing his back, massaging the tight muscles from his neck into his shoulders. It was a thing she often did when he was discouraged or distraught. There was a soothing magic in her gentle, affectionate hands. Before long, like a child, Mr. Sampsell put his head into her soft ample lap. Even after he was asleep she went on stroking him. . . .

The next day, while making his round, the conviction came upon Mr. Sampsell again. It happened very quickly. He was going down the long hill beyond the Crummitt place when he abruptly pulled to the side of the road and stopped. He had heard a single, unaccountable, clear whisper.

"In the packages!" the whisper said.

With amazing calm, without either hesitation or surprise, he stretched himself up over the seat and took from the rear cushion a package, from Sears, Roebuck and Co., addressed to "Mr. F. L. Bartley" and marked SHOES.

He held the parcel in his hands. With his right thumbnail he slit an opening along the double fold of paper. . . .

Mr. Sampsell said later that he "came to" in Cliff Updike's barbershop back in the village. He was lying in the chair getting a shave and Cliff was talking away about the hunting season, which had opened on November first. His mind was very cloudy. He could not even remember how he got there; he was like one trying to awake from a horrible dream in which someone posing as himself had frantically gathered up the contents and wrappings of a dozen ransacked parcel-post packages and hidden them in a blackberry patch in one of the fields of Miller Sands' farm.

Cliff was talking about hunting pheasants. He said there had been good cover last winter and there ought to be good shooting in the scrub. He ceased talking when another customer entered.

Mr. Sampsell lay in curious rigidity as Cliff finished shaving him, applied another hot towel and a scented astringent. Then the chair was pushed to the upright position. Even then Mr. Sampsell's muscles remained locked in a kind of rigor. He eyed the other customer in suspicion and alarm. He was a stranger in a business suit, small and sharp, with a leather bag on the bench beside him. There was something ominous about the man. He had too many pencils sticking out of his breast pocket. He had the quiet friendliness, the disarming ease of a postal inspector. (Actually, he was a brush salesman on a door-to-door canvass of the village.)

Mr. Sampsell's hands were trembling as he arose from the chair and put on his collar and tied his tie. He could not take his eyes off the stranger. He began searching for a particularly apt phrase, a penetrating comment on world affairs, to use before the other. He adjusted his tie and said with false airiness, "All right, Clifford, how much will that be?"

"Same as per usual," said Cliff, "—thirty-five."

Mr. Sampsell rammed his hand into his right trouser pocket and then into his other pockets in turn. He hadn't a cent.

"Dangnation, Clifford!" he said. "I've left my wallet at home."

"Aw, that's all right," Cliff assured him. "Hand it to me the next time you come in."

"I'm good for it, Clifford," he said. "You know I'm good for it, don't you, Clifford?" He was feverishly excited.

"Sure, I know you're good for it," Cliff said easily. "Any time—"

Mr. Sampsell whirled and said to the newcomer: "I should think I am good for a trifling amount like that. I have a very valuable diamond here in my coat. I'll show it to you. It weighs"—he winked at the astonished stranger—"thirty pounds."

His trembling hands reached for the coat and plunged into the empty pockets and suddenly he knew then what he had done. He had robbed the United States Mails. His face blanched and the coat fell to the floor. Like one deserted by all his sense, all his faith, all his hopes and all his gods, he burst out of the barbershop and went stumbling blindly down the road crying, "Clara! Clara!"

Mr. Sampsell was a patient at the State insane asylum in a town some fifty miles away for almost six months. On the day of his release he took a bus to Colonial Springs and there was met by Mrs. Sampsell and his daughter, Dora. He felt quite well and anxious to get on with the life he had swerved from when the delusion had overtaken him. One of the hospital psychiatrists, a young but sympathetic and remarkably perceptive man named Dr. Gordon, had done much to rebuild his self-confidence. Dr. Gordon explained that these things not infrequently came upon people "in their middle years" and then just as abruptly disappeared, often never to return, once the patient had determined to face reality. Such seemed to be Mr. Sampsell's case. He had had no hallucinations since the first week of his confinement.

During the early stages of his hospitalization he had lived in shamed and palsied dread. Once he had even refused to see his family when they came on one of their periodic visits. He had an obsessive belief he would be prosecuted as a mail thief. But no such thing happened. On the contrary, through the active interest and intervention of Dr. Gordon and a public petition signed by the villagers, Mr. Sampsell's daughter Florence had been allowed to keep on with his R.F.D. route against the day when he himself would be well enough to take it over again.

His homecoming was simple. The family had splurged a bit on a supper which consisted of two fried chickens, biscuits, mashed potatoes, gravy, artichokes, and fresh strawberries which Dora had bought in Colonial Springs.

Things were so-so in the household. Mrs. Sampsell had not been feeling too well since she had last seen him, having been bothered by a number of aches and pains, but she bore them without complaint, with the same gentle resignation that had marked her whole life. Mrs. Sampsell told him they had not been able to reduce the bills at any of the stores—in fact, they might be just a little bigger than when he had left—but Delbert had been willing to extend the bank note for another six months. Mr. Eckard had, as she had told him on her last visit, plowed the garden in March and they had set out lettuce and onions and tomatoes and had planted potatoes and snap beans. Florence had been managing fairly well on the mail route but it was a trial to the girl and she would be relieved to give it up now that her father was back.

In the evening Mr. Sampsell had one of the twins run up to the village and get him a pack of his favorite small-size cigars and then he and Mrs. Sampsell sat together in the swing on the front porch. It was warm. Fireflies flitted through the night under the poplars. A mock-orange bush in a corner of the yard threw off its heavy sweet fragrance and now and then, as the faint breeze shifted, there came an odor of honeysuckle and locust blossoms. Mr. Sampsell was glad to be at home and as he sat beside his wife in the spring evening his spirit seemed to relax and expand. She asked him about "that nice young doctor" with whom she had talked several times. And Mr. Sampsell reflected that the psychiatrist, in expressing sincere admiration for Mrs. Sampsell, had more than once subtly reminded him of the single name he had cried out that day he ran from Cliff Updike's barbershop in the deepest despair that had ever shaken his heart.

A little later Charlie and Eunice Stuart came over for a short visit and Charlie filled him in on the meager village news. A whole new roof had been put on the Methodist church. It was said that Pete Boyer had just about decided to give up the management of the Piggly Wiggly and build a store of his own right across from Willard's. . . . "Every durn' soul in this village signed that petition for you and people asked about you every day or two. . . ." Harry Frye had been pretty badly hurt by a tractor two months before and that character Cliff Updike, the barber, had himself been in the asylum again as an alcoholic for seven weeks around the first of the year when he failed to sober up from his Thanksgiving-Christmas drunk. Hadn't he run into Cliff there? . . . "By the way," Charlie wanted to know, "how do they treat you in that place anyway?"

Well, not too badly, Mr. Sampsell could answer honestly. He made no mention of his two months on Ward Four, the suicide ward. He spoke of his transfer to Sixteen (where smoking, letter writing and reading were permitted) and then told of being given the job in the hospital dairy. And soon after the first signs of spring came he had been taken from the dairy and put to work in the hospital gardens, pruning shrubs and hedges and planting flowers.

Mr. Sampsell had been cautioned by Dr. Gordon that he might expect unfamiliar sensations his first month or two at home—important and inevitable crises which he must understand and face and overcome—but he felt nothing of the kind except that once he abruptly arose without excusing himself and entered the house and found himself wandering aimlessly around in the living room. When Mrs. Sampsell came in to ask what he was looking for he had to think quickly to say "matches" because he hadn't the faintest idea. She reminded him that he had matches in his pocket and they returned to the porch together and in the darkness she sat beside him quietly, unobtrusively massaging the muscles from the base of his neck down his shoulder blades. Mr. Sampsell remained composed for the rest of the evening and even related with reminiscent humor several anecodotes concerning the hospital.

After Charlie and Eunice left, Mr. Sampsell sat on the porch with his wife for a last cigar. He felt a blessed awareness of the patient, rather dumpy little woman who had been his wife for more than thirty-five years and who had borne his children and most of his troubles. And he was touched by the interest and kindness of his neighbors. He reflected that, by and large, all people were generous and kind; he regretted being unable to perform some great deed to repay them. . . .

The Mr. Sampsell who set out upon his R.F.D. route the next morning seemed no different from the Mr. Sampsell who had driven over that road almost every weekday for more than a quarter of a century. He did not betray his nervousness; he had determined, as Dr. Gordon had instructed him, to push away from his feelings any undue excitement. He wore his old linen suit, which had grown threadbare around the pocket-edges but which still might do for two or three more seasons. And beside him, wearing a little round black straw hat and a clean dotted-swiss dress, sat Mrs. Sampsell.

It was a bright warm day, a glorious day. The apple and peach orchards were in full blossom. The fences along the road were heavy with honeysuckle. The banks were spotted with the varied colors of wildflowers. Jonquils and narcissus were peeping up in front yards and occasionally they saw blossoming japonica and mock-orange bushes. The pastures held an even lushness and fields of knee-high wheat were marked off in neat squares of deep green. To the west of them the slopes of three mountains—one running into another—rose brilliant and fulgent with the unbroken white and pink of dogwood in full flower.

Thus they rode along old #7, Mr. Sampsell drawing up to the mailboxes as they came to them and Mrs. Sampsell sitting with her hands in her lap and a benign smile on her face as she noted the beauty of the countryside. The fragrance of spring was in their nostrils and the rebirth of nature kindled their hearts.

When they came to Albert Vernon's, Mr. Sampsell saw a little girl of seven or eight in the front yard. He placed the paper and a postcard in the box and then lifted his metal-capped cane from the seat and held it out the window and waggled it at her playfully.

The child was hugging the fence, eyeing him shyly or sullenly, he could not tell which. He waggled his cane again.

"Don't you hit me with that thing, you crazy old coot!" the child yelled, and dashed across the yard toward the house in a pell-mell run.

"Don't be scared, honey!" Mr. Sampsell called after her frantically, straining far out the window. "Come back and I'll show you a—"

And then he was aware of a tight grip on his arm. It was an unyielding grip, not with the erratic strength of a man but with the constant, deeper strength of a woman. And a moment later he felt the patient, loving, understanding hand gently stroking his back. Mrs. Sampsell said not a word.

Clutching the steering wheel with all his might, his arms shaking, he was suddenly conscious that this was the first of the crises against which Dr. Gordon had warned that he must face and, *with help,* overcome. . . . Mr. Sampsell drove slowly and dully on down the road for almost a quarter of a mile before he pulled slightly off to the side and stopped and leaned forward and let the hot tears run down his face.

Never once did the calm and gentle hand cease its tender stroking of his back under the old threadbare coat. And still not a word did she say.

Presently he stopped crying. He took from his pocket a handkerchief and dried his eyes and blew his nose.

"Well, let's see," he said then. "Ed Tate's is next. There's the paper. And see if there isn't a letter in there for Ed's oldest boy."

So they drove on. Mr. Sampsell paid close attention to the old familiar intimate landmarks. The headstones in the little Lutheran Church near Amsterdam Hill needed straightening. Aubrey Beck had actually gotten around to repairing that piece of guttering on his stable that had been neglected so long. When they passed the blackberry thicket on Miller Sands' farm Mr. Sampsell glanced at it briefly —as at a spot where something unpleasant had occurred to someone of his acquaintance—and that was all. It even struck him as rather outlandish that anyone could have attached such importance to a thing, whether real or hallucinatory, so hard and impersonal and essentially worthless as a piece of crystallized carbon.

As she had done for all those years, and as she would do for years to come, her face cast in an expression of quiet courage and devotion, Mrs. Sampsell simply sat beside him, was simply there.

"My!" she said once, gazing out over the blossoming orchards toward the mountainsides pink and white with the dogwood that bloomed now and would bloom again and again, "it gets prettier every spring."

◈ Part 3

The Valley and the Mountains Beyond

The Silence of the Mountains

THE FIRST SLOW flush of gray came into the sky above Mill Mountain across the valley and gradually the hard outlines of rocks and trees chiseled their way out of night and snow into the cold winter dawn. The gaunt, big-framed man with eyes as frosty as the dawn itself had been there a half-hour already. He stood in the snow by the wire gate at the road lifting his feet now and then and putting his hands into his mackinaw pockets but not taking the flour sack with the forty pounds of shelled hickory-nut kernels off his shoulder. He had thought about doing so but did not consider it worth the trouble.

It had still been dark when he came down the hollow and it was about as cold a morning as they had had. Mountain winters were undependable. For two or three years hand-running there would be hardly any snow and only an occasional skim of ice over the river. And then a winter would come along when one snow would pile on top of another and water in the tanks on kitchen stoves would freeze solid while women were doing their cooking. But even hard winters like that were a natural part of the country and a man got through them, one after another. The only winter that had ever worked its way into his very bones was that of 1917–18 which he had spent in France in tents and in trenches. He had minded the unfriendly rain and mud. It seemed to him that his uniform was never dry and he was always worrying that his gas mask would not work and that his army rifle was going to rust. But worse than either weather or fear had been a kind of chronic and special and personal homesickness.

He lived just short of a mile and a half up on the side of Dunlap Mountain on a shelf of land cleared out of the laurel thickets and pines by his grandfather almost a century ago. In good weather he worked as a day hand for Mr. Will here at the old Craig English farm on the rich floor of the valley. He rarely asked favors and he had never "stilled"

148

or been in jail. He and his wife, Stella, had spent nearly every evening that early winter cracking the hickory nuts and picking out the kernels, and now he was going into town to dispose of them. He got into town once or twice a year. That was enough.

Down across the white meadow Mr. Will's house and barn and outbuildings assumed form, and in time (he had known it would be time because Mr. Will and his whole family stayed in bed until after daylight) blue smoke began rising from the rear chimney, quavering at first and then straightening itself into a delicate arrow, and he saw the oldest boy, bundled up and chin on collarbone to avert the bite of the cold, go out to the barn with the milk bucket and finally come back. At length Mr. Will himself, dressed for town and wearing his fur-collared flight jacket from the surplus store, went on his fast bandy legs through the yard to the automobile shed carrying a steaming teakettle.

When the car started up through the meadow he opened the gate and Mr. Will drove through and he closed the gate. He misjudged the way to open the car door, pulling the handle up instead of pushing it down, and Mr. Will had to lean across the seat and open it for him from the inside.

"Man alive!" Mr. Will said as he climbed in. "Whyd'n't you come on downt' the house, Journey? Cold enough to freeze your ears off!"

Mr. Will's round face was baby red. He could not stand cold.

"Right sharp," Journey agreed.

"Sharp!" Mr. Will said. "You know what that th'mometer on my back porch said? Three above!"

"I believe you," Journey conceded. "Sharp, all right."

Mr. Will had a fine car, equipped with a heater, but it was not built for a man six-foot-two. The roof was a mite low and made him duck his head. He sat toward the edge of the seat, his head angled forward, and they went on up the snow-covered valley, the chains grinding harshly as the car crawled along ruts through the drifts and over frozen chuckholes in the open places.

"What're you figurin' on buyin'?" Mr. Will asked presently.

"Well," Journey said slowly, "I thought I'd get me a hasp."

"Hasp! Is that all you're goin' to town for?"

"I mought look at paint brushes too," Journey said reluctantly.

He shifted on the seat and felt the moisture of perspiration on his palms. He had heard people claim they had trouble getting their breath in closed cars with the heater going. Cale Lowhatter swore up and down he had to cough and hock for a week from some kind of fumes that stayed with him after riding over to Tucker's Ford with Fletch Campbell the mail carrier. But he himself had ridden with Mr. Will quite a few times and never noticed any discomfort and he knew that his uneasiness now had nothing to do with the heater. He had to resist the temptation to feel in the buttoned pocket of his wool shirt and determine if there was still safely tucked in it the picture clipped from a magazine, the presence of which he could not have explained to Mr. Will and could scarcely explain to himself.

The car bounced steadily along. Man-on-Fence Valley was bounded on the west by the unbelievably even crest of Dunlap Mountain, as sharp and straight as the edge of a razor, and on the east by the irregular but easy rises and falls of the top of Mill Mountain above which today the sun would not appear until mid-morning. To the northeast old Tomahawk Ridge towered above the land, base and lower slopes white and upper ridges and peak lost in clouds and leaden gloom, remote and unassailable. Once it had been Indian country. Every time a man plowed bottomland he still turned up flint arrowheads by the score. In the oldest of the known times, probably before they even had tribal names and when only the silent panthers were their enemy, they had been there after bear and deer and lesser game. And later the Delawares, Cherokees and terrible Shawnees were there. By then the whites had converged on the valley to settle. They cut down trees and built log houses—the empty-handed ones cabins and the prospering ones forts with gun-slit windows—and chinked and dobbed them and built chimneys out of the native limestone and sandstone. And many of them had been dragged out of their houses and massacred and scalped. In time the Indians vanished, and of all those old lost days only stray remnants of the early pioneers remained: here a stone wall resisting battering wind or silent freezing and thawing and there an ancient cabin lonely in its laurel thicket or on the bank above the quiet river.

They met no one. The flat bottomland and the hillsides alike were lifeless under the heavy snow. They passed Shimlette's, Lockland's and Gatemyer's without seeing a stir. The valley had slipped back into a kind of unrelenting prehistoric gray coldness without life and upon which even historical memories had left not a trace.

At the Weeping Willow Church they hit the macadam and Mr. Will increased his speed. The throb of the chains became a light steady singing and they went that way through the village of Deer

Meadow where once he had lived and where he had done his courting and where, in the Baptist Church, he had married Stella.

Stella was a good deal younger than he was; he had married her when
she was sixteen. She was a Tuttle. She had the big peculiar fawn-
colored eyes that marked every Tuttle that ever lived. Her father
was old man Boyce Tuttle. Some people called him Hollerin' Tuttle.
His house still sat a little way up the stumpy hill at the lower end of
the village. When old man Hollerin' was alive he used to sit on his
front porch with his German police dog he had bought for a dollar in
Nag Alley in town and when anybody drove by in a car Hollerin'
would yell, "Deacon, you got any likker with you today?" or, "Sim,
what you doin' up here in God's country? Thought they had you
locked up in jail." And the dog would split across the creek and chase
after them until they were out of sight. Hollerin' never had any real
meanness in him but not everybody knew how to take him.

There was no sign of smoke anywhere in the village. The forty or
fifty houses, the school, the two churches and Walter Lange's store
huddled silent in the unending white of the snow.

As they passed the store Mr. Will said, "Gabriel won't be able to
get these people up on Judgment Day."

"They like to stay in bed, all right," Journey agreed. He did not
consider Mr. Will any world's champion early riser himself but he
said nothing about it.

He had kin people of his own, other branches of the Shelton family,
scattered around Deer Meadow. They either lived in the village or
had patch farms and some of them worked seasonally for the Forest
Service or on the road maintenance crew. He seldom got in touch
with them. He supposed that if the truth were known he liked the
woods better than kin people or any other kind of people. There was
something about people congregating together, whether it was living together in a village or marching together in an army, that made a
man lose his independence.

The chains of the car droning steadily, Mr. Will drove along. They
came in time to the upper end of the valley and turned abruptly east
on the modern highway, recently scraped, that once had been a pio-
neer trail and later a stage road and now was as level and straight as a
board. They left the somber mountains and proceeded through the
foothill orchard country and finally came into the rolling fox-hunting country that these days contained the white-fenced estates and
mansions of the Northern millionaires—as if within an hour they had

left one world and entered another—and there, from on top of Three-Mile Hill, they saw both the town of Colonial Springs and the sun. . . .

They parted on the Town Clock corner, at Central Avenue and Main Street, where for generations countrymen had parted to pursue their individual ways into the strangeness of the town. Mr. Will had already told him he would probably stand the best chance of selling the hickory-nut kernels at the big Supermarket at the foot of Wine Jug Hill.

"Now let's get our business over with," Mr. Will said, blowing on his hands, "and meet at Wilmer's Drugstore at two o'clock and get away from here. I don't want to get stuck in a drift after dark."

Mr. Will went bandy-legged down Main under the neon signs as if he not only belonged in the town but owned it. Journey knew he was headed as straight as a die for the office of Mr. Clint Chesterman, the County Clerk, to stand around smoking cigars and waiting until there was nobody else in the office so Mr. Clint could pull from under the counter two Coca-Cola glasses and a bottle of brandy. With all his talk of hurry, he would stand around down there half the day arguing politics with the county officials and tapping that brandy bottle that would keep him jawing all the time he was in town and make for reckless driving two-thirds of the way home.

Main Street had been scraped and the sidewalks shoveled and the snow left piled at the curb in a waist-high ridge like a breastworks. Cars were parked here and there along the snow ridges on each side of the street and a policeman, overcoated and muffler-wrapped and exhaling plumes of breath, was out in the intersection trying to keep the crawling traffic from getting snarled in the narrow channel of street that was left.

Journey started across against the red signal light and the policeman held up his gloved hand and said, "Take it easy there! Can't you see?" and he stepped back up on the curb, the sack balanced easily on one shoulder. The Town Clock went off with a sudden single iron boom and two or three people hurried across but confusion made him miss that opportunty. Impatiently the policeman said, "All right, all right!" Still he stood uncertainly, having already lost something, a measure of independence or dignity, not once thinking that in his habitat, the abiding mountains, where he was the equal of any man, no one—policeman or otherwise—would address him in that tone of voice, and most certainly and especially would not if he had in his hands his thirty-thirty rifle. It came to him then that he was waiting not for the color of green but for the iron intonation which, for that confused second or two, he had supposed set it off. He knew better, had merely forgotten how the lights really worked, and was rattled when he remembered. The boom, of course, had nothing to do with it. A man simply stood long enough for a walnut leaf to spiral to the ground on an October breeze, until the green was on in his direction, and then he went on across.

It was that way all along Main Street. He set off up toward Wine Jug Hill, the Negro section of cafés and beer parlors and nameless holes-in-walls, to the store Mr. Will had told him about. On along under the neons, like rigid overhanging abbreviated limbs of trees unseen, he walked with his deliberate, slightly stoop-shouldered gait.

He could not get used to the hard thump of his boots on the pavement; it made him feel as if he had planks for shoe soles. The uncertainty of his footing started him worrying about the picture in his shirt pocket. It was an advertisement for a nylon nightgown, a high-toned name for a piece of flimsiness, from a magazine one of Mr. Will's girls had found in a summer camper's cabin and passed on to Stella. It showed a slim young woman wearing one of the things and reclining on a sort of mist or cloud, and for all practical purposes she might as well not have had on anything at all. If he slipped and broke a leg and had to be taken to the hospital and some nurse found that sight. . . . A slow ooze of fine sweat broke out around his collar. On past the rhythm of plate glass and store vestibule he clumped.

At the foot of the Hill, just above the General Jubal Early statue that made the street curve around it there, he came to and entered the glass doors of the Supermarket. Orderly laden counters formed a neat and seductive maze of crisscrossed openings and aisles. In time a clerk was beside him, coming from where he knew not, wearing an apron, hands loosely to his sides, like one paused in flight, in his whole manner a single warning that he had just five seconds in which to be polite.

"Don't have any call for loose hickory-nut kernels—all that's in packages today," the clerk said briefly, in a kind of surprise, and almost immediately he moved away toward a woman customer wheeling along a metal basket cart piled with cans and packages.

Silently Journey turned and left the store. He clumped four blocks back down Main past the three banks, the Colonial Theater, the drugstores, Worthingham's Hardware and the Five and Ten. He came to the only other street with which he was at all familiar. It led by the Courthouse where, in summer, men came into town to sit, in shade or sun as fancy struck them, on the cement wall surrounding the Square. Just back from the sidewalk, on the lawn of the Square itself, was the big statue of General Lee on Traveller. A crust of snow lay upon the statue—on the horse's rump and the bow of the saddle and even upon the old General's bare head.

The street led in the direction of the railroad station. He set off up that way. This street he remembered. Along this same pavement one September day he and fifteen or sixteen other young fellows had walked in a loose untrained group, without being able to understand, much less follow, the barked commands of an officer in khaki uniform and leggings, to board a train and be taken eastward out of the mountains to Camp Lee, where he had spent a little less than three months before being sent to Norfolk and shipped across twenty-some hundred miles of unbroken ocean on a transport painted like a zebra.

Along this street were several grocery stores. He entered the first one he came to and a fidgety man wearing eyeglasses presented himself.

"Hickory-nut kernels?" said the man. "Well, I suppose we could handle them."

He took the sack and placed them on his scales.

"Thirty-six pounds," he said. "Forty a pound." He lifted a pencil from the counter and began figuring rapidly on a pad. "Fourteen-forty." He adjusted his nose glasses.

"You handle hasps?" Journey asked. He needed a good hasp to replace the rusty one that had broken when he tried to put a lock on his corncrib. He had the lock; what he needed was a hasp.

"Hasps! No sir. Try Worthingham's."

"I'll just take the cash," Journey said.

The man looked at him blankly and shook his head. "You'll have to take it out in trade," he said. "That was a tradin' price I quoted you."

Journey knew he was no hand with words. He did not know how to explain that he did his regular trading with Walter Lange in Deer Meadow and what he had come all the way to town for was cash. He was afraid that if he got into all that the man would want to know what he was so bound and determined to have cash for and he was not going to tell that to some stranger. Or to anybody. It did not even occur to him that the man might offer him a cash price if he asked about it. He picked up his sack and shouldered it and left that place too.

It had warmed up some. That September morning so long ago had been fine and warm. As he and the others marched in a ragged group toward the station, business people stood in their open doors and watched them; a good many waved and called out friendly words. There had been a regular crowd standing around on the broad cement platform in front of the station to see them off, kin people from out in the country and some of the highest and best-dressed people from right here in town. Up toward the station now a switch engine was shifting freight cars about, gray steam and smoke churning up above it.

In the next twenty minutes he clumped into three more stores, one after another, and could find no one interested in doing business with him. If they did not offer one excuse they offered another. The third store was within a block of the station. He had a strong notion to walk on up there and watch the switch engine for a while. Watching a locomotive was a steady and a sobering thing. But he knew that if he went up there it would be time wasted. Just then he heard the solemn booming of the Town Clock again and he turned and went back toward Main . . . a gaunt man, big of frame, stooped and frosty-eyed, the sack over his shoulder.

The loneliness of town seeped through him. There were a good many people on the street now but he recognized none of them. He wished he would run into somebody he knew. His Cousin Poke lived just a few miles up the railroad track at Chapman's Switch and one or two of Poke's boys were always in town on Saturday, but he had seen nothing of them. It might be that they were in jail; they got themselves in there sometimes.

It occurred to him to try his luck in Nag Alley. He clumped on down that way and turned into the alley where in the old days, even before the Civil War, owner of stiff-necked nag traded for spavined one and went home victorious and intoxicated. There were a one-chair barbershop and two or three stores along there and on up toward the end of the alley stood two loading platforms of wholesale groceries. He recognized and entered old man Jarrett's place, a structure that resembled less a store than a wooden cavern stocked and stuffed from floor to ceiling with secondhand suits, pasteboard suitcases, shoes, caps and helter-skelter odds and ends. They said that Jarrett, who had been skinning country people for almost fifty of his sixty-five or seventy years, owned half the property along the block.

Jarrett's pale crafty face peered out of a hole, a kind of rat's nest he had burrowed amongst his tatterdemalion stock and asked him what he wanted. Journey told him he had hickory-nut kernels to sell and Jarrett said, "I'll handle anything."

Like groundhog or fox gone into den or skeleton back into tomb, the old man took the sack and disappeared and Journey was left standing with the cheap suits hanging about his head and shoulders and a heavy odor of shoe leather in his nostrils. He knew Jarrett was back there figuring to cheat him but that was something a man just had to put up with. Reappearing, his face bright with honest dealing, Jarrett said, "Thirty-two pounds—thirty-five a pound. Makes . . . Here you are."

"Like to have my sack," Journey told him. He had to stand for being beaten on the hickory nuts but he was not going to throw a good sack into the bargain.

Back up on Main Street, in Worthingham's Hardware Store, amid the clean smell of machinery and oil, he spent the better part of two hours inspecting most of the things he had ever wanted or would ever want in his natural life. Worthingham's doors had been open for a hundred years; Stonewall Jackson's men and, some said, even Phil Sheridan's men, had been in there. The clerks knew how to deal with a man. They let him look around until he got good and ready to buy something and then one of them came up and sold it to him.

Journey spent a good deal of time at the gun case. Worthingham's handled fine guns: every kind of rifle you could think of and good Winchester and Remington .12-gauge and .16-gauge automatics, pumps and double-barrels.

He looked over the saws, wrenches, hammers, screwdrivers and shelves and tables of instruments a man would never learn the name of but, having the money, would be tempted to buy for the sheer pleasure of having around and picking up now and then to look at.

Eventually he got over to the paint brushes. He had had it in mind for a long time that he would do some painting. His property consisted of a sturdy cabin with a loft and lean-to, a board stable, chicken-house, pole corncrib and pigpen, and a good shed that could be used for anything. He had a garden site, a rocky corn patch and some apple and pear trees. He also had a fine part-Guernsey cow, a flock of chickens, a sow and two coon hounds. He owned all of it free and clear. He kept the buildings up but he had never gotten around to painting them. He believed a man ought to paint his buildings, and even his fences if he had the extra money.

Now a clerk came over. Journey took a four-inch brush off its rack and felt of it. The handle was sturdy. He stroked the brush over his palm, then over the back of his hand. The hair was as soft as down. It was as soft or softer than a woman-feel. It was the best brush and one of the best feeling things he had ever had in his hand.

"That'll run you seven dollars," the clerk told him.

Journey stood studying the brush for a while. Finally, slowly, he hung it back on the rack.

"I'm goin' to have to think it over," he said, "but I'll tell you what I'll do. I'll buy me a hasp."

The clerk showed him a hasp. It was a good steel one—none of that cast iron that broke with the first blow and almost the first look. It was a good satisfactory hasp. He bought it and paid the sixty cents for it and put it in the empty sack and made his way out to the street.

He had known he was not going to get the paint brush. All the time he had been examining it he had felt as if Stella were standing behind him. She was not nagging at him; she never did that. She had never even mentioned about the nightgown. He had simply seen her pick up that magazine a hundred times and turn to the picture again and again as she thumbed through it. She wanted that gown and she had a right to it. Most of the time she would keep it in a bureau drawer, but she would take it along when they went up to Deer Meadow to the two summer lawn parties and spent the night with her brother Wallace and his wife. And now and then, maybe, she would take a notion to wear it right there at home. But she would not complain if she never got it. It was only that, once in a very great while, in the winter deadness, when they had seen no one for a month or more, her fawn-colored Tuttle eyes would take on a dull expression, the pupils as big as hazelnuts, as she gazed out the window down over the ridge. It would only last for a day or so but during that time she would be dropping things in the kitchen, just letting them fall out of her hand and not picking them up.

He clumped slowly down Main until he was smack in front of the place. Out in the show windows in plain view—on forms made to look like women's middles—were the garments (white and black and pink and some sheer to the point of transparency) no man could be reasonably expected to contemplate. He barely paused, glancing

out of the corners of his frosty eyes, and had the notion that everybody on the sidewalk was looking at him. He walked on.

A door opening near him let out upon the sidewalk a smell of
cooking onions like a blast. He realized he was about starved. He
looked up above the high eaves of the buildings until he located the
pale disc of the sun. He judged it was well past noon. He started
moving toward the onion smell, then stopped and peered through
the steamy window. A man wearing an apron and white hat was
lifting, with a turner, little flat discs of meat and slipping them
into buns and slapping onions and relish on them and setting them
in saucers and sliding them across a greasy marble-topped counter
to a line of standing customers. He knew that, hungry as he was, he
could not eat anything and enjoy it right now.

He turned and made his way back up the block to the shameless
store with its flagrant display. He stopped and looked in, lifting first
one foot and then the other, shifting about uncertainly. He got a
glimpse of the interior and knew he would not enter the place on this
trip anyway. On past he went.

That put him in front of a fruit stand. He went in and bought a
dozen oranges and six bananas. He paid for them out of the ten
dollar bill and put them in the sack with the hasp and shouldered
the sack and went outside again.

He cast his eye down toward that women's store. He did not know
what a thermometer would read now but it seemed to him that it
had warmed up a good deal. He could feel sweat under his hatband
and around his shirt collar. He started walking back down the street,
reached the place—and went on by. He told himself he was too warm
to go in there now. He proceeded to the end of the block and paused,
leaning against the corner of Hoge's Drugstore. He unbuttoned
his mackinaw. For some time he simply stood and watched the
crawling traffic and the pedestrians. The street intersecting was the
one that went by General Lee's statue and led on up to the railroad
station.

It was the street that had led him to a foreign country and to a war
that had been so long ago that now he had trouble remembering the
place names. He could remember Paris, Bordeaux and the river
Marne. There was one smaller town, near the Marne, not much
bigger than Colonial Springs. The Americans had a hard time there.
They shelled it and fought their way into and took it. And then the
Germans shelled it and came back in with machine guns and tanks
and the Americans had to give it up. For two weeks they had a seesaw

battle for the place, winning it one day and losing it a day or two later. Four times or maybe five times he had fought his way along the main street of that town and then, with the others, was driven back until he thought he was going to spend the rest of his life there. And finally, for no special reason, they just took it and held it. That had been a long time ago but it came back to him fairly clearly now.

He straightened himself and buttoned his mackinaw. Once more he went up the street. When he reached the place, he adjusted the sack on his shoulder, screwed up his eyes and took a good grip on the doorhandle. In he clumped. Behind the counter a stylish-looking woman smoked a cigarette in a holder; her wavy hair was roached back somewhat like a man's. She placed the cigarette and holder in a tray on the glass counter and looked at him with her eyebrows arched.

"Yes?" she was saying. "Can I help you?"

Fingering the folded picture from his shirt pocket, he abruptly laid it on the counter and yanked his hand away as if it were hot. He scratched himself on the side of the neck and opened and closed his mouth. Then he opened it again.

"Mought consider buyin' one of them contraptions," he said brusquely.

The woman unfolded the picture and looked at it. "Yes?" she said. "What color would you prefer?"

"Whatever color they come in, I reckon."

"Well, peach is a nice color," the woman said helpfully. "Now what is the size?"

He could bring his gaze neither to the woman nor to the girdled and brassiered busts and torsos on counter and table. His frosty eyes —that could sight a wild turkey five hundred yards away or take the measure of any man coming up the hollow—batted and squinted. His hard boots felt insecure on the carpet. The place had a feel of pure nakedness.

" 'Bout the same size as you, ma'm," he said finally.

"Just a moment, please." The woman glided from behind the counter and vanished into a doorway at the rear.

Left alone, he got the panicky notion that he was going to be tricked. That woman had gone back there for some terrible purpose. She was staying a long time. Maybe she was putting that thing on and in a minute would stick her head through the door and call him back. . . . In Paris, when he went there with the bunch after the Armistice, they had gotten him into a place by one of the fellows claiming he was part French and that a family of his cousins lived in that house. They never acted like any cousins he ever saw.

Then the saleslady reappeared with a slender oblong package and was preparing to remove the filmy, fleshy garment for his inspection.

"Ain't no need to take it out and *look* at it, ma'm," he said miserably.

He paid her and jammed the package into his sack, really sweating now, like a man in a hayfield in midsummer. . . .

They left the town and rode through the millionaire country and then through the orchard country around the neat village of Cherry Glen and on into the mountains. It had not melted any out that way. The drifts were high beside the fences and every gatepost wore a cap of snow and the creeks they passed still had long thick icicles hanging from tree roots close to the water. Whatever there had been of the dull sun had already disappeared into the endless mountains to the west of them.

For a while Mr. Will was gabby about county politics and about nobody doing anything about the roads once you got off the main Highway, and then the liquor died out in him and he drove silently. Journey sat on the edge of the seat, his head ducked forward a little. They turned into the upper valley just as the first shades of twilight were settling. Smoke rose blue and heavy from every house they passed and when they came to and passed Deer Meadow a few lights were already turned on. It was not possible to see the top of old Tomahawk Ridge, towering up there in mist and cloud a mile above the earth.

"I expect Stell gets almighty tired stayin' home and nobody to talk to all fall and winter long," Mr. Will said suddenly.

"She's got me to talk to," Journey said.

"Yes sir," Mr. Will said, "I reckon so."

Over the valley still lay a pristine coldness without life. They left the macadam and Mr. Will slowed and they crept along through the ruts with the chains now throbbing heavily. On into the familiar lifeless gray coldness the car carried them.

When they came to the mouth of the hollow Mr. Will stopped to let him out and said, "I don't envy you that climb through that mile of drifts none."

"Ain't so bad on the north side," Journey said.

"Just up to yore navel on the north side. I guess they ain't no use askin' you all down to play setback, until this snow's gone."

"I ain't much of a hand at gettin' out in winter."

"I'll know when spring's here for sure," said Mr. Will. "I'll see you two down in the lower medder after cress greens. Well, you folks come."

"You all come," Journey said.

The hard outlines of rocks and trees were gradually fading back into night and unbroken winter coldness and silence. He went on up beside the creek, following the north side under the pines where in most places the crusted snow was not quite up to the tops of his boots.

It was good dark when he got up to the flat ledge that he owned free and clear. Stella had the lamp lit and he knew she had milked and watered and foddered the cow and had given the dogs their cornbread and had his supper on the back of the stove. She was sitting by the window patching a shirt, her accustomed place from which she could look down over the ridge. If they had been a half-mile closer she could have heard the car every day when Fletch Campbell went by with the mail.

When he went in he felt her big fawn eyes on him and he simply set the slender package down on the bench by the door and said, "Now I ain't goin' to get in no habit of buyin' these things."

Then he went into the kitchen and got the lantern and the lock and took the hammer and some nails and went out to the corncrib and put the hasp and lock on so no one could pry it off unless they did it with a crowbar. He just be damned if he was going to lay by a crop next fall and let some Gatemyer or Lowhatter sneak over there the following spring and carry it away to make liquor with.

He started back to the cabin. He could not see his property now but he was very much aware of it, of the buildings around him and of the fences that marked it off and even of the familiar and welcome feel of the very snow on his own ground under his own feet. As he moved toward the house through the cold black mountain silence there suddenly passed over him a profound longing for that paint brush. He proposed to get it on his next trip to town. He was going to buy himself some paint and he was going to paint his house, stable, shed, corncrib, henhouse and pigpen a pure white until they shone and glistened like the snow itself in the silent mountain moonlight for any man to see.

⊰ The Sound That God Heard

THAT WAS THE summer Cousin Mattie was staying with us. She was the postmistress down at Marble Valley where we had the other farm. I did not like Cousin Mattie. It was partly because, as Father said, her eyes were so keen she probably knew what was in every letter that went through the Marble Valley post office without even having to open the envelope. It was also because hardly a day went by that she did not promise, in a rather awesome confidential whisper, to pray for you; and when you are ten such uninvited intercession is in the nature of an outrage.

I did not like Cousin Mattie even before the episode at the revival meeting. We went to the revival meeting against Father's wishes and as a special courtesy to Cousin Mattie. Father said a man accepted God as he walked through his fields of wheat and corn and alfalfa, and that women and children did so by special appointment with the pastor of the Rocky Springs Presbyterian Church.

But we went to the meeting and how Cousin Mattie knew the instant that Scott Reed and I slipped from the last bench and out the door of the church I do not know.

Mr. Daffin had reached that point in his sermon where, standing with his right hand on the pulpit and his left hand pointing toward the smoking lamp in the northeast corner of the church, he was describing sin in the cities. I knew nothing about sin in the cities. I knew very little about sin anywhere.

I cannot explain how it came about. Scott suggested it to me. (Cousin Mattie said the Devil suggested it to Scott.) I thought that when Scott first phrased the proposal he would surely be struck dead. I felt the wisdom of edging away from him on the bench. I turned my eyes toward Mr. Daffin. He had now removed his pince-nez and was explaining that sin was a general category—that it existed in the town, in the village, on the farm, even in the hearts of the very young.

I ventured a glance at Scott. He had not disappeared in a sudden pillar of smoke and fire, nor had he turned to stone. He simply sat

there snickering quietly. Then he looked at me and said in a snickering whisper:

"They'll think it's the Devil! They'll think he's up prancin' around
on the roof."

I think it was the sheer extravagance and audacity of the picture
that excited me. (Cousin Mattie said I became an agent of Satan.) I
began to snicker too. I could not get out of my mind the fascinating
image of Mr. Daffin and the choir and the congregation frozen in
sudden incredulity and dismay by the supposed sound of the Devil
prancing around on the church roof. The more I thought of it, the
more I snickered and the more impractical it became to remain in
the church. So Scott and I slipped out the door.

We got outside under the three big oak trees and I was still in
that state of foolish, keyed-up excitement. I said, "You *really* goin'
to do it?"

The moon was bright. I could see Scott quite clearly. He was now
entirely collected and suddenly seemed mature and purposeful.

"Come on," he said. "I'll show you."

We climbed the old board fence behind the church and walked
directly down to the creek and started gathering the rocks in our
arms.

We picked small ones that could be easily thrown.

We walked back up nearly to the fence.

"Throw 'em real fast," Scott said, "Then run like fire!"

Fate or Scott or the Devil or whoever was the real entrepreneur
of the episode left me not one instant for possible reconsideration.
Scott's right arm began darting back and forth and his rocks started
raining on the crimped tin roof. Mr. Daffin's voice faltered just once
and then began again in what seemed to me greater and momentarily
puzzled exhortation. My own arm hurled just one stone. Scott was
already splashing through the creek and I was standing there alone,
with my arm upraised and drawn back for the second blasphemy,
transfixed by the incredible and outrageous sound of the single rock
I had thrown, a noise and deed postulated for me just an instant later
by Cousin Mattie's shocked and searing words:

"Tucker English—God heard that sound!"

As fantastic as the noise of my one hurled rock against the tin roof
was the swift materialization of Cousin Mattie there at the fence.
One moment she had been without form or existence; the next she
was there, an old and bony and screeching face implanted between

the two topmost boards—an avenging wraith and an eternal chastisement.

I was escorted, or rather propelled, back into the church as if by a spectral emissary preserved in an arid state in one of the forgotten graves out under the cedars and emerged and arisen dry and intact for this one special act in the world's conduct.

I remember little about reentering the church except Father's face, turned, shadowed by the ineffectual lamplight, grave and inscrutable. And then his head slowly turned away along with the rest and was lowered in prayer.

I sat beside Cousin Mattie on the hard oak bench in a stupor of shame and bewilderment. I stared at the little compartment on the back of the bench in front of us in which there were a hymn book and a Sunday-school quarterly as if it were a haven into which my being could crawl and hide. I began hearing each word that Mr. Daffin said—twice—through some mystic process of redistillation and echo. Like this:

Mr. Daffin—"Oh the Almighty loves and pleads with every miserable sinner among us . . ."

Echo—"Every miserable sinner among us . . ."

Mr. Daffin—"Will you turn aside from the Almighty?"

Echo—"Turn aside from the Almighty?"

Mr. Daffin—"Will you leave the Almighty pleading for your soul?"

Echo—"Pleading for your soul? Tucker, the Almighty is pleading with you tonight."

Not for ever so long did I realize that Cousin Mattie was leaning close to my ear, repeating every phrase just as Mr. Daffin finished it.

Mr. Daffin—"Will you dare leave this church tonight with your back turned upon the Almighty?"

Cousin Mattie—"Will you dare leave this church tonight with your back turned upon the Almighty?"

Up near the front of the church there was a peculiar sniffling sound. It was old Ben Coles. He had been drinking. He weaved to his feet. The revival meeting had been going on for more than a week. Each night Ben Coles weaved to his feet and stood asking for salvation. Each day in his little shanty, filled with odd pieces of antique furniture and knickknacks for which he scoured the countryside, he sat drinking hard cider until time to go to revival. It was a pattern that repeated itself year after year. Nobody paid much attention to

Ben—whether he stood up to be saved or remained somnolent in his seat. He stood there crying.

Mr. Daffin's voice rose and fell and then rode on an even hypnotic wave. Sonorous and hypnotic. "Oh-hh-h sinn-nn-er com-mm-mme." The words were no longer words: they were music, subtle and tender and compassionate.

"Stand and accept forgiveness for what you have done, Tucker." The words in my ear were soft and urgently imperious. "Stand up, Tucker, and walk forward!"

I was standing and being urged into the aisle. Once there I simply followed the old carpeting up toward the pulpit, slowly, my head lowered.

And so there in that shadowy church, with the choir singing, poor Ben Coles and I were the only two of that whole congregation to stand and admit our sins and undergo the clear and purifying catharsis of public confession.

Once before, when I was eight, I had received baptism. I remembered I had felt purified and what I had imagined was saintly. Now I did not. I felt only bewildered and ashamed. Mr. Daffin shook my hand, not, I thought, with any great enthusiasm, more as if he were embarrassed. Ben Coles and I stood there side by side, Ben weaving just a little. The choir was singing "Sinner, Won't You Come?" I suddenly wondered if I would have to do the same thing again next year. I wondered if Ben Coles and I would be the only two to come forward year after year. I wondered if he and I would form a kind of partnership. I began to snicker again. I also began to cry. I snickered—then cried. Then snickered. Then cried. Then did nothing. Just felt numb. Ben Coles was still sniffling. Mr. Daffin was very red in the face. He suddenly announced benediction.

When we got out to the car, Mother and Father got into the front seat and Cousin Mattie and I got into the back. Cousin Mattie put her arm around my shoulder. It did not feel good. I did not want her to touch me or say anything to me.

She said: "Tucker, I am so happy that you took your stand. There is rejoicing in Heaven tonight—rejoicing in Heaven."

Father said, "Mattie, we will discuss this matter later."

I could not see Father's face. Ordinarily there were tiny veins very close to the skin surface and they looked a little like red oak twigs made minute by distance. At certain times the veins could not be seen and Father's face looked as if it had been drained of something.

His face always looked that way when his voice sounded as it did now. I felt positive that I was going to be given a very severe switching.

When we got home and went into the house Father said, "Tucker, go to your room at once."

I was very scared. I went up to the top of the stairs and sat there on the carpeting with my face pressed miserably against the banisters. The door of the living room was open and I could hear every word they said.

Cousin Mattie said, "I am so very, very happy—"

"Mattie," said Father, "will you do me one tremendous, monumental favor?"

Cousin Mattie said, "You know quite well, Craig, I will do anything in my feeble power for you or any member of your family."

"Then—kindly—go—to—bed!"

Cousin Mattie marched stiffly through the hall to her room and Mother tried to say something to Father and Father said: "I don't feel like discussing this any further tonight. Will you please tell me where my short steel casting rod is?"

I heard Mother say, "What on earth do you want with your fishing rod at this time of night?"

I did not hear Father's answer. I did not think I had to hear it. I got up and crept into my room. The light was on and Poodle was lying on top of the covers. He wagged his tail, thumping it slowly and evenly against the covers as I undressed and slipped into bed. Poodle knew by my slow tears that something was wrong. He arose and stood on legs made uncertain by the bed covers and springs and began to lick my neck, healingly, faithfully, without question. I cried harder because Poodle had no soul and I could not have his companionship throughout eternity; I felt I should probably need it.

I kept my eyes closed as Father came heavily up the stairs and into my room. He stood for a moment at the foot of the bed and then said quietly: "Tucker, open your eyes. You are not asleep."

I said, "Yes sir."

I stopped crying. I always did in Father's presence.

"Tucker," Father said, "would you like to go bass fishing with me over on Benson's Run day after tomorrow? I am going to teach you to use a Dowagiac."

I sat up in bed and said, "Yes sir, but couldn't we go tomorrow?"

"No," said Father. "You will be busy practically all day tomorrow."

I said, "No sir, I haven't anything to do tomorrow."

"Yes you have," Father said quietly. "I believe you are familiar with the big rock pile at the lower end of the garden?"

I said, "Yes sir."

"Tomorrow morning," said Father, "I am going to have Stuart hook up the four-horse wagon with the grain bed on it and bring it down here. I am going to ask Taylor Reed to send Scott up here. I want you and Scott to load the wagon body level full and I want you to drive up in the far field and throw every rock just as far as you can throw it into the big gully. Do you understand me explicitly?"

"Yes sir," I said.

"The day after that," Father said, "I will take you fishing. Good night, son."

"Good night, Father."

He paused at the door. "One more thing, Tucker. You know what your conscience is?"

"Yes sir."

"Does it ever hurt you?"

"Yes sir."

"Will it hurt you about this?"

"I expect so, sir."

"Well, just remember that your conscience is less a punishment for the mistakes you have made in the past than it is a protest against the stupidity of repeating those mistakes in the future."

Father cleared his throat.

"It seems to me," he said, "the sooner a man learns that, the sooner he acquires the chance of moving with a measure of composure and a certain inner dignity in a world which frequently doesn't know its hat from a hole in the ground. Good night, Tucker."

"Good night, Father."

I listened to Father's steps going slowly down the stairs. They were the steps of a man with a measure of composure and a certain inner dignity.

৵ৡ Short Ride Up the Hollow

BY THE SHEER but natural chance of having been glancing now and then at the two boys across the creek, Plecker saw the very beginning of it. He was looking in that direction at the exact second the apple fell from the tree; thus, after that, he watched the whole episode develop step by step from its inception to its conclusion almost as a referee follows a tennis match.

Plecker was sitting on his front porch whittling shingles. It was a hot August afternoon and the hollow was filled with summer quiet. He could hear the alarm clock ticking inside his sitting room and the ripple of the creek as it flowed around the foot of the rocky hill across the hollow. His house, which once had been the community post office, sat on a low shelf jutting out of the hill about a hundred yards up the hollow from the public road. Below him, past a small wooden bridge at the wide mouth of the hollow, was the open valley. The hollow ran into the valley there at the bridge like the shaft of a T. From his bench Plecker could see not only up the hollow toward the abrupt side of the mountain but down through the mouth of the hollow in the other direction, the pastures and fields in the valley proper, over which a trace of smoky haze now lay.

Plecker was whittling not in the aimless time-passing fashion of a store-porch loafer but with the artistry and purpose of a man making a career of it for the rest of his life. He had a pile of shingles at the left end of the bench. He would pick up one, study it for grain-curve and knotholes, meticulously insert his knife blade and, with one flowing motion, peel off a thin sliver the entire length of the shingle. This sliver he would carefully place on a neat and growing pile at the other end of the bench. Occasionally he had been glancing across at the two boys under the apple tree.

The tree was diagonally across the creek, toward the mountain, on Edard Lowhatter's property. It was an old fallowwater with several dead limbs, standing in the lot below Edard's house, and had never been taken care of, never pruned or sprayed. Plecker had often thought it was a shame Edard did not take care of it because if the apples stayed on until fall they got as big and yellow and juicy as pippins. But most of them got wormy and dropped long before ripening; they had been falling one by one all summer.

The boys under the tree were Edard's oldest son, a thirteen-year-old with an overhanging lip, and Sim Gatemyer's boy of about the same age, and they were not supposed to be together there in the first place. Their fathers, Edard and Sim, were not speaking, having fallen out the summer before. Sim had let his cattle run loose and Edard had claimed they had wandered up the hollow and leaned over his fence and cropped off two rows of his early garden corn and that, moreover, they had made the creek water unfit to drink. Sim sent back the arrogant message that cattle never hurt any water and, as far as the corn went, he did not believe it because there was nothing on Edard's or any other Lowhatter's rocky and stumpy land that any human or any beast would want. Sim was overbearing and mean and Edard was stubborn and mean and each had vowed that if any speaking got done it would have to be the other who spoke first.

And the whole matter, Plecker knew full well, went back much further than the incident of the straying cattle. There was a saying throughout Mountain and Valley County that "if you want trouble, go out into the Gatemyer and Lowhatter country and you'll find it. If you want it with a Lowhatter you'll have to look him up but if you want it with a Gatemyer he'll bring it to you." They were the two big proud clans that populated the hills and in a sense ruled the hills and their history had been one of violence from the end of the Revolutionary War, when the original Gatemyers, as Hessian troops left stranded by the British, bore a name that was something like Gottmeier.

There was another tradition that Gatemyer and Lowhatter blood just wouldn't mix. There had probably never been a day in the past seventy-five years when one or more members of both clans had not been in the state penitentiary. They had a land of their own and they had a way of life of their own and in that way of life a store-porch cutting or a mountain-hollow shooting frequently was taken up by brother or uncle or cousin; retribution went on in a kind of sporadic chain reaction until it bore only the faintest connection with the original deed of violence.

When people had heard, three years before, that Sim had bought the old Shull place they thought it a mistake for him and Edard to be that close together. Sim was a man who was bound to have his own way. When he was in his thirties he was one of the Gatemyers reputedly mixed up in a notorious double stabbing in the church yard at Deer Meadow, an affair growing out of a dispute over where to hitch a horse. A Lowhatter was killed outright and a Dowdyshell bled to death even while preaching was going on. No one was ever convicted because there were no witnesses, but Sim was one of the four men who came back into the church while those two lay dying out there.

On winter evenings Edard often came down to sit awhile at Plecker's. After the falling out, whenever he heard Sim's step on the front porch, he got up, his face flushed a mean dark red, mumbled a goodbye and left by the back door. If Sim was there first and heard Edard coming in the back way, Sim simply sat, not even nodding to or glancing at Edard, talking arrogantly to Plecker as if they were the only two in the room, until at length he decided to go in his own good time. . . .

When Plecker saw the apple fall and hit Edard's boy on the side of the face, he remembered later that a quick sense of alarm ran through him and he wanted to get up and yell something to them but he could not make up his mind what it was he could yell. Edard's boy had been hoeing tomatoes in the patch next to the house when Sim's boy came wandering up the creek. The latter had hung down there over the fence for some moments and finally Edard's boy dropped his hoe and came through the gate and the two of them met in the shade under the tree. Edard's boy sprawled out on the ground and Sim's boy was squatting on his haunches, the way Sim could squat for hours without tiring, just six or eight feet away from the other boy. They were there for some time and then the apple suddenly fell.

Plecker saw Edard's boy rise to his knees glaring at Sim's boy. Again he wanted to yell at them. But he knew it was not enough simply to say that the apple had fallen by itself and had not been thrown. Even by then, he sensed, the matter had already assumed the old, outrageous, inevitable proportions . . . as if its course must be dictated not by right or reason but by some hidden command, almost Biblical in nature, suddenly heard and about to be obeyed here in the abiding hills.

Gazing steadily across the creek, Plecker went on with the enterprise he had started just after his wife died. He had come back up the hollow the afternoon of the funeral and the neighbors had gone away and he had sat alone on the porch through the twilight, hearing the whippoorwills, and on into the evening and he had known he had to do something with his time. The next day he had started tearing down his old barn and stable which he did not use anyhow. He had intended sawing up the seasoned oak logs for winter wood but the roof shingles had to come off first and he was struck with the idea of turning them into slivers with which to light the lamps, giving him no telling how much of a saving on matches. Now he had either forty-two or forty-three boxes full in the pantry and the spare room upstairs.

For several seconds the two boys remained motionless in the tableau that would often recur in Plecker's mind: Edard's boy on his knees, having picked up the apple and holding it in his hand, and the other still squatting there like a young image of his father Sim.

Then they were both on their feet and Edard's boy was shouting, "What'd you hafta go and hit me for!"

It was not a question or even an accusation but an indignant declaration of a circumstance already accepted as fact.

"I never hit you!" Sim's boy yelled back.

"You know damn' well you did hit me too!" Edard's boy shouted.

Plecker had one hope that Edard would come out of the house and put a stop to it, but then he remembered that Edard was up on the ridge, supposedly hunting ginseng roots. It might have been that he had gone up to the spring or the calycanthus patch to move his small still on which he occasionally made a run when he could get hold of sugar; he shifted it about every two or three weeks in the belief that if Sim ever ran across the still site he would inform on him.

Then Edard's boy drew back his arm and fired the apple. He threw it so hard that when it left his hand he went a little off balance and his right gallus slipped off his shoulder. His aim was at least a yard high. The apple sped over the other boy's head and came across the creek and the lane and hit the bottom of Plecker's fence. Plecker heard it thud.

Sim's boy began backing away, uttering some protest too low for Plecker to understand, all the way out into the glare of sunshine. Edard's boy was a rock thrower and Sim's boy already had his right hand and forearm up in front of his face in an attitude of self-protection. Edard's boy took two or three steps after him, hitching up his gallus as he moved, and then did what was instinctive to him: he stooped and picked up a rock his foot had found without his having to look for it.

He let fly with it almost immediately. It seemed to tip Sim's boy on the left arm or shoulder and the latter stopped backing away and even took a step forward before stopping again, at the edge of the shade, in a posture he must have thought menacing, his right fist doubled and held out from his side, as if he were going to lunge suddenly.

Edard's boy was already after another rock, bent over and digging around with one hand. He got one and brought it up, took a quick stance and threw. The Gatemyer boy seemed actually to stagger backwards and then threw his hands to his bleeding face. An instant later he bolted.

He started running down across the lot, still holding both hands to his jaw. He had apparently been hit in the mouth. When he reached the fence he stopped and leaned over and spat out blood and saliva. As he straightened up he yanked off his cap and threw it savagely to the ground.

He half turned and shouted hoarsely, "You'll git paid back! Don't you worry!"

Then he turned again, flopped over the fence and started on down the creek swiping one hand across the lower part of his face. Passing under the cedars, he leaned and spit again.

Plecker turned now and watched the Lowhatter boy. He was still standing at the edge of the apple tree's shade, planted with his arms akimbo like a man, looking in the direction in which the Gatemyer boy was disappearing. One of the smaller Lowhatter children must have seen part of the incident because Edard's wife had come out on the porch—two of the young ones around her—and was squawking at the boy to get back to the tomatoes. She was a woman with a nervous twitch to her shoulders and brilliant red lips, as if she constantly ate cherries. The boy paid no attention to her and in a moment she gave up and abruptly went on to the back of the house. Plecker saw one of the older girls streak out of the back yard toward the foot of the mountain, obviously sent to find her father.

Finally, with a bantam strut, the boy went around the yard fence to the tomato patch, grabbed his hoe and started digging with the blade flying high, in the manner of a conqueror.

Plecker's knife was systematically consuming a shingle. He watched the Gatemyer boy cross the public road and go down through the brown pasture specked with the yellow of goldenrod and the white of milkweed; even then he was still pausing occasionally and leaning to one side and spitting.

Sim Gatemyer's bay saddle mare was hitched down at the yard gate. Sim was a stockman; he had cattle and hogs at range over the mountains and he rode horseback looking after them. It was a standing joke that when Sim went from his house to the road to get his mail, he rode the mare. When he was not using the mare she was tied at the front gate ready for use. People said Sim liked to stay in the saddle because it set him above others.

Plecker saw Sim's boy reach the fence, go through the gate and the yard and enter the front door, which indicated his disordered state of mind, because back doors and side doors were normal means of entering for everybody in the community; they used front doors only when they had company or were excited.

Up on the slope a crow cawed and came flapping down the hollow and a moment later a squirrel began scolding irritably in the direction of the calycanthus patch and then Plecker saw the Lowhatter girl break out of the rim of woods and come running down toward their house and just behind her came Edard himself in the long deliberate stride that made his shoulders swing. Edard had an incredibly long neck; it actually looked as if there were extra sections in it, so that his head seemed to be on a platform eight inches above his shoulders. He swung on across the back clearing now; then the stable and house cut him off from view.

Plecker looked down across the pasture for some sign of movement at Sim's house, but nothing was happening down there yet. The mare at the gate stood switching peacefully at horseflies.

He carefully laid a sliver in the box at the end of the bench and was reaching for a new shingle when he saw Edard walk around a corner of his house and then heard him yell at the boy in the tomato patch, "Come here!"

The boy came out of the garden and up to Edard with that bantam strut. They said something to each other and Edard suddenly shouted, "God damn it! You done done enough already!" and let go a backhanded swipe that caught the boy across the neck and sent him sprawling. He got up and ran out of sight around the house. That was the last Plecker saw of the boy. Edard stomped up his front steps and disappeared into the house.

Turning his gaze back down the hollow, Plecker saw Sim coming out of his front yard adjusting his black felt hat. He unhitched the mare and swung his hard spare form up into the saddle. The mare wheeled and started up through the pasture at her steady plodding walk. Sim rode hunched over in the saddle, like a humpbacked man. Plecker could see that he had in his right hand the butt of the buggy whip which he carried both as riding crop and weapon. The lane through the pasture was powdery dry; even at a walk the mare's hoofs cast up dust spurts.

Edard was back out on his front porch by now. There was a straight chair beside the door and he sat down and wiped something along his pants leg several times. Then he held the object up before his mouth and spat on it. He reached in his pocket and brought out something else and fiddled with it a moment and then brought the two objects together, sliding one over the other in a systematic circular motion. Edard always owned a good knife; he said it was the handiest thing a man could have. This one was a bone handle triple blade, the main blade four inches long. It was the four-inch blade he was now whetting so deliberately.

Sim sidled the mare up to the big plank gate at the road in front of his house and leaned down and opened it. He backed her and then worked her forward through the gate, having a little trouble, and finally closed the gate after them. He was now in the main road and had something like a hundred yards to come to the entrance to the lane up the hollow.

Edard never once looked down toward the road. He simply sat honing his knife, pausing several times to bring the whetstone up to his mouth and spit on it for lubrication.

There was a dip in the public road between Sim's field gate and the wooden bridge. Sim's black hat went down into the depression and out of it and then the horse came into view and onto the bridge.

Edard must have heard the mare's hoofs when they hit the planks of the bridge floor, making a wooden ringing sound that burst into the quietness of the hollow like a succession of shots. Still he did not look down in that direction. But he did lay the whetstone on the porch and get up and walk down the steps into the high grass of the unmowed yard. The knife was held conspicuously in his hand and he was looking for something to test it on. There was nothing in the yard except a japonica bush and two lilacs, so he walked on over to the fence next to the creek and started sliding the knife along the top two-by-four inside the palings. Plecker could not have said what he was looking at; he might have been looking at the old chestnut orchard on the hill or he might have been standing there looking at nothing at all and pretending to notice nothing down the hollow. But his head was up in vigilance on the extraordinarily long neck.

Sim came riding up the lane. There were outcroppings of quartz and limestone in the lane and four different times the mare's iron shoes rang against them. Sim was still sitting slumped in the saddle with the brim of the black hat low over his forehead. As usual he had on his vest and no coat. He had a hard thin face and a drooping mustache. As he rode he chewed fast and steadily, his lower jaw moving back and forth under the mustache, and periodically he leaned down with his face close to the pommel and let go with a squirt of tobacco juice.

The lane came straight toward Plecker's house. At the yard it made a right-angle turn toward the creek and then another in reverse, around the fence, on up the hollow. Plecker kept wondering what he was going to be able to say when Sim got alongside the porch. He was certainly going to stay out of this but he supposed he ought to remark on how dry the season had been or, if Sim actually drew up the mare, ask him how the family was—just a polite greeting.

Sim was riding in the middle of the lane. He made the first turn, toward the creek, and then the second that led straight past Plecker's porch. Plecker had already cleared his throat for the greeting and was upon the point of uttering it when he saw that Sim was not going to speak. At first he thought Sim was not going to notice him at all; Sim leaned over the far side of the horse and spat tobacco juice and then settled in the saddle, looking intently on up the hollow. Then he turned his head toward Plecker and his button eyes stared at him from under the brim of the black hat. He did not speak a word or make a gesture. His beady eyes simply placed upon Plecker a demand: that Plecker, as a neighbor, admit in his heart that he, Sim, had the right to do what he was going to do.

The horse had not actually stopped. She seemed to be poised, a forefoot lifted, just long enough for the arrogant demand to be made, without Sim even having to pull on the bridle reins, and then she was moving again.

Sim went on up the hollow, hunched in the saddle and gazing ahead with the harsh, determined stare. Plecker could tell from the very way he rode that he was not even going to bother demanding that Edard punish his boy.

To all appearances, Edard might simply have been standing there whittling at his fence in sheer idleness, utterly unaware of the approach of the other. He never turned around. Sim rode by the wild cherry tree. Still Edard stood with his back to the lane.

When Sim was opposite Edard he reined in. For at least five or six seconds he said nothing. Then in a loud, gritty, overbearing voice he shouted:

"All right, Lowhatter! Come out here and take your medicine!"

Even then Edard did not look directly at him. His head seemed to go up a little higher and his hand went into his pants pocket, obviously with the knife still open, and he started walking up along the fence. He went through the gate and over the footlog. This brought him right up to the side of the horse.

Plecker saw the butt of the buggy whip go up and then come down. It went up and came down twice more, very fast. The mare was skittering by now, partly obscuring Edard, and Plecker could not tell where he was taking the blows. Edard had lunged in toward the horse with the apparent intention of dragging Sim out of the saddle. All Plecker could see for a moment was a general scuffle, Sim flailing with the whip end and the mare trying to wheel.

Then the mare broke away and Edard was standing alone in the lane, straight and tall. Plecker did not believe he had yet taken the knife out of his pocket.

Sim had ridden, or rather the mare had taken him, thirty or forty feet on up the lane above Edard. Then he got control of the horse and whirled her quickly and straightened in the saddle and was flogging her on the rump. He had her at a run almost by the time he had fully turned.

Edard knew, of course, that Sim was going to try to run him down and that must have been when he got out the knife. Because as Sim came charging down the lane he was standing with it in his hand, holding it quite high, almost on a level with the side of his face.

Plecker wondered if Sim thought, in his arrogance, that Edard was simply going to stand there out of sheer bitter stubbornness and pride—refusing to take a step out of the way—and let the mare run him down. Then Plecker himself thought the same thing.

Sim's real intention, apparently, was to knock Edard off balance before he could get out of the way and then wheel again and ride over him while he was on the ground. He was using the horse as weapon now and he must have supposed she would react precisely, like his own arm or leg, to his will.

Then they all came together and again, momentarily, the horse obscured Edard from view. But Plecker had the impression that Edard had not jumped away but had flung himself at mare and rider.

Edard must have caught Sim around the waist with his left arm ... holding and being dragged forward ... and at the same time stabbing and slashing. At last Plecker saw Edard's arm and knife hand going up and coming down and Sim being hauled out of the saddle.

A moment later, in what seemed no time at all, the horse was coming on down the lane at an excited trot, flinging her head and snorting, and Edard was stepping over to the edge of the creek and kneeling and doing something in the water with his hands.

By that instinct that will cause a man to try to stop a riderless horse when he would not try to stop anything else, Plecker arose and went down his steps and started toward the gate, calling: "Whoa, girl! Whoa now, girl! Whoa, there!"

He reached the gate. Sim's black hat was lying in the lane just above the corner of the yard. The mare gave another snort and shied from him and that was when he first realized Sim was being dragged, his left foot caught in the stirrup opposite Plecker, being dragged on his shoulders and the back of his head. Edard must have torn his vest partway off because it was clinging to only one armpit and trailing in the dirt. Plecker got one look at Sim's face: his mouth was wide open, as if he were trying to swallow some very large object.

Plecker was afraid he himself was going to be sick then and he quickly looked across the creek at the pines. That helped a little. Then he started moving cautiously toward the mare, holding out his right hand and saying, "Steady, girl! Steady!"

She bolted before he could get within ten feet of her. She made the two reverse right-angle turns around the yard and trotted on down the lane, still dragging Sim. Plecker knew that Sim was dying or already dead and there was nothing he could do for him; the mare would not let anybody get close to her now.

He looked back up the hollow. Edard had finished washing his hands and knife blade and had arisen, and taken his blue bandanna from his hip pocket and was drying the blade to keep it from rusting.

Plecker watched him going through the quick motion of closing the knife and putting it away and starting across the footlog while stuffing the handkerchief into his back pocket. Edard disappeared around the house. He had not looked down the hollow once.

At Sim's house they must have been watching because by the time the mare reached the road Sim's wife and some of the children were out on the front porch. The horse went on across the bridge and up to the field gate. There she sidled about, apparently trying not to step on Sim but still excited and confused now over not being able to get in the gate.

Sim's boy broke away from the group on the porch and came across the field at a run. A moment later Sim's wife ran up through the yard and reached the front gate and there caught hold of the post with both arms and emitted the first in a series of wails, like a Holy Roller convert. Plecker could hear them all the way up to his place.

Plecker was standing just outside his gate, still absent-mindedly holding his whittling knife open in his hand. He knew sooner or later he would have to go down and see what he could do for Sim's wife and children, but he could not seem to get started at once. Instead he walked along the fence for three or four steps and reached down and picked up the apple that had fallen from the tree and hit Edard's boy on the side of the face.

Mechanically slicing at the apple with his knife, he stood for some seconds looking down toward the field gate, where Sim's boy was trying to get to the horse, and the yard gate where Sim's widow was hugging the post and shrieking.

He continued to slice away at the apple, trying to summon the will to go on down there. Then the point of his knife dug out the worm that had undermined the strength of the twig. It was a tiny grayish-green worm about a quarter of an inch in length. It crawled out along the flat side of the knife blade, weaving in its blind search for the unknowable.

He flipped the worm off the knife and closed the blade and put it away and started on down the lane toward Sim's. He knew Edard was up at his place now, getting his .30-30 rifle ready. The authorities would be out before the day was over but it wasn't going to be any easy matter to get Edard out of that hollow. Plecker was glad he was not going to be the man to try it.

⤳ White Against Winter Dawn

THE GANGLING NELSON boy from just across the lane came ambling through Hunninger's yard and on around the house. Back there, he yelled toward the kitchen.

"Hey, Mrs. Hunninger! They're comin'! You might as well come on out here and pick yourself"—his voice cracked; his Adam's apple bobbed and he swallowed and tried again—"might as well come on out here and find a nice soft spot to—"

"Who's comin', Chester?" Mrs. Hunninger came out on the screened back porch and peered down at him through the door.

"*They're* comin'," Chester said. "Hun and Arthur Gore." He sat down on the steps, as if suddenly drained of energy, and shifted his blue corduroy hat around on his head. He was all elbows, knees and long neck held together by a single unseen string.

"What're they doin' outa the hollow? Ain't they up there cuttin' pulpwood?"

"No'm, and you wait'll you see what he's spent a hundred dollars on. You're goin' to have seven fits. You might as well go ahead and start in."

Chester squinted into the summer sky. He rarely talked to people directly; he talked to telephone wires and the topmost branches of trees.

Mrs. Hunninger pushed the screen door partway open. "Boy, what're you goin' on about?"

"You wait."

"Where're they now?"

"Stopped up there so's Hun could show it off to Gaylor. He's goin' to be showin' it off to everybody in the valley. You ought to make him borrow that big Holy Roller tent and charge admission. Least, he'd get his money back."

"He's showin' *what* off? What's that man done!" She pushed the door open and came out on the steps, looking down at Chester through her rimless glasses. She had an apron on over her print dress

179

and carried her graying head at a tilt, toward the left, as if her neck was slightly curved that way.

She often used that expression when speaking of Hun, placing special emphasis on the words "that man," infusing them with incredulity and alarm and glaring and thrusting out her chin as she spoke. "That man!" she would say, fixing a fierce gaze on a neighbor. "I'll tell you—there's never been a worker like him, and he's sixty-three. One of these days he'll just drop in his tracks. And even so, he's goin' to get up and he'p carry his own coffin. Did you ever look into that man's eyes? Well, you just try it sometime!" And she would move off, shaking her head, her expression something between a scowl and a grin, her feelings somewhere between disbelief and admiration.

"You wait," Chester said again, hauling himself up. "There they come now. They're comin' on down here." He started around to the front gate.

Mrs. Hunninger came down off the steps and followed him, looking suspiciously toward the road.

She saw it then for the first time. "My Lord!" she gasped. "Is that a mule?"

"It ain't no ostrich," Chester said.

"He's bought it! Did he go ahead and buy a mule?"

"Never nobody give it to him," Chester said.

They were both at the gate when Arthur's one-ton truck pulled up. Arthur was driving. Hun was sitting in the cab beside him.

"A white mule!" Mrs. Hunninger said. "I don't believe I ever saw a pure white mule."

"You done seen one now," Chester said. "You own one."

The mule was more than just white. His whiteness had a pristine quality, like midwinter snow; a rare and unique thing, a thing almost of greatness.

They drove slowly on past the gate and a few yards down the road, looking for the steepest part of the bank. Arthur concluded that the bank at the corner of the fence would have to do, and he stopped and came backing in a wide curve, putting the rear end up against it.

Hun got out the near side of the cab and came around the truck. He was a sinewy man with sandy hair and a wide, determined mouth and prominent jawbones. There were knots and cords about his shoulders and along the back of his neck. All of his movements suggested a powerful, driving energy that seldom, if ever, flagged. The only time people ever saw Hunninger at a standstill was on Sundays in good weather, when he sat out in his front yard in a rocking chair under the old oak tree, talking to his son-in-law from town. Even then he did not sit slack and slouch, rocking easily, like most men; he sat on the edge of the seat, his elbows on his knees, hands in front of him and his bony fingers interlocked. He seemed unable, ever, to free himself of the force and fire that pushed and drove him through every other waking moment of his life.

Arthur got out the opposite side of the cab and ambled to the back of the truck.

"Well," Hun said, "we might as well get him out of there."

Arthur took a cigarette and a kitchen match out of his shirt pocket and flicked his thumbnail against the head of the match and watched it flare and then lit the cigarette. "I guess he'll come all right," he drawled. "He went in."

The two of them together loosed the tail-gate chains and lifted out the gate and laid it on the bank.

"Boy," Hun said, "come on out. You're home."

He stepped up into the body of the truck and unfastened the halter rope. The mule came out readily and got his footing on the bank and they could all see him better then; or perhaps it was just that he looked better, more natural and imposing on the ground, where he belonged. He was a big mule, white as snow or cotton, simply standing there with no particular expression but with none of the sleepiness that usually goes with mules.

Now Hun turned toward Mrs. Hunninger, standing in the yard, glaring and scowling, trying not so much to think what to say as what to keep from saying, of all the things that crossed her mind.

"All right, Mama," he said not unkindly, "go ahead and bless me out." He stood waiting, looking at her. Hunninger had remarkable eyes: big copper eyes with pinpoint pupils, so that there seemed no division between pupil and iris, and they were laced with odd, tiny flames, sourceless and unexplainable. His gaze was very hard to meet.

Mrs. Hunninger simply turned and went back to the kitchen, shaking her head all the while she was in sight.

Arthur had gone over and picked up the tail gate from the bank and was fitting it back onto the truck.

"Arthur," Hun said, "I'll settle with you for goin' after him."

"That's all right," Arthur drawled, looking steadily at the mule. "I hope you got your money's worth."

"What?" Hun said. "What?"

Arthur gave his right hand a quick shake to spill the cigarette ash. "A mule ain't exactly famous for his reliability." He fastened the chains and then went on around and got in the cab of the truck. "Armentrout had some good reason for gettin' rid of him," he said out the window.

"I'll overcome it," Hun said.

Arthur started the truck and pulled on off up the road.

Leading the mule by the halter rope, Hun started around the yard toward the stable with his hard, plunging walk.

"Chester," he called, "come on around here and he'p me harness him. I want to get in that corn."

Chester stooped and found a pebble and underarmed it across the road. "On condition," he said.

"What kind of condition, boy?"

"That I stay at his front end."

Mrs. Hunninger went on with her morning housework, making the beds and then cleaning, leaving the breakfast dishes until later. She was sweeping the dining room when she heard Chester clomp up the back steps and come in the kitchen and yell:

"Mrs. Hunninger! Gimme a wet rag and some smellin' stuff! He says camphor or acromatic spirits of ammonia."

"What, Chester?" She hurried into the kitchen, carrying the broom.

"He's got the nose bleed."

"You tell him to come right on in here!"

Chester tilted his head and went, "Hah! Hah! Hah!"

"Don't you stand there brayin' like an idiot!" Mrs. Hunninger snapped. "You do what I tell you."

"It ain't practical," Chester said to the ceiling. "Just gimme the rag and the acromatic—"

"You tell him to come in here and lay down till it stops."

"It ain't practical," Chester said again.

Mrs. Hunninger went to the cupboard, opened the bottom drawer, brought out a cloth and took it to the tap at the sink and soaked it. "How come?"

"Well, I got a picture of that mule piled up in one of yore beds. Hah! Hah! Hah!"

"Mule!" She exclaimed. "You mean that mule's nose is bleedin'?"

"Yes'm. Soon's we got the harness on 'im and put 'im in front of that cultivator, it started drippin'. Gimme the rag. I got to get out there."

"You tell—"

"Yes'm?"

"Nothin'," Mrs. Hunninger said. "I got my own work to do."

"Yes'm," Chester said and went on out the door and toward the corn patch.

After a while Chester came in for ice water. Mrs. Hunninger was at the breakfast dishes by then. He took cubes out of the refrigerator and fixed a glass for himself and put more cubes in a gallon bucket and ran it about half full of water to take out to Hunninger.

"Well, say somethin'," Mrs. Hunninger said. "Did you all get it stopped?"

"Aw, yeah," Chester said. "It stopped."

"Did you use that wet cloth?"

"Aw, yeah, we used it all right," Chester said to the ceiling. "Didn't do any good, though."

"Well, how'd you get it stopped, then?"

"Unhooked him."

"Un-what?"

"Yes'm. Soon's we unhooked him it stopped."

Mrs. Hunninger snorted. "You mean that jackass's nose started bleedin' soon's you hooked him to that plow and then stopped soon's you unhooked him?"

"Yes'm," Chester said. He leaned across in front of her and drew himself a second glass of water. "Started right up again, though."

"Started up when?"

"Soon's we hooked him up again." He upended his glass into the sink. "Done that four times already. Looks like we ain't goin' to get much done today but hook up and unhook. Well, if that's what he wants to pay me for—" He picked up the bucket and started out.

"You tell that man I said to come in here. I want to talk to him."

"I'll tell him," Chester said, going across the porch. "I don't know if it'll do any good, though."

It was not until midday dinnertime that Hunninger came to the house. He was alone. Chester had gone on home to eat because he knew his mother had made fresh apple butter.

"All right, Mama," Hunninger said as he entered the kitchen, "come on in here and bless me out."

He went on through into the living room. Mrs. Hunninger was just getting ready to set things on the table but she pushed them back on the stove and followed him.

Hunninger was sitting on the edge of a straight chair, elbows on his knees, hands in front of him and the strong fingers interlocked. He was tired; his wide mouth was tight and his sharp jaw was set. But in the copper eyes the curious points of flame flicked and laced. Halted now, he could have been carved from oak or stone except for the movement of those tiny flecks of fire in his eyes.

"You come on in here and eat your dinner, Hun."

"I'm too tired right this minute, Mama," Hunninger said, shaking his head slowly. "Just go ahead and bless me out."

"How come you to buy that mule?"

"Needed him," Hunninger said stubbornly. "We got seven acres here and it's good land. I mean to work it. I'm goin' to put the field and that back lot both to taters. Used to see that mule every day up there in Armentrout's field when Arthur and me was goin' back and forth to Covington to work on that road bridge. He looked like a good strong mule and I made up my mind to have him."

"You made up your mind to have him, all right," she said, "but you needed him like you need a hole in the head, the way they say."

"All right, Mama," Hun said soberly and thoughtfully, "I'll tell you. It was rough last winter. I never missed a day carpenterin' on that bridge. We worked at five below a couple of days and we worked in wind and rain and sleet. Goin' back and forth, it was bare. There wasn't a leaf. Great God A'mighty! I don't reckon there was a leaf or a blade of grass for 500 miles around—" He unlocked the strong fingers and gripped both knees, trying to find the words to express the grim starkness of the mountains in wintertime. He stopped and stared at the floor.

"I don't know what that's got to do with your needin' a mule," Mrs. Hunninger said.

"Mama," Hun said, suddenly holding out his hands palms upward, "look at these. I've had calluses on 'em since I was thirteen years old. How long is that? That's right around fifty years, ain't it? You know I always been a hard worker."

"I don't deny that," she said, because he spoke the truth, not only for himself but for thousands of men throughout all the valleys and hollows and hills of the old Allegheny mountains. They cut timber or built roads in Virginia. They worked on section gangs in Tennessee. They mined coal or smelted ore or constructed dams in Kentucky. They ran the mills and refineries and the great hydroelectric plants of the Kanawha Valley. They were the driving force behind all the industry of that mountain empire. They were the lasting men of sinew, making hard and almost impossible things go.

"I'm not any hand at listenin' to the radio or watchin' TV or settin' around the post office the way some people are. I enjoy 'em once in a while but I just never taken to 'em. The children are all growed up and gone. We give three boys to the service and we never complained. Now there's just you and me and we ain't as young as we once was. Winter and summer, I get up before day." He unlocked the fingers again and let them droop over his knees as he tried, now, to speak of the pervading loneliness that comes with winter dawn. "It's awful gloomy before daybreak and a man puttin' a little age on him feels a kind of chill goin' through his bones— Well sir, I saw that mule out there in Armentrout's field—by dog! he's *white* ain't he, Mama?— and I made up my nind I just wanted that white fellow standin' out here in the stable where I could go out there at daybreak them gloomy mornin's and see him and lay my hand on him. Mama, that's the only excuse on earth I've got for buyin' that mule."

"I never heard the like," Mrs. Hunninger said. She started for the kitchen, calling over her shoulder, "Now you come on in here and eat." Then Hunninger got up and went to the table and began eating his dinner, and that's all the talk there was of reason or beauty either.

They were out there all afternoon. Chester came in only once for water and that was around three o'clock.

He took off his corduroy hat and wiped his brow with his sleeve. "Man!" he said. "Am I tahrd!"

"Has that man got you workin'?" Mrs. Hunninger asked.

"Yes'm."

"Has he got that jackass goin' yet?"

"No'm, but I believe he's weakenin'."

"What're you all doin' out there—hoein' it?"

"No'm, we ain't hoein' it. We're plowin' it."

"Well, how you plowin' it? I thought you said—"

"We're just plowin'."

"Who's plowin'?"

"We are. Wup! I wasn't supposed to say. Hun tole me I wasn't to tell."

"What's pullin' the cultivator?"

"I ain't goin' to break my promise," Chester said, looking away. "But it ought not be too hard to figure out. They ain't but three of us out there. The mule ain't pullin' that plow and I ain't got the stren'th for it. So you can add two and—"

"Chester, is that man pullin' that plow?"

"I tole him I wouldn't tell nobody."

"I'm goin' out there," she said.

"You better not take a chanct," Chester said. "He'll hook you up too. And that'd be worse'n ever. I can't manage a team."

"No I won't neither," Mrs. Hunninger said in afterthought. "I've been married to that man thirty-seven years and I never interfered. I ain't goin' to start now. I got them dresses to fix for Vera, for when she comes out here Sunday."

She went into the front room to the sewing machine and began letting out the three dresses her daughter had left with her. Vera had been taking on weight that summer. . . .

About an hour later, Mrs. Hunninger saw Chester ambling through the yard in the direction of home. She stopped the machine.

"Chester!" she called through the window. "Did you all give up?"

"I give up long ago," Chester said. "He never, though."

He came over and settled down on the front steps.

"Has he quit for the day?" she asked him through the screen door. "No'm."

"Did he get the mule goin'?"

"Finally."

"How'd he do it?"

Chester drew in a breath. "Never saw anything like it," he said in a kind of wonderment. "Every time we'd finish a row and get back to where the mule was tied, he'd stop. I mean Hun would stop. He'd walk over and put his face right up to the mule's face and just stand lookin' at him, real hard, not sayin' a word."

"I never heard—" Mrs. Hunninger began.

"I never either," Chester said. "First, it didn't 'mount to anything. The mule just looked back at him. So we kept on goin' down that patch and back again—back and forth—Hun pullin' that cultivator, then stoppin' and lookin' the mule in the eye. Hun begun wearin' him down. First, the mule just begun to look off. Then, later on, you could tell it was makin' him fidgety and uneasy—he couldn't meet Hun's eyes at all. He'd sort of shift about and shuffle his front feet. Mrs. Hunninger, I swear he just outlooked him, that's all!"

"Is he workin'?"

"The mule? He sure is. About a half an hour ago we come around once more and that big white mule had a kind of hangdog look. Hun walked over to him and said, 'You ready to come out here now and earn yore keep the way everybody has to do?' It looked to me like that mule nodded—I don't know. Anyway, Hun untied him and he just stepped out in front of the plow waitin' to be hitched up. Hun hitched him and he went right on off. No nose bleed or nothin'. Hun just outlooked him."

"That man!" Mrs. Hunninger said, shaking her head. "One of these days he'll just drop and even then—"

"I know," Chester said. "He'll get up and he'p 'em carry his own coffin. It wouldn't surprise me none if he did. I got to be gettin' on home."

It was almost dark when Hun left the patch and headed for the stable with the mule. Mrs. Hunninger was in the kitchen by then. She could hear him whistling; he seldom whistled. When Hun saw her through the window he called: "We got us a good mule, Mama. A real good mule. Mama, how about you namin' this mule?"

"I swear!" Mrs. Hunninger said, flustered but pleased. "I never named a mule in my life. He is a kind of pretty, old no-'count thing, though, ain't he?"

"That's a fine name, Mama," Hun said. "Come on here, Purty Thing."

Mrs. Hunninger watched through the window as Hun went on to the stable, whistling lightly, leading the big white mule.

For just a moment she thought of those bitter cold winter mornings when Hun would get up before daybreak and walk out to the stable and feed the mule and run his hand along his white flanks before going off to some job or other that would keep him on the run until evening's dark.

Without warning, she began to cry. The warm tears came easily, comfortably. It lasted less than half a minute. Then she took off her rimless glasses and wiped her eyes dry. She fitted her glasses back on, turned to the stove, and went on with getting supper.

Cindy Thacker's Christmas Dinner

It HAD NOT yet begun to snow when the two children slipped out of the shanty into the night and picked their way quietly under the dark scrub oaks and then down the shale bank toward the swinging footbridge that crossed the river.

It was a peculiar night. From the top of Mill Mountain on the east to the top of Dunlap Mountain on the west the sky was sheeted with high thin white clouds which screened the moon so that only the palest light filtered down among the valley's shadows; but occasionally the moon—itself high and racing—broke through the clouds and Cindy thought it was like a sled flying along over a skim of snow, and then in another moment it was obscured as denser and darker clouds moved in directly under it.

"Why didn't you bring Guy?" Bud asked in his curiously deep voice, almost a baritone, startling from the throat of a five-year-old.

"Guy's asleep," Cindy said gently. "I covered him up good. I covered up Guy and Maybelle both. They're both asleep. You come on."

"He'll kick the covers off," Bud said.

"No he won't kick the covers off," Cindy said. "I tucked them in good."

"He'll kick them off just the same," Bud insisted. "If Papa and Mama come back and he ain't got any covers on him they'll whup—"

"You hush up!" Cindy said without heat. "We'll be back before Mama and Papa do. You come on."

When Papa and Mama went to town on Saturday night they stayed late. They went to see the movie and Papa shot pool and drank beer because Papa said what was the use of a man living if he could not do that. Even when they lived in Albemarle County, where Papa worked in an orchard, and they went to Charlottesville on Saturday night they stayed late and on their way home people sometimes ran into Papa and left a new dent in the car. Mama went

188

along to see that too many people did not run into Papa and sometimes they both slept late the next morning. And Papa could not get along with the man who ran the orchard and they upped and put everything in the car and on a two-wheel trailer behind the car and they came across the mountains and through Staunton and Colonial Springs and now they lived here.

They went around the corner of the board stable and then under the two old white-oak trees. When they reached the footbridge Cindy took Bud by the hand. One spring flood after another had made the bridge lean a little farther downriver so the footplanks were tilted thirty or more degrees. With her free hand Cindy grasped one of the thin suspension cables. She proceeded carefully across the unsteady planks, sliding the lightly closed hand along the cold cable, with Bud edging sidewise along behind her.

The valley was about a mile wide there. Behind them the great bulk of Mill Mountain sheered up and became lost in the night sky. From the far ramp of the bridge, before they had ascended and descended the two cleated diagonal boards that served as a stile across the immaculately white-painted fence into the pasture where Mr. Rinehart sometimes grazed his blooded two-year-olds, they could see the blazing lights in the restored brick mansion, on an elevation as flat as a table top, that dominated the whole valley. They climbed the fence and started walking directly across the pasture toward a stately hickory and a gate at the creek that flowed around the elevated land on which the house stood. On ordinary occasions, such as the daily journey to catch the school bus at the upper road, Cindy would have gone all the way around Mr. Rinehart's pasture and followed the lane that was a public right-of-way through the adjoining place of Mr. Andy Jessup.

Crossing the cropped stubble field, Bud still held onto Cindy's hand and walked slightly behind her.

"Is he goin' to count his money?" he asked.

"Guy ain't got any money to count," Cindy said. "Papa give him a nickel last week and he lost it out in the yard. Papa said he wasn't goin' to give Guy any more money if he couldn't take any better—"

"Not Guy!" Bud said. "Mr. Winehart."

"What money you talkin' about?"

"That money he brings home every day from the bank."

"He don't bring home any money from any bank that I know anything about."

"He do so!" Bud said. "Papa thed he brings home the back end of that thtation wagon full of money every day and spends all night countin' it." On certain words Bud lisped slightly but inconsistently.

"He ain't goin' to count any money tonight," Cindy said. "They ain't goin' to have any time to count any money. They're goin' to be too busy."

"You know what they'll do if they catch us?" Bud said. "They'll sick them dogs on us."

"They won't any such thing," Cindy said with absolute conviction. Bud believed and the children at the village school believed that to step within the confines of the white-fenced estate was to invite instant pursuit, by baying foxhounds and shouting riders, and perhaps to die a mangled death in some remote thicket of chinquapin or hazelbrush. But *she* did not believe. Because she had seen them and in her fancy she had joined them. In Albemarle she had seen them and here she had seen them—the strange Northern people who on confident and reckless horseback, sometimes poised and sailing like birds, galloped about the countryside behind yelping hounds chasing real or pretend foxes—male and female scarcely distinguishable in their extravagant, beautiful garb of black and green and especially red. She had seen the flying people and it was her dream and her secret that she had flown with them.

"Uhhh-hunh," Bud contended. "They'll feed us to that ghost too."

"Ghost!" Cindy scoffed. "What ghost? There's not any such thing as ghosts. Miss Prufer said there wasn't."

"There is so too," Bud said expansively. "They got a ghost in the cellar with a chain around his neck guardin' all that money. Papa *thed* so!"

"You forget all about that ghost," Cindy told him. "You learned your poem yet?"

" 'Merry, Merry Kwithmas—' " Bud began automatically.

" 'May we repeat,' " Cindy prompted. "You forgot the 'May we repeat.' Here, I'll say it for you:

> " 'May we repeat—
> Merry, Merry Christmas!
> Peace, goodwill to men.
> Merry, Merry Christmas!
> We'll say it once again.' "

Again the moon broke through the cloud skim and went racing high above them and they moved across the field—small and almost lost in the mountain country and the night.

They came to the second white board fence and climbed over it and then crossed the footlog at the creek and set out up toward the mansion itself.

"You warm enough, Bud?" Cindy said, looking around at him. "You ought to have your sweater on."

"I couldn't find it," Bud said. "Guy took it out somewheres and never brought it back."

He had on a pair of overalls, worn through at both knees, and a once-bright cotton shirt made in imitation of plaid wool. Cindy wore a fairly good jumper suit of red corduroy with a matching jacket. Both were bareheaded. Bud had fair hair but Cindy's was the color of ripe chestnuts. Cindy was already slim and graceful-bodied at nine and by the time she was eighteen she would be long-legged and unusually pretty.

They climbed the sharp, steep side of the flat-topped hill to the low thick limestone fence wall running around the brow of it like a parapet.

"Don't say a word," Cindy said gravely, drawing Bud down beside her against the bottom of the wall.

"I ain't thayin' nothin'," Bud protested.

"Hush!" Cindy whispered. "You make any noise, I'll send you home. You don't want to be sent home *now*, do you?"

"I ain't thayin' nothin', I tell you, Thindy!" Bud protested again. "Where's all them dogs?"

"Locked up in that kennel down there the other side of the barn where they belong. They're all asleep. They ain't goin' to bother you."

"They ain't all asleep neither," Bud said. "I can hear 'em growlin'."

"Hush!" Cindy said. "They ain't growlin' at you. They're just whinin' in their sleep."

Holding Bud by the hand, she began moving along the fence almost on tiptoe, as if to lighten her step for fear it would be heard in the house. They came to the point where the wall virtually touched the corner eave of the three-car garage and there Cindy pulled herself to the top of the wall and helped Bud up beside her. They crawled warily over the tile roof to the ridgepole line and lay there

side by side looking over across the yard, like snipers in a camou-
flaged nest.

It was a very big yard bordered by boxwood and filled with maple
and oak trees under which, in summer, the Rineharts and their guests
could sometimes be seen lounging in chairs and hammocks, with
iced drinks in their hands or on the grass beside them. That was
when they were not swimming in the long pool they had dammed in
the river and posted about with signs saying PRIVATE and KEEP OUT.
They lived in the water and on the lawn then, and it was only in cool
weather that they dressed in black or brown pants and red coats and
mounted their horses and flew behind their hounds.

There were no leaves on the maples and oaks now and Cindy and
Bud could see clearly, through the bare branches and the broad windows beyond, in the paneled, high-ceilinged dining room, the dozen
men and dozen ladies—the latter wearing dresses that left their
shoulders bare—sitting at the longest table that either of the children
had ever seen in their lives, with the exception of a table at a lawn
party they had once attended with Papa and Mama at a lake in the
mountains above Waynesboro before Bud had begun to remember
things and so long ago that even Cindy could no longer recall it
clearly. Light exploded from the chandelier and fell and disintegrated
and then recreated itself in lamp and candelabra and roaring fireplace
until it seemed to Cindy that this room must be the very heart of
all light, all warmth and all cheer in the universe.

"See!" Cindy said. "Didn't I tell you? What did I tell you, Bud?"

"What're they doin'?" Bud asked.

"What's it look like they're doin'? They're eatin'! Didn't I tell you
Mama told me they'd be eatin' that big bustin' dinner?"

"I know they're eatin'. They ain't eatin' no dinner though. It's done
'way past thuppertime."

"That's what they call it," Cindy said. "Mama told me that's what
they call it. They eat it 'way at night and they call it dinner."

"Papa thed they don't take time off from countin' their money
to eat."

"They do, though. They come in from fox huntin' and they eat
about a ton. *Every night!* Christmas Day they don't even go fox
huntin'. They get up early and start eatin' and eat all day long."

Bud thought about that.

"What're they eatin'? They ain't eatin' weeds, am they?"

"I don't know what they're eatin'. I bet it's good, though. I bet it tastes good."

"I bet it don't," Bud said contemplatively. "If I was rich I still wouldn't eat no weeds. You couldn't hire me to eat no weeds."

"I'm goin' to be rich some day," Cindy said. "I've got a secret I'm never goin' to tell anybody but I'll tell you that part of it. I'm goin' to have a house with a porch on it. You want to come to my house and swing on the porch, Bud? You and Guy and Maybelle want to come?"

Bud did not answer. He was shivering a little.

"You warm enough, Bud? You get over here closer to me and I'll hold part of my jacket around you."

Bud moved over against Cindy and she unbuttoned her jacket and tried to cover his shoulders.

All up and down the long table, people were talking to one another. A colored man and a colored woman brought things in through a door and took other things out, walking fast but carefully with their heavy loads. A large tureen was brought in and placed at the head of the table and individual bowls were ladled out and passed among the diners, the steam rising up into the laughter and the glitter from rings and brooches.

"I know what that is," Bud said. "That's thoup."

"Don't that look good, Bud? Can't you feel that goin' down into your stummick?"

"I guess so," Bud said doubtfully.

"I'm just *nuts* about soup!" Cindy said.

"I ain't so crazy about thoup," Bud said disparagingly.

"What're you crazy about? If you could wish for anything you wanted, what would you make a wish for?"

"Nothin' thept that big box of candy Papa's goin' to bring home."

"How do you know Papa's goin' to bring home a big box of candy?"

"He *thed* maybe he would."

"Mama didn't say so."

"Papa's goin' to bring the whole back end of the car full of things for Kwithmas," Bud said.

"Papa might not do any such thing," Cindy said.

"He am too. He's goin' to see Santy Claus."

"He's goin' to drink too much beer. He always drinks too much beer. Mama said so."

"Hunhh-uh," Bud said stoutly.

"I don't care. That's not what I'm wishin' about. I'd tell you my secret only you'd go and tell— Look, Bud! Look at that! You know what that big thing is, Bud?"

Bud stoically contemplated the huge form of the turkey, in basted *rigor mortis* on the immense platter, borne carefully by the colored man to the head of the table and placed before Mr. Rinehart.

"What?" Bud asked.

"That's a turkey, Bud! Did you ever saw anybody eat a turkey?"

"That don't look like any turkey to me."

"That's what it is, all right."

"It looks nekkid," Bud said.

"That's a cooked turkey. I'm just *nuts* about cooked turkey."

"You never ate any cooked turkey."

"I'm just nuts about it anyway. I'm goin' to have a house with a porch and—"

"They don't cook them nekkid, do they?" Bud asked in faint shock.

"Now you're just lettin' on. That's just silly."

"No it ain't either. I want to—"

"That's the way *to* cook them. You don't cook a turkey with the feathers on. You know very well you don't."

"Papa's goin' to bring home a turkey for Kwithmas."

"How do you know Papa's goin' to bring home a turkey?"

"He *thed* so!" Bud hissed.

"He said maybe."

"He *thed* he would."

"You don't know whether Papa's goin' to bring home any turkey or not. He ain't got but three tickets on the drawin'. Mama said he might not win it."

Almost simultaneously the two of them felt the first sting of the snow on their necks and ears.

"It's snowin', Bud!" Cindy said with a peculiar gentleness. "I'm just nuts about snow. Ain't it nice to lay here and feel the snow and watch them?"

Bud seemed to have no particular reaction to snow.

"Watch them, Bud!" Cindy coaxed. She was afraid he was going to start complaining. "Look at that man standin' up with that glass in his hand. I know who that man is. You know who that man is, Bud?"

"No," Bud said, all interest gone from his voice.

"That's Dr. Coulter. He keeps some horses here and he comes out here fox huntin' all the time. You remember that time his horse threw him over across the river and he stopped over home and asked Mama for a drink of water and said you ought to have your chest examined and your tonsils taken out?"

"He ain't goin' to take my tonsils out," Bud said. "Papa thed, he didn't quit gettin' drunk and fallin' off his horse and tellin' uvver people—"

"I don't care what Papa said! You want to know another part of my secret, Bud? When I get big I'm goin' to let some doctor like Dr. Coulter marry me! He's goin' to have gray hair and part it in the middle and have—"

"I'm cold, Thindy!"

"Look! —Bud. Look there! You know what that red stuff is? That's cranberry sauce. Can't you just taste all that—"

"I want to go home," Bud said.

"Stay a little while longer, Bud," Cindy pleaded. "Let's be real quiet and see if we can hear what they're talkin' and laughin' about. I'll lend you my whole jacket. How'd you like me to take off my jacket and hold it around you?"

"I'm cold."

"I'll give you somethin' nice if you'll stay," Cindy said.

"What'll you give me?" Bud asked with slightly revived interest.

"I'll bring you somethin' real nice from school. I'll slip a piece of chalk in my pocket and bring it to you. How about that, Bud?"

"I don't know," Bud said.

"I'll get a piece of red chalk. I'll get you a whole big piece. I swear I will! Would you like to have a nice long piece of red chalk, Bud?"

"Will you bring it tomorrow?"

"There ain't any school tomorrow, Bud honey. You know that. We're out for Christmas. But I'll bring it the first day school takes up and I'll tell you my whole secret. Will you be quiet now and try to hear what they're laughin' about?"

"If you swear about that chalk."

"I swear. Here, put this on." She arose to her knees and took off the corduroy jacket and slipped Bud's arms into the sleeves. "Ain't that warm and nice now, Bud?" she said gaily. "Now you just lay there and try to get that poem right. You see if you can learn to say the whole thing before we get home."

Bud lay absolutely quiet as the snow settled thinly about them. Cindy lay in rapt concentration, without uttering a sound, until the flaming plum pudding was brought from the serving pantry and then she exclaimed:

"Bud! Look, Bud! It's on fahr! I bet you never saw anybody eat anything on fahr! Bud, I tell you it's on fahr!"

Bud was by then beyond comment upon even that miracle. He lay with his teeth clenched. Cindy watched while the flame vanished and the pudding became an eaten and forgotten thing and the guests were arising and moving out of sight. Still she had not heard a word from inside the house and gradually she accepted the fact that she would not know what they talked about until the day she herself entered the world of these people who in the daytime flew and after dark laughed as they ate fiery food.

Silently she got up and helped Bud down off the roof and the wall. Bud's legs were so stiff he could hardly walk until the blood began circulating again. They set out down over the hill, Bud still wearing Cindy's jacket.

Cindy could feel the swelling of her heart. A warmth and glow extravasated from her inmost being. If she missed the jacket at all its absence was far more than made up for by the dazzling extravaganza she had witnessed, a vision climaxed in pure flame.

"You want to hear my secret, Bud?" she asked in a curiously small, strained voice. "I'll tell you if you swear you won't ever in your life tell anybody. We're all goin' to live in that big house. You and Papa and Mama and Guy and Maybelle. One day when I'm comin' back from school and I see their station wagon comin' I'm goin' to wait till it gets real close and I'm goin' to jump out in front of it and get hurt. I swear I am! They'll take me up there and put me in bed and bring me all them things to eat and have Dr. Coulter come and sit by me and they'll love me so much they'll want me to stay forever and ever and you and Mama and Papa and Guy and Maybelle can come over and we'll all live there together. I swear that's what I'm goin' to do!"

"Don't you forget about that chalk," Bud said.

They walked on and came to the creek and crossed it.

"You know how to say your poem now?" Cindy asked finally, in a normal tone. "I'll say it once more for you:

> " 'May we repeat—
> Merry, Merry Christmas!
> Peace, goodwill to men.

Merry, Merry Christmas!
We'll say it once again.' "

"You be sure that's red chalk," Bud said.

It had stopped snowing. The moon had come out again and the two children could see the faint tracings of their shadows as they walked back across the pasture toward the dim light of the shanty in pale relief against the dark brooding surface of the mountain.

✑§ A Warm Day in November

HIS TRIAL WAS held at the January term of the Circuit Court before a jury of twelve of his fellow Virginians and with silver-haired Judge Estes presiding. Outside the Courthouse windows snow lay white upon the square and the park with its statue of General Robert E. Lee astride Traveller and facing south in the dignity of defeat. Snow covered the nearby hills and on beyond it lay deep in the valleys and hollows out in the Allegheny Mountains where we people came from.

The courtroom was filled with lean weathered men, hard and quiet and intent. Every seat was taken and back against the walls men were standing. Men from the rolling hills and the orchard country were there, and men from the patch farms and the valleys and the remote hollows. Some had driven their old cars thirty or forty miles into town or had gotten rides with neighbors. The very fiber of our country was there.

I watched the thin, gentle figure of Uncle Gene McCantland, my mother's brother, as he took the witness stand in his own defense. It is a deeply distressing thing to see one of your own kin on trial for a serious crime. The witness chair looked too big for him. The whole proceeding seemed too big for him.

I looked at Uncle Gene's face. He had clear blue eyes and a long nose, a wide straight mouth and abnormally large ears. They looked artificial, as if they were made of papier-mâché and pasted to his head. Even with the long nose and large ears his face had a quality in it that made you think of a woman's face—a restraint and gentleness and silent outrage that is largely feminine.

One of Uncle Gene's lawyers, Mr. Frank Waller, had arisen at the defense table, leaning forward a little, his fingertips just touching the edge of the table.

"Now Mr. McCantland," he said, "I'm goin' to ask you about meetin' Perlater and his friends there in the road. Perlater was left-handed, wasn't he?"

"Yes sir," Uncle Gene said in his soft-spoken voice.

"You knew he was lefthanded?"

198

"Yes sir."

"You saw him reach with his left hand toward his inside coat
pocket?"

"Yes sir," said Uncle Gene.

I sat with the members of my family, watching and listening. My
mind kept going back to that Sunday morning in the early part of
November when Uncle Gene came riding sadly down the clay and
gravel road on his black horse Eagle with his dog lying across the
saddle in front of him.

He came around the turn under the big poplar below the Gaylor
house. Eagle was walking slow. Uncle Gene had him reined in. He'd
probably had trouble with the horse at first, but he was all right now.
Uncle Gene had the reins in his left hand and had the dog's head and
shoulders cradled in his right arm.

It was about mid-morning. My family was up at the Weeping
Willow Presbyterian Church listening to Mr. Glendye's sermon.
The Reeds and Hamiltons and Locklands and the other old families
of the valley were also there, all of them listening to a sermon and
singing hymns and praying, just as they had been doing every Sunday
morning almost since the time there was a Mountain and Valley
County.

I was down at the barn. I waited for Uncle Gene to turn in at the
big gate and come on into the pasture, but he rode on past and kept
to the road until he got opposite the barn. Then he pulled Eagle up
and called down to me, "Go to the blacksmith shop and bring a pick
and shovel up to the orchard."

"What do you want with a pick and shovel?" I called back.

Uncle Gene's quiet voice came down through the field to me.
"I'm goin' to bury my dog," he said.

There was a little echo against the side of the barn. It was almost
a whisper: 'Goin' to bury my dog.'

I went around to the blacksmith shop and got the pick and shovel.
I went up through the field toward the road with the pick over my
shoulder and the shovel balanced level in my hand. The field was
dry and brown. Uncle Gene had ridden on ahead of me, slowly, still
holding the dog in the crook of his right arm. I could hear Eagle's
shoes on the gravel and the outcroppings of limestone rock in the
road.

It was a soft gentle day, a day a little like my uncle's voice. It was
what some people called Indian summer; others said Indian summer

did not come until December. Anyway, it was a warm day for November. The valley was still full of color, for fall had come late.

The slopes of the mountains on each side of the valley were ugly and barren where the Company had been cutting the trees. They had come into the valley, they said, to take out only white oak for barrel staves, but they took everything as they went—chestnut oak, red oak, poplar, even cedar and pine. Fifteen sawmill camps were scattered around in the hollows and they were taking everything but the stumps and the huckleberries. If you have ever lived in mountain country and seen that you know what it is like. It makes you wonder what is so important in the world that a thing like that has to be done.

It had been crisp earlier that morning. It must have been crisp when Uncle Gene got up just after daylight and went out into the yard and called the dog after he had heard the two shots close together.

We had heard the other dogs running since a little after midnight. They must have raised the fox somewhere on the other side of Dunlap Mountain because the first time we heard them was when they crossed the top of Dunlap running south. We recognized the owp-owp-owp of Perlater's fast bitch and the deeper boom of his older hound mingled with the yap-yap of the other dogs. We knew it was Perlater himself and that crowd of Company men wearing riding breeches and shiny leather leggings, men with unfamiliar names that belonged back in Pittsburgh or Cleveland or wherever the hell they had come from.

Uncle Gene rode ahead of me over the top of the hill. He stopped Eagle at the orchard and slowly got off the horse with the dog in his arms. He laid the dog down on the bank and looped Eagle's reins over a fence post and picked up the dog and carried him to the edge of the orchard where three cedars grew in a row beside the fence. I climbed the fence at the road and went up into the orchard where Uncle Gene was standing beneath one of the cedars.

"That Jess Perlater killed my dog," he said quietly.

I said, "How do you know it was him?"

"It was his dogs we heard," he said. "He's the only man in this country who carries a revolver when he's fox huntin'. He's the only man in this country who'd do that kind of a thing."

That was the first time in my life I had ever heard of a man killing a dog unless the dog had gone mad or was running sheep or cattle or had gotten so mean he was a danger to children or to people passing along the road. I had never heard of a neighbor wantonly killing another neighbor's dog. I had never heard my father speak of it, or my grandfather. I had never heard of it in any of the old stories. White men had been living in that valley for two hundred years and before that the Indians had been there, and in none of the handed-down stories, not even about the Shawnees or Cherokees, had such a thing ever been mentioned.

Uncle Gene was standing there with the dog lying at his feet. There was a wound around the dog's left eye that had been put there with a heavy-calibered gun. It was an ugly wound. Part of the ear had been torn away. There was still blood around the wound. I could not get over the strangeness, the wrongness of it.

He was a rust-colored young hound that had been sent to Uncle Gene by a big right-handed pitcher for the Washington Senators named Jack Sterling who used to come down for fox hunting. Uncle Gene named the dog Jack.

But it was not merely that Uncle Gene was proud because he was the only man in that country who had ever been given a dog by Jack Sterling the big-league baseball pitcher. It was something else.

It was the relationship that Uncle Gene had with all living things. There was some subtle communication that came out of the heart of his gentleness—a thing that children and animals seemed to recognize and respond to. I believe he saw all life as a kind of flowing— through himself, through other men and women, through animals, through trees. It was a sense of continuity, I think, that is often lost in more articulate people. I think he had the greatest respect for life as such of any man I have ever known.

"I think I will bury him about here," Uncle Gene said.

Leaves had blown over under the cedar from the other trees. He took the shovel and scraped them away. He scraped the ground bare and pushed the shovel into the earth. He didn't need the pick. The earth was loam and clay and the rain had made it soft and the leaves had kept it that way.

I looked at Uncle Gene's hands. They were small and white. They had none of the moles and brown spots that cover the backs of the hands of most farm men. They looked white and small and delicate on the handle of the shovel.

Uncle Gene started digging a grave for the body of his dog.

He was wearing a canvas hunting coat. He stopped once and took off the coat and folded it carefully and laid it on the ground. I offered to take a turn with the shovel, but he shook his head. He wanted to dig the grave himself.

I went over and sat down on a big limestone rock near a clump of sumac.

Uncle Gene finished digging the grave and put the shovel aside. He stood there a little while looking down the valley in the direction we had last heard the hounds running. We couldn't hear them any longer. They must have caught the fox somewhere below the Davenport place where the valley narrowed and the river flowed over a bed of black rocks below the road. Maybe they had run the fox into a den in the rocks on the side of Dunlap. That meant that the Company crowd and their hounds would be coming back up the valley after a while.

Uncle Gene picked up the dog and laid him in the grave. He stood looking down at Jack for the last time, his face restrained and gentle like a sorrowing woman's.

"I can't hardly stand to throw the dirt onto him," he said.

He said it low, so low I could hardly hear him, almost as if he were talking to himself. It was almost as low as the echo against the side of the barn: 'Goin' to bury my dog.'

"I think I'll just put my coat over top of him," he said.

He picked up the canvas coat and put it over the dog, covering his head and face and tucking it under his sides. Then he took the shovel and eased the dirt in around the dog and rounded out a little mound over him.

"I like to think about Jack bein' able to hear the rest of them when they run on clear cold nights with the stars out," Uncle Gene said.

We stood for a minute looking at the fresh dirt. Then I took the pick and shovel and we walked on down to the fence without looking back.

Uncle Gene untied Eagle and we started walking back up the road under the poplars and oaks, Eagle following along behind.

"I guess I'm goin' to hafta face that man before the day is over," he said quietly.

We walked up the hill. There was a great white-oak tree on top of the hill and when we came to it we stopped. We stood in the road and Uncle Gene began telling me what had happened.

"I found him behind a log beside that path that goes up the side of Betty's Hill," he said. "I think he went up there and got in the chase just about daylight, just about the time they crossed over from the other side of Dunlap the second time. I could hear him after that. I think the fox led the dogs north for a while and the men were sittin' there on top of Betty's. Then the fox must have doubled back and run right by the men as they sat there on their horses. I expect that Jack, bein' fresh, was in the lead and Perlater knew it by his bayin'. I expect Perlater was sittin' there with his pistol in his hand and his mind made up to take a shot at him. He must have shot him as he slowed to jump the log."

As Uncle Gene was talking, the strangest feeling came over me. We were standing there in the road under the big oak tree. Scarlet leaves were scattered over the road. Uncle Gene was talking in a low voice. His blue eyes did not leave mine all the time he was speaking. They were unwavering, and there was something inexorable in them. I got the strange feeling that I was taking part—that the two of us were taking part—in something that had already happened. And I knew that Uncle Gene was feeling the same thing.

We started walking on down the hill, Uncle Gene still leading Eagle.

"I don't expect Perlater was even mad," he said.

I knew what he meant. The two Perlater brothers had come from West Virginia. Maybe they had been with the Company in other parts of the country. They were both tremendous, swaggering men. Up at Deer Meadow the story was told about what the two Perlater brothers said to each other the first day they came into the valley and stopped on the brow of Calhoun hill and looked down at the little village that was to become a boom town.

"I'll take the hotel, the poolroom, and the movie house," Harold Perlater was reported to have said.

"I'll take the poker and dice game and the bootlegging," Jess said.

"We'll divide up the wimmen," Harold Perlater told his brother in that bluff, swaggering way that had the strong undercurrent of truth to it.

They were that kind of men.

My Uncle Gene and I walked on down the gravel road toward the rusty iron gate that led into the meadow.

The Company itself had done something to the valley in which our people had lived for generations. It is hard to say just what it was. It was not that they took land without paying a just price or that they exploited the men who worked for them. They paid their way as they went and they paid a fair price for the land. Men with trucks and teams of horses made more money with the Company than they had ever made before in their lives. In fact, the Company was openhanded about money. They would see a piece of mountain land they wanted and they would go to the owner and say, "How much is it worth?" And they would pay the asking price.

Perhaps that was it. The money. Or that and other things not so easy to put your finger on. There was, for example, a very pretty valley girl named Ida Gibson whom Harold Perlater got into trouble and whose father took money from the Perlaters. And there were the scarred mountainsides and the roads broken and gutted by the heavy lumber trucks. There was the exodus from the valley of wild turkey and quail and small game that had always used the mountains for cover. There was a solemn old Negro named George Wayland who used to preach every Sunday in an old warehouse until Jess Perlater bought the building and tore out the floor and converted it into a bowling alley.

It is a hard thing to express. Most of the Company men were likable enough when you met them. They were openhanded men with a breezy, casual way of doing things. It is very hard to object to a casual way of doing things. The arrogance was not so much within the individual men as within the collective enterprise itself.

How much for this right-of-way? . . . We're going through your property but we'll pay you for it. . . . How much for a building in which an old Negro preached to his few people? . . . . How much for ruining the mountains and the roads? . . . How much for a horse? A daughter? . . . Name the price and we'll pay you.

My Uncle Gene and I walked down the road and went through the gate and into the meadow.

"It used to be," he said, "that a man could sit on his front porch in the evenin's and listen to the whippoorwills."

As we were going through the field the Company crowd came into sight farther down the valley. They were riding up along the quiet river, coming up our way, eight men on horses with their tired hounds trotting along beside them. We could hardly see the hounds from that distance.

"I might get into a little trouble over this thing," Uncle Gene said to me in his quiet way, "but I'm goin' to face that man. I want to hear what he's got to say."

We emerged from the field and Uncle Gene went into the house.

I led Eagle past the cedars to the creek and let him drink, and then I took him back up and tied him at the front gate. I went through the gate into the yard and walked along the slate walk under the maples to the house. I sat down on the porch. I watched the men coming up the valley.

In a little while I heard Uncle Gene coming through the hall outside the house. He had his .30-.30 Winchester rifle in his hand. He sat down on the front steps and took the cartridges out of the magazine and looked at them. He looked at each cartridge carefully before slipping it back into the magazine. He pumped one into the cartridge chamber.

He had changed clothes. He had on his black felt Sunday hat and his blue serge suit and a white shirt and a dark red necktie that wasn't tied well. Uncle Gene never could tie a tie well. The knot was a sort of complicated lump under the right side of his collar. I don't know how many times I have seen my mother go up to him and straighten his tie. I wanted to do that now.

I made a clumsy effort to talk to him.

"If you're bound to go up there and meet them," I said, "why don't you leave your rifle here?"

I was too young to talk to him; I didn't know enough.

Gene looked at me with his unwavering blue eyes. He did not answer me.

I thought about Uncle Gene standing alone in his room on that quiet Sunday morning, on that warm November day, looking into the mirror on his dresser and putting that tie on. I thought about him adjusting it and shifting it about deliberately with his sensitive hands, his calm blue eyes watching his hands in the mirror, and not able to do it right; and finally giving it up and taking the rifle down from the closet.

As I watched him there on the front steps, examining the cartridges, I had the sudden desperate wish that this was happening instead to my father's brother, Uncle Jerome English. Uncle Jerome would have let out a holler they could have heard up at the church, three miles away. He would have given Jess Perlater one of the worst cursings one human being ever gave another. He probably would have bought a jug of moonshine whisky and stayed tanked-up for two or three days and he would have gotten it out of his system. It would have been very simple to explain to my family what had happened while they were at church had Uncle Jerome been involved. And I had again the sick feeling of watching Uncle Gene in the re-enact-ment of something that had happened long ago.

He arose slowly. "You stay here," he said a little sternly. "I don't want you mixed up in this."

He started out through the yard under the maples. Then he turned and came back.

"I might have to go away for a while," he said. "I'm not sure, but I might. If I do, I want you to look after Eagle till I get back."

He reminded me about stabling Eagle if there was a cold rain and told me how much oats and corn to feed him. He shook hands with me, quickly. I stood there and watched him walk out through the yard, not fast, and untie Eagle and mount and ride up through the field to the road a half-mile from the house.

The way they told it later—the way a man named Whiting testified to it—they were coming up the road when they saw the slight gentle-faced man with the long nose and large ears sitting astride the black horse in the middle of the road ahead of them. To say that he was blocking the road seemed the wrong way to put it; he did not seem big or imposing enough to block anything, much less to keep that Company crowd from going anywhere or doing anything they wanted to do.

"I didn't know the man," Whiting said in court. "I didn't know who he was or what he wanted or what he was trying to do. I got the notion he was trying to get us to do something, maybe to go back down the road."

Perlater knew him—knew him less by name than as the owner of the rust-colored hound he had seen and killed earlier in the day. So Perlater rode ahead of the others, spurred his two-year-old roan and trotted on up the road ahead of his friends.

Perlater must have thought the whole thing would take only a minute. He was perfectly prepared to be generous.

"About that dog," Perlater said. "How much would you say he was worth?"

And already he was changing the reins in his hands and automati-cally reaching with his left hand toward his inside coat pocket.

Uncle Gene did not even wait for Perlater to complete the gesture. Nor did he say a word. He threw the rifle to his shoulder and fired the single shot that took away the side of Perlater's head in almost exactly the same way that Perlater's bullet had torn away the dog's head.

Uncle Gene said only one thing during the whole confusion, after Perlater's horse had turned and galloped back among the others, with some of the other horses now pitching and lunging and the reverberation of the shot already evaporating. I heard that part of it as I was running across the field toward the road.

"You heard him!" Uncle Gene called out. His voice was strangely clear above the clamor. "You all heard him offer me money! You saw him reachin' . . ."

And now Uncle Gene was on the witness stand, accused of murder in the first degree.

And the people from the farms and valleys and Allegheny hollows were there listening. Twelve men, people like ourselves, were listening and watching before filing into a room and searching their hearts and taking a vote on what to do about my Uncle Gene. The fiber of our country was there. Its justice was there and perhaps its compassion.

Outside, the snow lay on the ground, on the parks in the town and on the hills beyond the town and on the granite face of old mountains—the Alleghenies, standing there stately and somber, devoid of either mercy or misgiving.

✑ The White Circle

As SOON AS I saw Anvil squatting up in the tree like some hateful creature that belonged in trees I knew I had to take a beating and I knew the kind of beating it would be. But still I had to let it be that way because this went beyond any matter of courage or shame.

The tree was *mine*. I want no doubt about that. It was a seedling that grew out of the slaty bank beside the dry creek-mark across the road from the house, and the thirteen small apples it had borne that year were the thirteen most beautiful things on this beautiful earth.

The day I was twelve Father took me up to the barn to look at the colts—Saturn, Jupiter, Devil, and Moonkissed, the white-face. Father took a cigar out of his vest pocket and put one foot on the bottom plank of the fence and leaned both elbows on the top of the fence and his face looked quiet and pleased and proud and I liked the way he looked because it was as if he had a little joke or surprise that would turn out nice for me.

"Tucker," Father said presently, "I am not unaware of the momentousness of this day. Now there are four of the finest colts in Augusta County; if there are four any finer anywhere in Virginia I don't know where you'd find them unless Arthur Hancock over in Albemarle would have them." Father took one elbow off the fence and looked at me. "Now do you suppose," he asked, in that fine, free, good humor, "that if I were to offer you a little token to commemorate this occasion you could make a choice?"

"Yes sir," I said.

"Which one?" Father asked. "Devil? He's wild."

"No sir," I said. "I would like to have the apple tree below the gate."

Father looked at me for at least a minute. You would have to understand his pride in his colts to understand the way he looked. But at twelve how could I express how *I* felt? My setting such store in having the tree as my own had something to do with the coloring of the apples as they hung among the green leaves; it had something

also to do with their ripening, not in autumn when the world was
full of apples, but in midsummer when you wanted them; but it had
more to do with a way of life that had come down through the generations. I would have given one of the apples to Janie. I would have
made of it a ceremony. While I would not have said the words, because at twelve you have no such words, I would have handed over
the apple with something like this in mind: "Janie, I want to give
you this apple. It came from my tree. The tree stands on my father's
land. Before my father had the land it belonged to his father, and
before that it belonged to my great-grandfather. It's the English
family land. It's almost sacred. My possession of this tree forges of
me a link in this owning ancestry that must go back clear beyond
Moses and all the old Bible folks."

Father looked at me for that slow, peculiar minute in our lives.
"All right, sir," he said. "The tree is yours in fee simple to bargain,
sell, and convey or to keep and nurture and eventually hand down to
your heirs or assigns forever unto eternity. You have a touch of
poetry in your soul and that fierce, proud love of the land in your
heart; when you grow up I hope you don't drink too much."

I didn't know what he meant by that but the tree was mine and
now there perched Anvil, callously munching one of my thirteen
apples and stowing the rest inside his ragged shirt until it bulged out
in ugly lumps. I knew the apples pressed cold against his hateful
belly and to me the coldness was a sickening evil.

I picked a rock up out of the dust of the road and tore across the
creek bed and said, "All right, Anvil—climb down!"

Anvil's milky eyes batted at me under the strangely fair eyebrows.
There was not much expression on his face. "Yaannh!" he said. "You
stuck-up little priss, you hit me with that rock. You just do!"

"Anvil," I said again, "climb down. They're my apples."

Anvil quit munching for a minute and grinned at me. "You want
an apple? I'll give you one. Yaannh!" He suddenly cocked back his
right arm and cracked me on the temple with the half eaten apple.

I let go with the rock and it hit a limb with a dull chub sound and
Anvil said, "You're fixin' to git it—you're real-ly fixin' to git it."

"I'll shake you down," I said. "I'll shake you clear down."

"Clear down?" Anvil chortled. "Where do you think I'm at? Up
on top of Walker Mountain? It wouldn't hurt none if I was to fall
out of this runty bush on my head."

I grabbed one of his bare feet and pulled backwards, and down

Anvil came amidst a flutter of broken twigs and leaves. We both hit the ground. I hopped up and Anvil arose with a faintly vexed expression.

He hooked a leg in back of my knees and shoved a paw against my chin. I went down in the slate. He got down and pinioned my arms with his knees. I tried to kick him in the back of the head but could only flail my feet helplessly in the air.

"You might as well quit kickin'," he said.

He took one of my apples from his shirt and began eating it, almost absent-mindedly.

"You dirty filthy stinkin' sow," I said.

He snorted. "I couldn't be a sow, but you take that back."

"I wish you were fryin' in the middle of hell right this minute."

"Take back the stinkin' part," Anvil said thoughtfully. "I don't stink."

He pressed his knees down harder, pinching and squeezing the flesh of my arms.

I sobbed, "I take back the stinkin' part."

"That's better," Anvil said.

He ran a finger back into his jaw to dislodge a fragment of apple from his teeth. For a moment he examined the fragment and then wiped it on my cheek.

"I'm goin' to tell Father," I said desperately.

" 'Father,' " Anvil said with falsetto mimicry. " 'Father.' Say 'Old Man.' You think your old man is some stuff on a stick, don't you? You think he don't walk on the ground, don't you? You think you and your whole stuck-up family don't walk on the ground. Say 'Old Man.' "

"Go to hell!"

"Shut up your blubberin'. Say 'Old Man.' "

"Old Man. I wish you were dead."

"Yaannh!" Anvil said. "Stop blubberin'. Now call me 'Uncle Anvil.' Say 'Uncle Sweetie Peetie Tweetie Beg-Your-Pardon Uncle Anvil.' Say it!"

"Uncle Sweetie . . . Uncle Peetie, Tweetie Son-of-a-Bitch Anvil."

He caught my hair in his hands and wallowed my head against the ground until I said every bitter word of it. Three times.

Anvil tossed away a spent, maltreated core that had been my apple. He gave my head one final thump upon the ground and said "Yaannh!" again in a satisfied way.

He released me and got up. I lay there with my face muscles twitching in outrage.

Anvil looked down at me. "Stop blubberin'," he commanded.

"I'm not cryin'," I said.

I was lying there with a towering, homicidal detestation, planning to kill Anvil—and the thought of it had a sweetness like summer fruit.

There were times when I had no desire to kill Anvil. I remember the day his father showed up at the school. He was a dirty, half crazy, itinerant knickknack peddler. He had a club and he told the principal he was going to beat the meanness out of Anvil or beat him to death. Anvil scudded under a desk and lay there trembling and whimpering until the principal finally drove the ragged old man away. I had no hatred for Anvil then.

But another day, just for the sheer filthy meanness of it, he crawled through a classroom window after school hours and befouled the floor. And the number of times he pushed over smaller boys, just to see them hit the packed hard earth of the school yard and to watch the fright on their faces as they ran away, was more than I could count.

And still another day he walked up to me as I leaned against the warmth of the school-hack shed in the sunlight, feeling the nice warmth of the weatherbeaten boards.

"They hate me," he said dismally. "They hate me because my old man's crazy."

As I looked at Anvil I felt that in the background I was seeing that demented, bitter father trudging his lonely, vicious way through the world.

"They don't hate you," I lied. "Anyway I don't hate you." That was true. At that moment I didn't hate him. "How about comin' home and stayin' all night with me?"

So after school Anvil went along with me—and threw rocks at me all the way home.

Now I had for him no soft feeling of any kind. I passionately hated him as he stood there before me commanding me to stop blubbering.

"Shut up now," Anvil said. "I never hurt you. Stop blubberin'."

"I'm not cryin'," I said again.

"You're still mad though." He looked at me appraisingly.

"No, I'm not," I lied. "I'm not even mad. I was a little bit mad, but not now."

"Well, whattaya look so funny for?"

"I don't know. Let's go up to the barn and play."

"Play whut?" Anvil looked at me truculently. He didn't know whether to be suspicious or flattered. "I'm gettin' too big to play. To play much, anyway," he added undecidedly. "I might play a little bit if it ain't some sissy game."

"We'll play anything," I said eagerly.

"All right," he said. "Race you to the barn. You start."

I started running toward the wire fence and at the third step he stuck his feet between my legs and I fell forward on my face.

"Yaannh!" he croaked. "That'll learn you."

"Learn me what?" I asked as I got up. "Learn me what?" It seemed important to know. Maybe it would make some difference in what I planned to do. It seemed very important to know what it was that Anvil wanted to, and never could, teach me and the world.

"It'll just learn you," he said doggedly. "Go ahead, I won't trip you any more."

So we climbed the wire fence and raced across the burned field the hogs ranged in.

We squeezed through the heavy sliding doors onto the barn floor, and the first thing that caught Anvil's eye was the irregular circle that father had painted there. He wanted to know what it was and I said "nothing" because I wasn't yet quite ready, and Anvil forgot about it for the moment and wanted to play jumping from the barn floor out to the top of the fresh rick of golden straw.

I said, "No. Who wants to do that, anyway?"

"I do," said Anvil. "Jump, you puke. Go ahead and jump!"

I didn't want to jump. The barn had been built on a hill. In front the ground came up level with the barn floor, but in back the floor was even with the top of the straw rick, with four wide, terrible yawning feet between.

I said, "Nawh, there's nothin' to jumpin'."

"Oh, there ain't, hanh!" said Anvil. "Well, try it—"

He gave me a shove and I went out into terrifying space. He leaped after and upon me and we hit the pillowy side of the straw rick and tumbled to the ground in a smothering slide.

"That's no fun," I said, getting up and brushing the chaff from my face and hair.

Anvil himself had lost interest in it by now and was idly munching another of my apples.

"I know somethin'," I said. "I know a good game. Come on, I'll show you."

Anvil stung me on the leg with the apple as I raced through the door of the cutting room. When we reached the barn floor his eyes again fell on the peculiar white circle. "That's to play prisoner's base with," I said. "That's the base."

"That's a funny-lookin' base," he said suspiciously. "I never saw any base that looked like that."

I could feel my muscles tensing, but I wasn't particularly excited. I didn't trust myself to look up toward the roof where the big mechanical hayfork hung suspended from the long metal track that ran back over the steaming mows of alfalfa and red clover. The fork had vicious sharp prongs that had never descended to the floor except on one occasion Anvil knew nothing about.

I think Father had been drinking the day he bought the hayfork in Colonial Springs. It was an unwieldy, involved contraption of ropes, triggers and pulleys which took four men to operate. A man came out to install the fork and for several days he climbed up and down ladders, bolting the track in place and arranging the various gadgets. Finally, when he said it was ready, Father had a load of hay pulled into the barn and called the men in from the fields to watch and assist in the demonstration.

I don't remember the details. I just remember that something went very badly wrong. The fork suddenly plunged down with a peculiar ripping noise and embedded itself in the back of one of the work horses. Father said very little. He simply painted the big white circle on the barn floor, had the fork hauled back up to the top, and fastened the trigger around the rung of a stationary ladder eight feet off the floor, where no one could inadvertently pull it.

Then he said quietly, "I don't ever want anyone ever to touch this trip rope or to have occasion to step inside this circle."

So that was why I didn't now look up toward the fork.

"I don't want to play no sissy prisoner's base," Anvil said. "Let's find a nest of young pigeons."

"All right," I lied. "I know where there's a nest. But one game of prisoner's base first."

"You don't know where there's any pigeon nest," Anvil said. "You wouldn't have the nerve to throw them up against the barn if you did."

"Yes, I would too," I protested. "Now let's play one game of prisoner's base. Get in the circle and shut your eyes and start countin'."

"Oh, all right," Anvil agreed wearily. "Let's get it over with and find the pigeons. Ten, ten, double ten, forty-five—"

"Right in the middle of the circle," I told him. "And count slow. How'm I goin' to hide if you count that way?"

Anvil now counted more slowly. "Five, ten, fifteen—"

I gave Anvil one last vindictive look and sprang up the stationary ladder and swung out on the trip rope of the unpredictable hayfork with all my puny might.

The fork's whizzing descent was accompanied by that peculiar ripping noise. Anvil must have jumped instinctively. The fork missed him by several feet.

For a moment Anvil stood absolutely still. He turned around and saw the fork, still shimmering from its impact with the floor. His face became exactly the pale green of the carbide we burned in our acetylene lighting plant at the house. Then he looked at me, at the expression on my face, and his Adam's apple bobbed queerly up and down, and a little stream of water trickled down his right trouser leg and over his bare foot.

"You tried to kill me," he said thickly.

He did not come toward me. Instead, he sat down. He shook his head sickly. After a few sullen, bewildered moments he reached into his shirt and began hauling out my apples one by one.

"You can have your stinkin' old apples," he said. "You'd do that for a few dried-up little apples. Your old man owns everything in sight. I ain't got nothin'. Go ahead and keep your stinkin' old apples."

He got to his feet and slowly walked out of the door.

Since swinging off the trip rope I had neither moved nor spoken. For a moment more I stood motionless and voiceless and then I ran over and grabbed up the nine apples that were left and called, "Anvil! Anvil!" He continued across the field without even pausing.

I yelled, "Anvil! Wait, I'll give them to you."

Anvil climbed the fence without looking back and set off down the road toward the store. Every few steps he kicked his wet trouser leg.

Three sparrows flew out of the door in a dusty, chattering spiral. Then there was only the image of the hayfork shimmering and terrible in the great and growing and accusing silence and emptiness of the barn.